DEATH
AT
PARADISE
PALMS

ALSO BY THE AUTHOR

WRITING AS STEPH BROADRIBB:

The Retired Detectives Club series:

Death in the Sunshine

The Lori Anderson Bounty Hunter series:

Deep Down Dead

Deep Blue Trouble

Deep Dirty Truth

Deep Dark Night

WRITING AS STEPHANIE MARLAND:

Starke and Bell series:

My Little Eye

You Die Next

DEATH
AT
PARADISE
PALMS

STEPH
BROADRIBB

THOMAS & MERCER

Text copyright © 2022 by Steph Broadribb
All rights reserved.

Published by Thomas & Mercer, Seattle

www.apub.com

Amazon, the Amazon logo, and Thomas & Mercer are trademarks of Amazon.com, Inc., or its affiliates.

ISBN-13: 9781542027526
ISBN-10: 1542027527

Cover design by @blacksheep-uk.com

Printed in the United States of America

To Mum and Richard – for always being awesome

1

MOIRA

This is not how most days start. Usually right about now Moira would be on her way home after her early morning swim, or already back at base and dropping her kitbag in the kitchen before heading out for a brisk walk across the grasslands with her three dogs. Instead, she's in the passenger seat of Rick's boneshaker of a jeep, racing up the near deserted streets of the Ocean Mist district of The Homestead Retirement Community. They're heading towards the biggest house in one of the neighbouring districts – Paradise Palms. It's one of a handful of mansions that sit high up on the crest of the ridge with views across the whole community. Those homes are premium real estate – the most expensive houses in The Homestead. Locally, they're known as the Millionaires' Row.

Rick reaches a four-way stop and takes a right without braking. Moira curses under her breath and grips the handle above the window for balance. She glances across at Rick. 'You missing those car chases from back in the day?'

'Something like that,' he says with a boyish grin.

Even though she hates being shaken around like a martini at a James Bond convention, Moira can't help but smile; Rick's grin is rather disarming. The jeep's a big vehicle, but with Rick in the driver's seat it looks like a child's toy being driven by a giant – a giant wearing cargo shorts, a navy polo shirt and sandals. Even with the two-month compulsory medical rest imposed by his doctors after taking a bullet, Rick has lost none of his muscular bulk. Moira wonders if he's been defying the doc's orders and working out in secret. She wouldn't put it past him.

As if sensing her appraising him, Rick glances her way. 'You know who Olivia Hamilton Ziegler is, right?'

Moira shakes her head. 'Never heard of her.'

Rick raises his eyebrows. 'For real? Well, you'll recognise her when you see her, that's for sure. She's a fine actor. Been in a whole bunch of box office hits. *Towards the Devil, After the Sun Dies, Jasmine Dreaming, A Bucketful of Courage, Tomorrowlandia* – any of those ring a bell?'

'Not really,' Moira says, gripping the handle tighter as Rick bounces the jeep over a couple of speed bumps. 'I've never been into watching films much.'

Rick stares at her over the top of his shades. 'You aren't into movies . . . ? Wow.'

'It's not a big deal. I prefer a good book or the telly, that's all.'

'Sure.' He pushes his shades back up his nose. 'So you might not recognise her, but you should know she was a big deal in her heyday, still is to a lot of people. She's married to a younger guy, Cody Ziegler. They're well known as one of the happiest married couples in the film industry.'

'Got it.'

Moira's never been one to follow celebrity lifestyles and news. All the glitz, glamour and Instagram filters do her head in – it's not real life, it's not even the celebrities' real lives but a fake story made up to make themselves look great and their lives look perfect. Real life isn't like that. Real life is seeing how much shit you can cope with and then having a whole lot more piled on top of you until you break. As a DCI in the Metropolitan Police, Moira had experienced first-hand what *that* felt like. That's why she retired out here in Florida: to forget and to heal. Mind you, with everything that's happened recently, she doubts there's any chance of forgetting or healing anytime soon. Still, she's not had a panic attack since she moved here early last year. Just the one scare a couple of months back – but she'd managed to get her breathing under control and had avoided a full-blown episode. It's progress and she's happy to take any win, no matter how small.

Rick makes a left turn into the street that marks the end of the Ocean Mist district of The Homestead and the start of the Paradise Palms district. There's a squat one-storey building on their right – a gatehouse that houses the security team who monitor the comings and goings across The Homestead community. Rick takes the lane on the far side for residents, slowing down to allow time for the cameras to pick up the jeep's licence plate, and then speeds up as soon as the light changes from red to green. He steers the jeep through a chicane bend and out on to a main road, then floors the gas again.

'How'd you know this Olivia Hamilton Ziegler anyway?' asks Moira.

'I've never met her. She got my number from Hank at the CCTV station. She asked him how she could get in contact with the people that solved the murder at Manatee Park. He gave her my cell. She called. And here we are.'

'Right.'

It's been just over two months since they solved the murder of a young woman whose body Moira had found floating in the lap pool in Manatee Recreation Park surrounded by thousands of dollar bills. Ex-DEA agent Rick, married British couple Philip and Lizzie Sweetman – an ex-DCI and ex-CSI respectively – plus Moira herself, an ex-DCI who specialised in undercover work, had joined forces and solved the case before the local cops. The local papers and The Homestead Retirement Community residents' Facebook page had gone crazy for the story. Moira guesses Olivia Hamilton Ziegler found out about them from one of those sources.

'And her husband is missing?'

Rick makes a left on to a wide tree-lined boulevard. Nods. 'That's what she said.'

'And she wants our help?'

'She said that too.' There's a smile in his voice as he says it. 'And that it was urgent.'

Moira nods. She knows that feeling: the promise of a new case. It feels good. Today is not a normal day, and Moira is thankful. Retirement can be pretty boring, and she only has one investigation on the go at the moment. 'An investigative journalist contacted me.'

Rick's jaw tenses. He looks over at her. 'About your bad news blackout theory?'

'It's more than just a theory. The Homestead management are deliberately shutting down any negative news stories or questions raised. We saw it in how they responded to the murder at Manatee Park, and the burglaries before that. Also, this journalist has had personal experience of getting his story shut down.'

'You know what story?' asks Rick.

Moira shakes her head. 'He didn't say. Said he wanted to talk details face to face rather than on the phone.'

'That's smart.' Rick runs his hand across the stubble on his jaw. He steers the jeep around another bend and starts to climb a steep incline. 'But be careful, yeah? The management of The Homestead seem to have a real big influence – certainly over the press, maybe even with the cops. Tread lightly, you know what I mean?'

'I haven't even decided if I'm going to meet the journalist yet,' says Moira, fighting the urge to tell Rick she can take care of herself. She knows she doesn't need to, that he's telling her to tread lightly because he cares, not because he doesn't think she's capable. She also knows that Rick's right, she does need to be careful. Far more than he can possibly imagine.

From the way the press reported the Manatee Park murder a couple of months back – first as an accident and then as a crime perpetrated by someone from out of state, when really it had been a resident of The Homestead – she knows The Homestead management have influence. The cops had acted disengaged with the murder case and she suspects there was pressure put on them to stall the investigation. The intel Rick gathered from his police contact, Hawk, also indicated there was something odd in the way the cops treat this place.

Since then, Moira's made it her mission to find out the truth, but getting behind the *happy ever after* retirement rhetoric has proved harder than she'd anticipated. This journalist could help her dig deeper, but involving him is a risk. What if he gets curious and wants to know more about her? Everyone has secrets, and some are more deadly than others. What if he discovers 'Moira Flynn' doesn't really exist? She doesn't want to have to run. Again.

Rick takes a sharp turn off the street and brakes to a halt. 'Here we are.'

Jolted away from her concerns into the here and now, Moira looks up at the high-barred black metal gates blocking their way. There are spikes on the top of the gate, and along the top of the high walls. CCTV cameras fixed to the wall on either side of the gate stare unblinkingly down at them. 'That's a lot of security.'

'For sure,' says Rick as he winds down his window. Pressing the button on the intercom, he looks into the camera and says, 'Rick Denver and Moira Flynn here to see Mrs Hamilton Ziegler.'

There's no answer over the intercom speaker, but a few seconds later the gates in front of them slowly start to open.

'I guess we're allowed in then,' says Moira, squinting against the sun to see past the gates and up the long driveway. As Rick manoeuvres through them, Moira sees a small gatehouse to the left of the driveway and a double tennis court across the neatly mown lawns to the right. The driveway curves around to the left and Rick brings the jeep to a stop in front of an ornate fountain whose three white marble horses are shooting jets of water high into the air before splashing down into the bubbling pool below.

The water looks tempting. The temperature is already hitting the mid-thirties – or mid-nineties as she should say here in the USA – unseasonably warm for the time of year, even in central Florida. As she climbs out of the jeep and follows Rick towards the house, white pea gravel crunching underfoot, Moira feels sweat forming on her skin. Right now she wishes the long-sleeved, heavy cotton T-shirt she's wearing was a little lighter.

As they reach the front steps, she pauses a moment and looks up at the house, taking in the vaulted glass atrium held up by whitewashed oak pillars, the double-height windows and the turrets – one in each corner of the mansion – and lets out a long whistle. Houses up here on Millionaires' Row really are something.

Rick looks at her with a smile. 'Cool, huh?'

'Interesting how the other half live,' says Moira, following him up the three marble steps to the huge double-width, double-height oak front door.

He nods, and steps forward to the door, giving two assertive raps with the knocker. There's a twinkle in his eyes as he says, 'Yep, real interesting.'

Moira tries not to let the twinkle distract her. She ignores the jolt of electric she feels from Rick holding her gaze just a moment too long. Disregards the way his tan accentuates his silver quiff and brings out the lighter flecks in his dark brown eyes. She breaks eye contact; can't afford to get too close. There's no way she'll ever be able to let her guard fully down with anyone again, not even Rick. It's too dangerous, for both of them.

Her mobile buzzes. Moments later the electronic ringtone blasts out. Pulling the phone from her pocket, she looks at the number on the screen. She doesn't recognise it, and it isn't the journalist – she's already saved his number. It's probably a cold-caller trying to sell her something she doesn't need and doesn't want. Rejecting the call, she switches the ringer off and shoves the phone back into her pocket. She needs to focus on learning what she can about this actor, Olivia Hamilton Ziegler, and why it is that she thinks they can help.

Behind the door there's a succession of clicks as locks and bolts are unfastened. With multiple locks and all the cameras, it's clear Olivia Hamilton Ziegler is highly security conscious. Moira glances at Rick. 'It's a big place. Does she live here just her and her husband?'

Rick shrugs. 'I guess we're going to find out.'

He smiles that wide, generous smile of his and Moira feels her stomach do a little flip.

That's when the door starts to open.

2

MOIRA

'Cody didn't come home last night.' Olivia Hamilton Ziegler clasps her hands together, her knuckles whitening from the pressure. 'And he didn't let me know he was staying out. That never happens. Never. Not in all the years we've been married.'

They're in the kitchen, sitting at the island unit that separates the food preparation area from the sofas at the other end of the room. It's a vast space. *The whole ground floor of my house is probably smaller than this one room*, thinks Moira. Although the cabinets are dark blue, the white walls and marble countertops and splashback, along with the bifold doors that flood the room with light, make the room feel bright and airy. The place is clearly high end, but it's lived in too. Homely. The stack of mail on the end of the counter, the plates and mugs on the drainer beside the sink and the fridge magnets depicting places from all over the world stuck higgledy-piggledy on the front of the massive double fridge all give hints about the people who live here.

It's not what Moira expected from a celebrity home. And Olivia Hamilton Ziegler isn't what Moira expected either. Firstly, she seems like a regular person rather than a movie star. Stressed, yes, but down to earth. Real. Someone you can't help but warm to. And secondly, she's dressed like a regular person too – blue jeans, a white shirt, minimal jewellery: diamond studs and her wedding ring. Her make-up is naturally done, and her white-blonde hair is cut in a long bob that skims her jawline. She's barefoot, and her toes are the most dramatic thing about her, painted a bright fuchsia pink. It's hard to tell how old she is, but Moira guesses she is probably somewhere in her mid-sixties.

'Here you go.' Olivia puts two mugs of coffee down on the counter and pushes them across to Moira and Rick. 'It's rocket fuel strong. I don't know how to make it any other way.'

'That's perfect, thank you, ma'am,' says Rick, turning the mug handle to the right. He waits until Olivia has taken a seat opposite them before asking, 'Now, how can we help?'

Olivia takes a breath. Her eyes turn watery. 'Like I said, it's my husband. He's gone missing and I can't get hold of him.'

'Have you called the cops?' asks Rick, his voice soft, kind.

Olivia nods. 'I have, but they treated me like I was some hysterical woman. And, Jeez, I came really close to being one on the call with them.' She clenches her fists. 'They just wouldn't take me seriously. Didn't listen. Told me he was a grown adult and he'd probably stayed at a friend's place or taken a trip I'd forgotten about. And their tone, it was like they thought I was wasting their time, making a fuss about nothing, you know? They were disrespectful.'

Moira knows. They'd experienced it with the Manatee Park murder – the cops making out she and her friends were the problem rather than the person who'd killed the young woman in the pool. 'I'm sorry you've had to go through that.'

'Thanks.' Olivia pulls a tissue out from the sleeve of her shirt and dabs it under her eyes. 'I'm sorry about this, I . . .'

'Please don't apologise,' says Rick. 'How did you leave things with the cops?'

Olivia continues to dab the tissue under her eyes. 'They said they'd send someone over.'

Moira glances at Rick. 'The police are coming here?'

'Yes,' says Olivia. 'That's why I needed you to come right away. So you're here when they arrive.'

Rick frowns. 'But if you've got them coming out, why do you need—'

'Okay, look. I don't like cops. I called them, yes, because in this situation I figured I had to, but I don't trust them one bit.' She looks from Rick to Moira. Exhales hard. 'Early on in my career, you know, about a million years ago, I got pulled over because my tail light was out. The traffic cop should have written it up and given me a warning or a fine or whatever, but he and his partner didn't do that. They wanted to breathalyse me and said they had to take me downtown to do it. I told them I was on my way home from shooting all day on set and I hadn't had one drink, but those young-blood cops had recognised me and seemed all set on making a big performance out of it. They made me leave my car on the side of the highway and took me in the back of the cop car to the precinct. When we arrived, they took me in through the front in handcuffs and the paparazzi were waiting. It was almost 2 a.m. and there was no good reason for all those photographers to be there. The story in the press the next day was that I'd been arrested for a DUI. It was bullshit. No charges were brought against me because I had zero alcohol in my system. But those cops didn't care. They'd set me up.'

Moira shakes her head. 'Arseholes.'

'They were that for sure,' says Olivia. 'Since it happened, I've never trusted cops.'

Rick gives an awkward smile. 'So you know we're ex-cops, right?'

Olivia nods. 'Not beat cops, though. I've done my research. You, Rick Denver, are from out of state and worked for the DEA your whole career.' She looks at Moira. 'You're British, and worked London streets as a detective. And your two friends, they're another detective and a CSI. I've always liked the British – you have good manners.' Olivia smiles. 'And anyways, all of you are retired. I doubt you've got paparazzi contacts.'

'I can promise you that we don't,' says Rick.

'So tell us about your husband,' Moira says. 'When did you realise he'd gone missing?'

'I got worried when he wasn't home by ten last night. Sure, he often works late or goes out for dinner, but he always lets me know. So when he didn't come home or call last night, I thought it was weird.'

'And did you call him?'

'Of course, but it went straight to voicemail. I thought that was odd – Cody always has his cell phone on and charged. The movie business never sleeps so he's glued to the thing. For it to go to voicemail didn't seem right.' She sighs. 'You know, I thought about calling the cops last night but I figured they'd say he was probably out having fun, so I waited. Maybe I should have gone with my gut.'

'Your husband's in the movie business?' says Rick.

'The independent movie business, very different to Hollywood,' Olivia says a little sharply. 'He's a producer and owns the company – DVIZION. He's all about ethical moviemaking and the pure art of the moving picture rather than making box office hits at any cost. It's refreshing, quite frankly, and there's a big cult following around him and the movies he supports.'

There's a buzzing in Moira's pocket. Her phone is going. Ignoring it, Moira notes the language Olivia uses – cult following – and immediately thinks of crazed fans and obsessed stalkers. She doesn't mention this to Olivia, though. Instead, she asks, 'Do you know when he left yesterday morning?'

'Around ten, ten thirty, I'd expect. He'd started work early from the study, and I heard him on a call when I was leaving the house at nine thirty to go shopping with a friend, so he was still at it then.

But he'd told me he was going into the office for an eleven thirty meeting, so I don't think he'd have left it later than ten thirty to set off.'

'And whereabouts is his office?' asks Moira.

'It's out towards Orlando,' says Olivia. 'The drive takes about forty minutes.'

The buzzing in Moira's pocket stops. She exhales. 'Was there anyone else here yesterday morning who could've seen your husband leave?'

'No, we live alone, although people come in most days. We have the gardener on Tuesdays and Thursdays, our housekeeper on Monday and Friday, and the pool guy on Friday too.'

Yesterday was Wednesday. It seems that's the only weekday someone doesn't come in. Moira wonders if that's relevant. Suspects that it is. 'And the gatehouse, that's unoccupied?'

Olivia takes a sharp intake of breath. Bites her lip. Nods. 'Yes. It is, now.'

Moira catches Rick's eye. Olivia's stress reaction at the mention of the gatehouse is interesting. Moira wants to know more. She's about to ask a follow-up question, but her phone starts buzzing again.

Rick jumps in. 'And is your husband's car missing?'

'Yes. It's not here, and when I called his office first thing this morning, his PA – Donna Neale, such a nice lady – went out to the parking lot and checked. She said that it's not there either.'

Moira tries to stay focused on what Olivia is saying but the vibrating in her pocket is distracting. She should've turned the phone off rather than just the ringer. She wonders if the caller is the same person who rang as they arrived here, and then again just a moment ago – the unknown number. And if it is, why they're calling again almost immediately. It gives her an uneasy feeling.

'Has Cody ever done anything like this before?' asks Rick.

'No. Never.' Olivia shakes her head. 'Something's wrong, I can feel it. Cody's a good man, he'd never just disappear off somewhere without telling me.' Her voice catches in her throat. 'Someone has done this. Taken him. We have to find him.'

Moira notices Olivia hasn't said once that she loves her husband. In her experience, the wives or husbands of those missing always emphasise how much they love their lost spouse, even if it's them behind their disappearance. Olivia's reaction is different. Her anguish seems genuine enough, but there's something about the situation that's not ringing true. Moira glances at Rick. She bets he's thinking the same: what isn't Olivia telling them? She opens her mouth to ask a question, but her words are drowned out by a loud alarm coming from an intercom unit over by the door.

'That's the front gate,' says Olivia, her eyes widening, suddenly fearful. Hurrying across to the intercom unit, she peers at the small video screen and then presses a button on the control panel beneath it. Turning back towards Moira and Rick, she glances at the front door and shudders. 'The cops are here.'

3

MOIRA

The atmosphere is totally different with the cops here. Rather than take them into the kitchen, Olivia has led them into the formal dining room. Now they're sitting at the huge oak table – Olivia, Moira and Rick on one side, and the two uniformed officers on the other. Olivia's behaviour has changed. She's brittle and formal. The atmosphere feels adversarial even though they haven't got past introductions. The tension makes Moira's teeth itch.

At that moment, she feels her mobile vibrating in her pocket again. Trying to ignore it, Moira watches as the older of the two cops takes out a notebook, sets it on the table and opens it to a fresh page. He has a stocky build and a no-bullshit expression, along with blond cropped hair and a ruddy complexion that looks more down to a regular use of alcohol and fast food than an outdoor lifestyle. Moira guesses he's in his forties.

The officer clears his throat. 'I'm Officer Schofield, ma'am, and my colleague here is Officer Rodriguez.'

Officer Rodriguez smiles. She's very different to her colleague – petite, probably in her twenties, with long brown hair pulled back into a low ponytail. 'I'm pleased to—'

'We're here in response to the call you made earlier this morning,' continues Schofield, talking over Rodriguez and ignoring his colleague's irritated glare. 'About your husband.'

Olivia sits up straighter. 'As I said on the call, my husband has gone missing.'

'Can you tell us when and where you last saw him?' asks Rodriguez. Her tone is softer than her colleague's, more sympathetic.

As Olivia explains the timeline, Moira notes that Olivia hasn't introduced her and Rick to the cops. It doesn't bother her. It's easier if the cops don't know their names; limits the potential that they'll realise they solved the murder at Manatee Park case. There was bad blood between Philip and the lead detective on that case – Detective James R Golding. If these cops make the connection, it could raise the tension even further.

Again, her mobile starts to buzz in her pocket. Moira clenches her teeth. Doesn't want to pull the phone out during the conversation, but it's really distracting. After eight buzzes it switches over to voicemail. Moira glances at Rick. His expression is neutral. His eyes are focused on Olivia as she tells her story.

'. . . and so, as I said before, his car is gone and his cell phone is going straight to voicemail. When I tried to find his location on the Find My Cellphone app, the cell didn't appear, so I guess it's switched off.'

'What type of car?' asks Schofield.

'A silver Lexus,' says Olivia. 'The registration is a personalised one – 100 CTZ. It's on a palm trees plate, not a standard issue.'

Schofield nods. 'Okay. And tell me about your husband – age, description, that kind of thing.'

'He's about six foot, athletic, fifty-five years old. Attractive.' Standing up, Olivia takes a silver-framed picture from the dresser behind them and brings it back to the table, setting it down in front of the cops. 'This was taken last spring.'

Schofield looks at the framed photo of Cody and Olivia standing side by side under cherry trees in full blossom. He glances towards Rodriguez. Raises his eyebrows.

Olivia narrows her eyes as she sees the look pass between the two officers. She glances from Schofield to Rodriguez. 'You're not going to write any of this down?'

'I've got a good memory, ma'am,' says Rodriguez.

Olivia turns to Schofield. 'And what about you?'

'My memory is just fine,' he says, his tone surly.

Olivia frowns. 'Your notebook sitting there on the table tells me something different.'

'Look, ma'am. Your husband is a grown man, and he's barely been away twenty-four hours. From what you've told us, there are no signs of foul play. It seems more likely that he's taken a business trip, or had an evening out that's turned into a full night, rather than something bad happening to him. He's a man in his prime, an attractive one, as you say. In my experience, husbands don't tell their wives everything they're doing all of the time.'

Olivia exhales hard. 'So you don't believe me. You think he's playing away?'

Rodriguez gives a little shake of her head. 'What my colleague means is—'

'What your colleague means is that there's a big age difference between me and my husband and so he probably has another woman.' Olivia's voice falters as she says the word 'woman'. She points at Schofield, making stabbing movements with her finger, anger causing her voice to rise in volume and pitch. 'Yes, there's an age gap but we've been happily married for thirty-five years. I might be eighty-five years old, but don't you go discounting me. Don't you dare.'

Moira's surprised. She'd guessed Olivia to be twenty years younger. She's obviously had some work done but it's subtle. And fair play to her for having a husband thirty years her junior. Why the hell not?

Schofield shrugs. 'Like I say, ma'am, your husband's an adult and there are no signs of foul play here. I recommend you give it forty-eight hours, and if he hasn't come home or made contact by then, give me a call.'

Olivia narrows her eyes. 'And if I don't want to follow your recommendation?'

Rodriguez looks sympathetic. 'We can—'

'Ma'am. I suggest that you do,' says Schofield, shooting a dirty look at Rodriguez, who blushes. He takes a card out of his top pocket and slides it across the table to Olivia. 'You can reach me on these numbers, but after forty-eight hours only, you understand?'

'I understand just fine,' says Olivia, her tone heavy with sarcasm. 'You don't believe me when I say my husband's in trouble, and you don't give a damn if he is.'

Rodriguez shakes her head. 'No, ma'am, that's not what my—'

'Yes, it's exactly what he meant, and I won't tolerate you coming into my home and insulting me.' Olivia's voice is steel hard. Getting to her feet, she gestures towards the door. 'It's time you both left.'

As Olivia ushers the two cops out to the front door, Moira and Rick hang back. Pulling her phone from her pocket, Moira checks the screen. She's had five missed calls, all from the same number that she didn't recognise earlier. Again, they haven't left her a voicemail.

She frowns. If they're that keen to get hold of her, why haven't they left a message? It doesn't make sense. The unease she'd felt earlier grows. Five calls in quick succession seems excessive even for the most insistent cold-calling salesperson. Moira wants to know what they want, but she can't risk calling back or answering the call until she knows who they are. It's too dangerous. She screens her calls for a reason: she has to guard her privacy to stay safe.

'You doing okay?' asks Rick. He's watching her with concern in his eyes.

'Yes, fine.' Moira forces a smile. She doesn't want Rick to worry about her. She shoves her phone back into her pocket. 'Shall we debrief with Olivia? Things got a bit heated in there.'

'Good plan,' says Rick.

As Moira leads the way out to the atrium to find Olivia, she pushes the thoughts of the missed calls from her mind. There's nothing she can do about it right now, and she needs to focus on Olivia and the case.

If this mystery person wants to talk to her, they need to reveal their identity first.

4

RICK

With the cops gone, Olivia leads them out of the dining room and along a wide hallway towards Cody Ziegler's study. Both sides of the hallway are lined with floor-to-ceiling bookshelves all stuffed with books; there must be thousands of them.

Rick glances at Moira – he knows she likes a good book – but she's looking down at the parquet floor. Distracted. She's worried about something, he can tell from the tension in her expression, even though when he asked if she was okay she told him she was fine. He tries not to mind. Moira's a real private person and he doesn't want to pry into her business. Still, he kind of wishes she'd talk about it to him. Maybe it's a British thing; the Brits are known for their tight-assed ways, for sure. But then, sometimes, when it's just the two of them and they get to talking, it feels like Moira's starting to trust him, and open up, a little more.

'It's along here, right at the end,' says Olivia, gesturing down the hallway.

'Great,' says Rick, pausing to allow Moira to go in front of him.

Moira says nothing. As she passes him, she looks deep in thought.

They continue on along the hallway. As he walks, Rick thinks about the time a couple of months back when Moira visited him in the hospital, and that night walking around the lake a week or so afterwards. She'd opened up to him then; told him stuff about her life back in London and the operation that'd gone wrong and forced her into retirement. He figures he's gotten to know her better than Philip and Lizzie have, but oftentimes he wonders if he's even scratched the surface. The way she is, it's intriguing, and it makes him real curious. Maybe the mystery is part of what makes her so alluring.

'Those officers won't help me, will they?' says Olivia, turning back to look at Moira and Rick, her tone implying she already knows the answer to her question.

Rick shakes his head. The rookie, Rodriguez, had seemed a good sort, but her partner, Schofield, hadn't given a damn about Cody Ziegler or letting Rodriguez speak. Rick hates guys like that. 'Not until at least forty-eight hours have passed.'

'And let's face it, probably not even then.' Olivia frowns. 'They thought I was some hysterical woman time-waster.'

'Officer Rodriguez took you seriously,' says Moira.

Olivia considers Moira's point for a moment, and then nods. 'Yes, true, she did. But her brute of a partner discounted me on sight and overruled her.'

'Well, we're here to help,' says Moira. 'And we're taking you seriously.'

'And I'm grateful for that,' says Olivia, opening a door at the end of the hallway. 'The CCTV system is linked up to a dedicated computer housed in the purpose-built closet over on the far side of the room. I don't know how it works, but you're welcome to take a look.'

'Thanks,' says Rick. 'I'm sure between Moira and me we'll be able to figure it out.'

Olivia nods. 'Okay, I'll leave you to it then and fetch us some more drinks.'

'Appreciate it,' says Rick.

As Olivia walks back along the hallway towards the kitchen, Rick takes a look at Cody Ziegler's study. It's nothing like he'd imagined. Instead of a den-type room with dark wooden bookcases lining the walls and one of those big heavy oak desks dominating the space – a professional man cave – this study is utterly modern. Bright white walls, bold modern art prints, big bifold patio doors looking out on to neatly maintained gardens, a glass-topped desk and ergonomic grey mesh chair. It's neat and tidy – there are no papers on the desk or the filing cabinets. In fact, other than a computer screen and a cable that must be used to plug it into a laptop, there isn't anything on the desk. There isn't even a trash can. Rick's a tidy guy – he doesn't like clutter and gewgaws – but still he doesn't think he could work in this space. It's too sterile. Where's the paper to write on, or some sticky notes at least?

While Moira goes to find the CCTV closet on the opposite side of the room, Rick pulls his cell phone from his pocket and taps out a message on the Retired Detectives Club group message chat. Lizzie and Philip knew they were meeting Olivia Hamilton Ziegler this morning. He needs to update them.

> Rick: Meet with Olivia Hamilton Ziegler interesting. Husband of 35 years – Cody Ziegler. 55. Missing since yesterday morning. No signs foul play. Cops not acting – said wait 48 hours. Olivia wants us to find husband. Worried something bad happened. We're checking house CCTV now. Will revert after.

Three dots appear to show someone is typing. Rick watches the screen, waiting to see the message.

'Found it,' calls Moira. She's standing in front of a shallow walk-in closet with her back to him. The doors are open and he can see computer screens in the cubby beyond.

Rick looks back at his cell; the person's still typing a message but it hasn't appeared. Doesn't matter, he'll read it later. Shoving his cell phone back into his pocket, he heads over to join Moira. Just as Olivia had said, the closet has been altered to make a bespoke CCTV monitoring station. There are two levels of shelves, each holding two computer monitors. Each monitor shows four different camera feeds. There are sixteen in total. Beneath them is a narrow desk that's set to standing height just a few inches deeper than the shelves. On it sit a wireless keyboard and mouse.

'You know how to work it?' asks Rick.

'Maybe,' says Moira. 'It's showing the feeds live on screen. I just need to figure out how to access the saved recordings, if it does record.'

She pulls the keyboard and mouse closer to her. After studying the system a few moments, she clicks the mouse a few times and brings up the main menu, then selects 'History'. A folder appears with thumbnail stills of video clips stored by camera number and date.

Moira scans the list. Frowns.

'Problem?' asks Rick. He squints at the screen but the text is real small and it's hard to read it without his glasses.

She frowns. 'This is the recording history. It goes back a month.'

'That's good news.'

'No, it isn't.' Moira turns to face him. 'Because yesterday's recordings from all the cameras aren't here.'

Rick runs his hand over his jaw. 'Someone deleted them?'

'Perhaps,' says Moira, clicking the menu and bringing up 'Settings'. She scrolls and clicks through a couple of menus. 'Damn.

The auto-record setting has been switched off. The cameras are on live-feed-only mode.'

'Do you know who switched the recording off?'

Moira shakes her head. 'Doesn't say, but it must have been done early yesterday morning as there's no recordings beyond midnight the night before.'

Rick nods. 'If they live here alone then—'

He stops talking as Olivia enters the study.

Olivia looks from him and Moira to the CCTV monitors. 'Did you find everything you need?'

'There are no recordings saved for the last twenty-four hours,' says Moira. 'The system looks like it was reset to live feed only around midnight the evening before.'

Olivia looks thoughtful. 'You know, there was a power outage that night. I was heading to bed, and it must have been just a little after midnight, when everything turned off. We were in darkness for around a minute then the power came back on. Do you think that could have affected the CCTV?'

Rick doubts it – high-end security systems usually have work-arounds for power outages – but he wants to be sure before he tells Olivia that. If the outage didn't cause the change in the system, then only Cody and Olivia were in the house at the time the system configuration was changed. That means one of them must have been responsible, and the motives each might have had for doing it could be very different. He masks his suspicions with a smile. Keeps his tone light, easy. 'Could be. We'll need to check it out with the manufacturer to know for sure.'

Olivia purses her lips into a thin line. She puts her hands on her hips. 'I'm an actor, and I've spent my life studying people – how they act when they're acting, and how they act when they aren't. So don't treat me like I'm some kind of idiot. You suspect I killed my husband and stopped the recordings to cover it up, am I right? Or,

23

just like those cops, do you suspect Cody ran off and so he altered the feed first to try and hide the fact?'

Rick feels warmth spread up his neck and across his cheeks. 'I didn't say . . .'

Olivia keeps her gaze on Rick. Shakes her head. 'Honey, you don't need to use words, your face says it all.'

'You called us here to help you,' says Moira, her tone friendly but determined. 'And that's what we're doing. We're looking for anything that will give an indication of why and where your husband has gone. Now, if you've changed your mind and you don't want us here, you can ask us to leave at any time and we will. But if you do want our help, we need to check out anything and everything that could help us locate your husband.'

Olivia says nothing. She holds Moira's gaze and narrows her eyes. Moira doesn't flinch or look away. She keeps looking straight back at Olivia.

Rick tries not to smile. Moira has true grit, he reckons. It's one of the many things he admires about her.

Olivia is the first to break the stand-off. Exhaling hard, she says, 'Look, either the power outage caused the CCTV to stop saving the recordings, or someone came into this house and tampered with the system, because I can guarantee one hundred per cent that neither Cody nor I did one thing to change those settings.'

Rick sees Moira glance at him. He guesses she's thinking the same as him – usually the most likely explanation is the truth, and here there are three most likely explanations. The camera feed changed because of the outage or because Cody or Olivia changed the settings. He looks back at Olivia. 'What was the sequence of events yesterday morning?'

Olivia sighs. 'It's like I told you already, Cody worked here in the study from early in the morning. I went out to meet a friend for shopping around nine thirty, and Cody was due to leave for the office a little while after. When he didn't come home before I went to bed, I was worried and I called his cell phone but it went straight to voicemail. I did think about calling the cops then, but told myself maybe he was having a late dinner out or something. Still, it didn't feel right. He *always* lets me know when he isn't coming home so I can bolt the doors. He never deviates from our agreement.'

Rick hears Olivia's words and knows there's more to this than she's letting on. She clearly cares for her husband and the concern that something's happened to him seems genuine, but when she talked about him staying away from home, and their routine for when that happens, her voice changed. He can't put his finger on it, but he's damn sure there's something Olivia Hamilton Ziegler isn't telling them.

Moira shakes her head, and Rick can tell she's getting the same read on the situation he is. Moira looks at Olivia and says, 'If you want us to help you, you need to be honest. Tell us what's really going on here.'

Olivia looks away and says nothing for a long moment.

Rick glances at Moira, hoping the direct challenge approach will work.

Moira keeps her eyes on Olivia. Her tone is firm. 'Look, Olivia, for this to work we need to know everything. If you're not upfront with us, it could hinder us finding Cody.'

Olivia sighs. She looks at Rick, then Moira, and gives a single nod. 'Okay, so here's the thing. Cody and me, we've been together almost thirty-five years but our relationship – me the cougar, him the gold digger – it isn't at all like everyone thought.' She laughs, but there's no joy in the sound. 'The press, the studios, other actors, everyone – we've had them all fooled.'

5

PHILIP

Philip rereads the message from Rick on their group chat thread and smiles. They've got a new case. Perfect. This is exactly what he needs.

He glances across at his wife, Lizzie, sitting at the island in their kitchen, reading the latest Michael Connelly thriller. She's wearing the bright blue maxi dress he always thinks looks stunning on her, and has twisted her white-blonde hair into a bun on the top of her head and secured it with one of her paintbrushes. She's frowning, as she always seems to be these days when it's just the two of them. He wishes she'd cheer up. He misses her smile.

Yes, yes, a new case is just what they *both* need. It'll give them something important to focus on – a shared purpose. It will help to patch things up, them working together again, he's sure of it. After all, working on a case together all those years ago was how they first met and fell in love. They need to rekindle that feeling, and forget about the other stuff. What's done is done. He needs Lizzie to recognise that.

He clears his throat, then says loudly, 'We've got the case.'

Lizzie looks up from her book. 'The Olivia Hamilton Ziegler one?'

'The very same,' says Philip, grinning. 'Rick and Moira are there now. Apparently the cops weren't helpful, so the job is ours. They're checking the CCTV at the moment.'

'Is there a plan?'

'Once Rick and Moira have looked at the CCTV footage, they'll get back in touch. We'll probably regroup here later today.'

'Okay,' says Lizzie, looking back at her book.

Philip doesn't understand how Lizzie can be so calm about this. He's been on tenterhooks ever since Rick said there might be an investigation in the offing, and he'd thought Lizzie would be keen to get going on a new challenge. 'I've been doing some background work on Olivia Hamilton Ziegler. She's a very interesting lady.'

Lizzie says nothing. Giving a little shake of her head, she continues reading her book.

Philip tries to ignore Lizzie's obvious irritation with him. They're on the same team here, and they need to be able to communicate about the case at least. As DCI in the Thames Valley, he led hundreds of high-profile operations. He might be retired now, but he's highly experienced and he's good at this stuff. Lizzie always used to respect that. Still, he ploughs on, hoping he'll pique her interest.

'She was born in rural Virginia and ran away at seventeen to California wanting to be an actress. She worked as a waitress and model for a few months before being spotted by a talent scout and given a small role in her first film – *Don't Hold Back*. After that her career took off and she made over twenty films, including the big blockbusters – *Towards the Devil, After the Sun Dies, Jasmine Dreaming, A Bucketful of Courage, Tomorrowlandia.*' Philip refers to his notes on the spiral-bound pad beside him on the countertop. 'What's really interesting, though, is that unlike most actresses of her era, her career got stronger and she became in even greater demand as she got older, not the other way round. She was in her sixties when she won her Oscar – one of the oldest women ever to win one.'

'Because women are has-beens once they start getting wrinkles?' Lizzie looks up at him and narrows her eyes. 'Nice.'

'That's not what I'm saying at all,' says Philip, rushing to correct himself. 'It's the industry – it's well known for being ageist.'

'I guess that's true,' says Lizzie, putting her book down on the white quartz countertop. 'So what else do we know?'

'She met and married her husband when she was fifty. It was a three-month whirlwind romance. All the media reports said it wouldn't last but they've been proven wrong. Olivia and Cody have been together ever since and are said to have the strongest marriage in the business.'

Lizzie rolls her eyes. 'Just because they're still married, it doesn't mean the relationship is strong.'

Philip tries not to take the comment personally. 'Yes, yes, true. But they've been married thirty-five years.'

'Lucky them,' says Lizzie, her tone suggesting anything but.

This isn't going well, thinks Philip. He needs to get them on to safer ground. 'They moved to Paradise Palms, district four of The Homestead, five years ago. Olivia Hamilton Ziegler had retired from films a few months earlier and the media coverage from around that time says she'd always intended to retire in Florida and that Cody Ziegler was relocating his business from LA to Florida as they didn't want to be apart.'

Lizzie purses her lips and twists the trio of rings on her wedding finger around as she thinks. 'So they live up on Millionaires' Row? It sounds very perfect, doesn't it – the perfect career, the perfect marriage and the perfect retirement?' She shakes her head. 'Life is never that perfect, there has to be something else going on.'

Philip shrugs. 'I'm just going on what I've discovered through my background searches. I can't—'

'What have Rick and Moira discovered?' says Lizzie, cutting Philip off.

'Not much yet.' Philip glances at the WhatsApp message again and then back over to Lizzie. 'Apparently the husband, Cody Ziegler, has been missing since yesterday morning and there are no signs of foul play.'

'Could be he's gone off somewhere without telling his wife,' says Lizzie, looking pointedly at Philip. 'As we know, not all husbands tell their wives everything.'

Philip looks away as heat flushes up his neck and across his cheeks. He runs his hand over his bald pate, smoothing the imaginary, long-gone hair down into place. That was a cheap dig, a low blow. A clear sign that he's still nowhere near being forgiven.

He hopes the couples counselling will help. They've got their first session with the therapist later and although he knows Lizzie is reluctant, at least she's agreed to attend. He's hoping it'll help them get back to how they were – happy.

He glances at Lizzie. She's picked up her novel and is reading again, seemingly unconcerned that she's hurt him. She's always been so kind, warm-hearted and forgiving. He hardly recognises this cold and uncommunicative version of the wife he's loved for so many years.

Philip knows he's the cause and he hates it. He really hopes the counselling helps.

If it doesn't, he's not sure what else to try.

6

MOIRA

They're in the lounge, or great room as Olivia calls it. Everything in this room is a shade of cream – the walls, the furniture, the curtains and the rugs. The dark wood floor and the modern brass and blown-glass chandelier are the only contrasts. It's so pretty, Moira hopes she's not transferring dog hair from her leggings on to the sofa.

'So tell us, what is the truth of your relationship?'

Olivia clasps her hands together. Gives a small nod. 'Ours was a manufactured love affair, but it was based on a genuine affection. It was platonic rather than romantic, and we've had a great friendship and a strong business partnership for thirty-five years.'

Moira isn't surprised. Rick told her Olivia and Cody allegedly have one of the happiest marriages in the film industry. Nothing that perfect could be real. Life just isn't like that. She glances at Rick and sees that he's frowning. Maybe he really had believed the hype about the couple. If he had, he should've known better. No matter what people say, they always let you down. Especially those you trust the most.

Olivia seems to interpret their silence as disbelief. She looks from Rick to Moira.

'Look, thirty-five years ago I was pushing fifty. Do you know how many great roles there are for female actors in their fifties, especially back then? I'll tell you how many – virtually zilch. And of the few parts that are on offer there's rarely anything challenging or ground-breaking, they're all sweet grandmother or "old woman with cat" or whatever.' Her voice is getting louder, angrier. 'You know, back then my agent told me I should be happy. I'd had a good run, played some iconic characters, and been nominated for more than one Oscar. But I wasn't happy. I wanted to *win* an Oscar, and I wanted to keep working – doing what I loved and was good at – until *I* decided to retire, not until I was forced into the shadows by a bunch of chauvinistic suits governing an industry that only wants to show young, beautiful women on screen, and thinks nothing of pairing a sixty-something leading man with a twenty-something leading woman. I refused to let them limit me and I had enough smarts to see how the movie world works.' She gives a sly smile. 'And so I found a way to make them want me again.'

Moira's read about the horrors endured by those who inspired the Me Too movement, and the plentiful stories about gender and age inequality in Hollywood. She has no doubt Olivia is telling the truth.

'How did you do it?'

'By being a good actor,' says Olivia, smiling. 'I sold them a story – a wild love affair between a rich fifty-year-old woman and a handsome gold digger barely out of his teens. The press loved it and couldn't get enough of me. Instead of an ageing has-been, I was viewed as a sexy cougar. My picture was everywhere. Within days my agent was getting calls offering me work. The rest is history – I got some great parts, and I won my Oscar.'

'Didn't either of you feel trapped – like you were unable to find actual love because you had to keep up the pretence?' Rick says. 'Thirty-five years sure seems like a long time.'

'Fair question,' says Olivia. 'But I did have love, I just couldn't go public with it.'

Rick frowns. 'What do you mean?'

31

'Look, I'm telling you this now because it doesn't matter for my career and things are changing anyways. Back then I wasn't allowed to go public with the love of my life if I wanted to keep my career, because she was a woman – a total marvel of a woman. Her name was Tamsin Fields and she was beautiful, vivacious, smart . . .' Olivia's voice trails off. Her eyes become watery. 'She's been dead nearly three years now. Cancer took her at its third attempt.'

Rick's jaw is clenched. His fists too. Moira knows his wife died of cancer. It must be hard hearing Olivia's story.

'That must have been really tough,' says Moira.

Olivia nods. 'When we lived in LA it was harder, we had to be very careful, but once we moved out here things were more relaxed. Tamsin moved here with us. We told people she rented the gate-house, but the reality was we all lived together in the big house.'

'And how did Cody feel about that?' says Moira.

'He was happy. He loved Tamsin too.'

Rick frowns. 'And what about him, did he have anyone else?'

Olivia nods. 'Sometimes. It was all very harmonious. They stayed here on occasion, if he wanted them to. We're very open with each other. We don't have secrets.'

'And does he have anyone special at the moment?' says Moira.

Olivia thinks for a moment. Shakes her head. 'No, I don't think so. He's been so tied up with work recently that he hasn't had time for socialising.'

'Okay,' says Moira. Olivia seems genuine enough but there's something needling her, something that tells her this isn't the whole truth.

Olivia seems to pick up on her doubt. She grasps for Moira's hand. Squeezes it tightly.

'Look, Cody's my best friend. We tell each other everything. And he'd never disappear without telling me. Those cops aren't going to do anything useful, you saw the way they were.' Olivia looks from Moira to Rick, her eyes pleading. 'You *must* find him.'

7

LIZZIE

Lizzie doesn't want to be here. The place is pleasant enough, she supposes; the waiting area is painted a calming pale blue, and the couches are inoffensive antiqued brown leather. Over towards the entrance, the pale wooden reception desk is neat and tidy, and the black-suited, short-haired young receptionist sitting behind it had been friendly and professional as she'd welcomed them and asked them to take a seat. It's not the place that Lizzie doesn't like; no, it's the reason for being here.

'I'm sure they won't be long,' says Philip, his tone hearty and bolstered with what is obviously faked confidence. He gives her a smile, but it doesn't reach his eyes. No matter how much he's trying to pretend, he seems unusually awkward, nervous, as he sits, poker straight, on the couch beside her.

'Sure,' she says. It would be fine with her if they never came to collect them. She only came because Philip wouldn't shut up about them trying couples counselling, and in the end the only way to stop him pestering her was to agree. She regrets that now and wishes she'd stood her ground.

The clock on the wall ticks loudly as the seconds pass. The receptionist's fingernails tap against her keyboard.

Lizzie hears the click of a catch and a door opens on the far side of the waiting area. Clasping her hands together in her lap, she fights the urge to leap up from the saggy-bottomed leather couch and run away. Instead, she smiles when the therapist comes out to the reception area to greet them, and then inwardly curses her innate politeness and for not speaking up and leaving.

'I'm Dr Sanderson,' says the therapist by way of introduction, holding out her hand. 'And I'll be working with you this morning.'

The therapist looks from Philip to Lizzie expectantly. She's tall and younger than Lizzie had expected, although, she has to admit, *most* people are younger than she'd expected these days. She looks to be in her late thirties – younger than Lizzie's son and eldest daughter. But unlike her daughter, Vivien, who favours long floaty dresses, Doctor Sanderson is wearing a lightweight brown trouser suit with a cream blouse. Her long dark hair is smoothed back into a low ponytail and she's wearing oversized black-framed glasses.

Philip stands first and grabs the woman's hand, shaking it vigorously. 'Philip Sweetman, and this is my wife, Lizzie.'

'Pleased to meet you,' says Lizzie, even though she's anything but. She gets to her feet and shakes the therapist's outstretched hand. It feels soft, not cracked by turpentine and paint like Lizzie's own.

'Let's go through to my office,' says Doctor Sanderson with a smile. 'This way, please.'

They follow her across the waiting area to the office, both of them walking slower than usual. Lizzie wonders if Philip's regretting them coming, now they're actually here. After all, she's the one who has wanted to talk about what happened, what he did, and what he's kept from her all these years. He's the one who constantly refuses to speak about it.

Inside the office, Doctor Sanderson gestures to two chairs on the far side of a large, pale wood desk. 'Please, take a seat.'

They sit, and the therapist settles herself in the swivel chair on the opposite side of the desk to them. As the therapist makes her introduction and launches into a spiel about how the session will work, Lizzie casts her eye around the room. It's bland and beige – as impersonal and inoffensive as a mid-price hotel, and equally uninspiring. At least the blinds are closed so no one can look in and see them. She'd been worried when they arrived and she realised the therapist's office was on the ground floor.

Still, she doesn't need to worry. They've come to Clermont for the session and no one knows them here, not like back on The Homestead. She'd hate for their neighbours and friends to know they're having problems and to ask her about them. It's embarrassing that Philip's been lying to her for so long. The only person she's told is Moira.

When the therapist asks for some more details about them, Philip seems eager to talk. He keeps the conversation on safe ground – where they met, how long they've been married, their children, and their old careers. Lizzie sits back in her chair, happy to let him waffle away. She just wants the time to pass quickly so they can leave.

'And why don't you talk me through what's brought you here,' says Doctor Sanderson. Her voice is calm and melodic. Soothing.

'We've been having a problem,' says Philip. He glances at Lizzie.

Lizzie nods, although 'problem' feels like far too small and simple a word to describe what's going on with them.

'And why is that, do you think?' says the therapist, looking over her glasses at them in turn.

Philip says nothing and glances again at Lizzie. She looks away. Let him talk; he's the one who harangued her into coming.

He looks uncomfortable and starts mumbling about differences of opinion and blocked communication channels. It's so bland and impersonal that it sounds more as if he's talking about a problem between two work colleagues rather than husband and wife.

The therapist lets Philip ramble on for a few minutes and then clears her throat. She looks pointedly at Lizzie. 'What was it that you think started the "problem"?'

Lizzie takes a breath, disappointed that Philip can't even say what he did out loud, and meets the therapist's gaze. 'It was because he lied to me.'

Doctor Sanderson jots some words in her notebook. 'In what way?'

Lizzie looks at Philip, wondering if he'll tell the therapist what he did, but he's looking down at his feet and doesn't meet her eye. She exhales hard. 'Philip was a DCI in the police force back in England. He was in charge of an abduction case – a young girl – but he delayed acting on a tip-off and as a result the team got to the child too late and she'd already died.'

Doctor Sanderson tilts her head to one side. 'And you blame him for this death?'

'Yes I do,' says Lizzie, a hint of irritation creeping into her tone. 'But I blame him more for why it happened and the fact that he lied about it.'

'Continue,' says the therapist, noting something down in her book.

Lizzie feels anger rising inside her. She clenches her fists. 'He told his team, his boss and me that the tip-off had come in just before lunchtime and he'd gone out for a two-hour lunch before following up, but that wasn't true. Yes, he delayed acting on the tip-off for two hours, but he wasn't stuffing his face at lunch all that time. He was in hospital having tests.'

Doctor Sanderson nods. Her voice maintains the air of calmness. 'And you didn't know he was having these tests?'

'That's right. Apparently he'd been having health issues for months, but he didn't tell anyone around him – not me, his wife, and not his employer or colleagues.'

'And is that your recollection, Philip?' asks Doctor Sanderson.

Philip nods. His voice is quiet, barely a whisper, as he speaks. 'I didn't want to worry her and—'

'That's bullshit and you know it,' says Lizzie, her voice rising in volume. 'You did it for *you*, not for me, or your family, or for the victims of crime or your team. Why can't you just admit it? You loved the pomp and kudos of being a senior police official and you didn't want to lose that status if you had to move to a desk job or take medical retirement. So you were selfish – told no one and had secret tests done – and as a result a child died.'

The therapist tilts her head again and says in her melodic voice, 'Lizzie, what is it you're more angry about, the loss of the child's life or that he kept his health issues from you?'

'What kind of stupid question is that?' snaps Lizzie. 'I'm angry about both.'

'But you said this happened ten years ago. So why is it causing you a problem now?'

'Because I only found out the truth recently.' Lizzie exhales hard and glares at Philip. 'I read it in some paperwork. *He* was never going to tell me. And the reason it was documented was that he had a heart attack shortly after the child was found dead, but rather than letting him return to work once he'd recovered, they forced him into retirement. I'd always suspected there was more to it than him making a mistake with a tip-off, but he'd assured me that hadn't been the case. He *lied* to me.'

'I see,' says Doctor Sanderson, nodding. She turns to Philip. 'And how do you feel about this?'

Philip's face is flushed but he has that obstinate look in his eye and his chin is tilted up defiantly. 'That paperwork was filed away. She went through my private things.'

'*That's* what you're focusing on? That I went in your room and looked in your precious filing box?' Lizzie throws up her hands. 'You wouldn't talk to me about what happened. You'd kept the truth from me for ten years. It's like you think I'm an idiot, or some delicate flower who can't handle the truth . . . or you just don't respect me enough to tell me the truth. I just . . . I just . . .' She shakes her head. 'What's the point?'

Doctor Sanderson writes down another note and then looks at Philip. 'Is that why you did what you did?'

He stays silent. Doesn't respond.

Lizzie raises her eyes to the heavens. 'Of course he won't—'

'Philip?' interrupts the therapist.

He looks down, away from the therapist's gaze. Doesn't speak.

As the seconds turn into minutes, Lizzie fights the urge to throttle him.

'Philip,' repeats the therapist. 'It's important that you acknowledge what Lizzie has shared.'

'Sorry. I do acknowledge it. I . . . it's . . . it's hard for me to talk about. I had to be strong, you see, I had to be the man, and provide for Lizzie and my family.' He glances over at her. 'To look after you like I promised in our wedding vows.'

'I didn't need you to look after me, I wanted you to be my partner – for us to be equals in our marriage – and I thought we were. But then I discovered you'd been lying to me for ten years and I . . .' Lizzie sighs. 'I just don't know how I can believe you, or trust you, any more.'

'Good, this is good, Lizzie,' says Doctor Sanderson, making a note on her pad. 'Philip, what do you say to that?'

Philip is silent a long moment. His right leg jigs up and down, and there's a muscle pulsing in his cheek.

Lizzie shakes her head again. 'He won't say anything. I've tried to get him to talk about it often enough.'

'Philip?' says the therapist, leaning closer. 'Tell us what you're feeling right now, it's important that you share.'

'Sad,' says Philip, his eyes watery. He blinks. 'I loved my job, I didn't want to lose it because of ill health.' Philip looks at Lizzie and puts his hand on hers. 'I love my wife too.'

He's looking at her like he wants her to tell him she loves him, but she can't. He isn't forgiven, not even close. Looking across the room, Lizzie resists the urge to snatch her hand away and allows his hand to rest on hers for a moment even though his touch is making her skin crawl.

The telephone on Doctor Sanderson's desk buzzes once. She looks back at it, then at Lizzie and Philip. 'Well, that's the end of our time today and I think we've made a good start. I'll see you same time next week, okay?'

Philip gives the therapist a small smile. 'Thanks, Doctor Sanderson.'

Lizzie says nothing.

◆ ◆ ◆

As he drives them home, Philip prattles away about the session and how nice the therapist was. He keeps talking and talking, not pausing long enough for her to get a word in. Over half an hour later, as they approach the entrance to The Homestead and make their way along the ring road towards the Ocean Mist community, Lizzie is getting increasingly irritated.

From the way Philip's talking, it's as if he thinks he deserves a prize for telling the truth. And, yes, he did tell the real story in the therapist's office, but only because she'd found out already. He's lied to her all these years. Lizzie clenches her fists. How can a relationship filled with lies be worth saving? And why can't he tell her he's sorry? He's never said once that he's sorry for hiding the truth from her, not once.

'. . . and so if we keep going to these sessions I think you'll find that we'll be fine, and that's great because with the new case for Olivia Hamilton Ziegler it's important that we focus and—'

'Philip, will you shut up, for God's sake.' Lizzie's voice is loud when she speaks, cutting off his endless monologue.

He looks at her, surprised. 'What? It was a good session, though, wasn't it? And Doctor Sanderson, she was helping, yes? You thought that too, didn't you? It's going to—'

'No, Philip, I didn't.' Lizzie shakes her head and tries to harden herself to the look of pain and fear in her husband's eyes. 'I tried it, okay, but this isn't going to work.'

8

MOIRA

She's a mile from home when it starts pouring. Rain here isn't at all like the British drizzle – it's far more dramatic. One moment you're strolling along in bright sunshine, the next the sky has darkened and you're caught in the middle of a tropical monsoon. It's still hot, though, and humid with it.

There's no sense in running. Moira knows she'll be drenched in seconds anyway. So she keeps walking across the open grassland of Misty Plains, heading towards the line of tall oaks in the distance that marks the border between the Ocean Mist district of The Homestead and the as yet unnamed district eleven. Marigold, the leggy juvenile Labrador, runs on ahead with Wolfie, the mixed-breed terrier chasing at her heels. Pip, the elderly sausage dog, trots at Moira's side, stopping to sniff at an interesting smell every now and then. The rain, heavy as it is, doesn't seem to bother them at all.

As she walks, her phone vibrates in her pocket. Pulling it out, she checks the screen and sees it's the unknown number again. This is ridiculous; it's the fourth call she's had since leaving Olivia Hamilton Ziegler's house. As with the other calls, Moira lets this one go to voicemail, but the caller must have hung up as the phone doesn't alert her to a new message.

It's unsettling. Surely a cold-calling salesperson wouldn't be this persistent? And if it isn't a random sales call, who is ringing her and why don't they leave a voicemail? She's googled the number but it's not coming up in the search as a telemarketer or nuisance caller – even though it's more than a nuisance to her.

Moira shudders. She moved here to The Homestead – to Florida – to get away from danger and a life of constantly looking over her shoulder. But now, with these persistent calls from this unknown number, the fear is returning.

Making a new life here was supposed to give her a fresh start – a tabula rasa – and in some ways it has. She's swapped the cold dampness of London for the bright sunshine and tropical downpours of Florida, and exchanged the fast-paced, high-pressured life of an undercover DCI for the steadier-paced world of the recently retired. And although she'd done her best to keep people at arm's length, she's become closer with Lizzie than she'd ever intended, and despite her better judgement she's growing ever closer with Rick.

Moira exhales hard. Whoever this unknown caller is, they've served as a reminder that she can't afford to get too close with the people here. She needs to hide the truth of who she is for her own sake, and for theirs. She can't have people like Rick and Lizzie caught up in the crossfire if her past finds her out here. She cannot have their blood on her hands too.

She's still thinking about what to do when the phone rings in her hand. Moira flinches, almost dropping it, and mutters, 'What the hell?'

Pip, the sausage dog, looks up at her, wide-eyed with concern. The hair on the top of his head has been dampened by the rain and is sticking up in spikes.

'It's okay, baby,' she says, soothing him with her voice. 'It's just the stupid phone.'

As Pip continues trotting along beside her, Moira clenches the handset tighter in her fist. Damn caller. Enough is enough. She's going to answer the call and challenge whoever it is about who they are and what they want from her.

She looks at the screen and that's when she realises the number is different this time. It belongs to the investigative journalist who'd made contact the other day, not the unknown caller.

Taking a breath, Moira swallows down the fierceness she was about to unleash, and presses answer. 'Hello?'

'Is this Moira Flynn? It's Jake Malone here, we spoke the other day.'

'Yes, hi,' says Moira, watching Marigold and Wolfie chasing each other in speedy circles around her.

'Are you okay to talk?' His voice is affable, with a slight Boston accent.

The rain has eased off a bit. Turning slightly, Moira angles her face so she's not getting the worst of it head-on. 'Yep, go ahead.'

'Okay, great, so I've been doing some digging and there's an interesting pattern emerging around how criminal activity that's occurred in or close by to The Homestead has been reported. It's like you said about the murder being reported as a tragic accident initially – it seems that whatever happened is buried in the least accessible part of the paper or news outlet, and the facts are dumbed way down.'

Moira frowns. 'I thought you said you had personal experience of a story getting shut down?'

'I have, but one incident doesn't make a good article.' There's the sound of talking in the background, and the clicking of fingers against a keyboard. 'I need a depth and breadth of evidence to conclusively prove what's going on here.'

'Okay, I get that. So what else do you need?' Moira knows she sounds suspicious, but she can't help it – she is suspicious. After what happened in London, she's learned the hard way that even the people you think you're closest to will betray you. And she doesn't know this Jake Malone at all.

'When we last spoke, you said there'd been unrest in the residents' groups?'

'There has,' says Moira, watching as Wolfie does a one-eighty turn and chases after Marigold in the opposite direction. 'Any negative stories or questions asked by residents on social media or in The Homestead online discussion groups are immediately shut down and deleted.'

'And you have proof?'

'I have some screenshots.'

'That's great.' There's the sound of more typing. 'Are there any other residents I could speak to about it?'

Moira hesitates. She thinks about Peggy Leggerhorne, the woman whose house had been the first to be burgled a few months ago, and whose information had played a big part in Moira and the others uncovering both the burglar and the killer of the young woman in Manatee Recreation Park.

It had been Peggy who'd first alerted Moira to the way The Homestead management policed the discussion forum, deleting posts they felt weren't positive enough in nature. She was a very private person, even more so after the burglary, but as she'd helped Moira before maybe Peggy would be willing to speak to Jake.

'Perhaps, but I can't give you their names now, I'd have to see if they were okay with it first.'

'Sure, that's no problem. If you could speak to them, and then let's get together with a face-to-face meet. I'll look through my schedule and message some potential dates over.'

'Sounds good,' says Moira.

'Great,' says Jake. 'I'll be in touch then.'

Moira ends the call. Jake seems on the level but she's still not one hundred per cent sure she wants to meet him face to face. Earlier, Rick had asked her to tread lightly and she knows it's good advice. Although she's been focusing on the bad news media black-out aspect of what seems to be happening, it's very possible, as Rick said, that The Homestead has some sway over the local cops too. Moira wants to get to the truth of what's going on, but she has to be careful and not risk exposing herself. It's a fine line to tread.

'Come on, guys, this way,' calls Moira, turning back across the grasslands towards home. She picks up her pace and beside her Pip speeds up too. Wolfie and Marigold continue to caper around them. The rain has stopped now, just as suddenly as it began, and the sun on the damp grass is causing steam to rise and makes the air smell like a freshly mown lawn.

As she walks, Moira thinks about Olivia Hamilton Ziegler and her missing husband, Cody. Olivia's dislike of the cops seemed real enough, and Officer Schofield seemed about as much use as a chocolate teapot, but the missing CCTV footage really bothers Moira. It seems too convenient that a power cut caused it to switch off auto record during the exact period Cody Ziegler went missing. Yet from what Olivia said, Cody and herself were the only people in the house at the time the system was switched to live play only. Of course it's possible someone else broke into the property and then erased the footage of themselves, but surely there'd have been some signs of a break-in? As she walks, Moira continues to puzzle over it.

She's almost back to the white gravel path that marks the start of the Ocean Mist district when her phone buzzes in her pocket. She calls the dogs back to her so she can put them on their leads, then pulls out her phone, expecting it to be Jake Malone getting back to her with some dates to meet.

But it's not. It's a text from the unknown number.

Her heart rate accelerates. Her mouth goes dry as she rereads the words.

I KNOW WHO YOU ARE

Moira's stomach flips and she thinks she's going to be sick.
Her worst nightmare is coming true.
They've found her.

9

RICK

They're due to meet at Philip and Lizzie's place, but Rick still has a couple of calls to make before they regroup. As he turns down Wild Meadow Drive, he presses call on his cell phone and waits to be connected.

It's answered after two rings. 'Good morning, EQS Alarms, how can I help you today?'

'Hi there, I have a question about your EQ1000 model, would you be able to help me with that?' says Rick, taking a left into Sunshine Harbor Boulevard.

'No problem, sir,' says the lady at EQS Alarms. 'I'll put you though to our customer assistance team, please hold.'

Rick waits as a tinny instrumental version of a famous Aerosmith song is played over the line. It takes a half minute before the music cuts off abruptly and a man answers. 'EQS Alarms, you're speaking with Bob.'

'Hi, Bob. I'm looking at your alarms and I'm thinking of buying one, but to help me decide the right model I've got a quick question about your EQ1000 alarm.'

'I'm happy to help you with that. What's your question?'

Rick takes a right into the street Philip and Lizzie live in. He slows the jeep to allow an oncoming car to overtake a parked vehicle and then continues on. 'Can you tell me if a power outage will cause the system to reset?'

'I surely can,' says Bob. 'If there's a break in the power supply for more than thirty seconds, the system will go offline unless a backup battery pack is installed to safeguard for that type of emergency. With the EQ1000 model you'll need to purchase yourself the backup battery pack separately, but if you opt for the EQ2000+ model you'll get the pack as an added-value bonus.'

Rick nods. He doesn't know whether the Zieglers have a backup battery pack but he's sure he can find out. 'That's good to know, Bob. And if I was to buy the EQ1000 and the system reset itself after a power outage, would it be in live-play or auto-record mode?'

'Live-play mode, sir. That's the standard out-of-the-box factory setting on the EQ1000 model.'

'Thanks, Bob, you've been real helpful,' says Rick, indicating right and pulling the jeep close into the kerb outside Philip and Lizzie's place.

'No problem at all, you have yourself a nice day, sir, and give me a call back anytime if you have any other questions about our products.'

After ending the call and parking up, Rick doesn't get out of the jeep right away. Instead, he scrolls through his contacts and makes another call.

'Hey, buddy, I've got a favour to ask.'

'Always the way,' says Hawk, chewing loudly on his gum as he speaks. 'What you got going on this time?'

Rick smiles. Him and Hawk go way back – they'd trained together back in the day and had worked on the same team for a little while before Hawk took a job based out of Miami. Since Rick retired and moved to The Homestead they've been meeting up on a semi-regular basis for a few beers and a trip down memory lane. Hawk's a good guy and he's well connected with the local law enforcement, highly discreet, and easily persuadable with tickets to the game or his bar tab getting picked up.

'Can you run a plate for me and see what traffic cameras it's been picked up on in the last forty-eight hours?'

'Yep, that won't be a problem,' Hawk says, still chewing. Rick's never seen him without a piece on the go. 'You're working another case, huh?'

'Looking into something – a misper the local cops don't seem too interested in.'

There's a crackle of paper, as if Hawk's opening up a notebook. 'What's the plate?'

'It's personalised. 100 CTZ. Registered to a Cody Ziegler.'

'Okay, got it. I'll have it run through the system and let you know.'

'Appreciate it.' Rick pauses as he spots Moira a little way along the sidewalk, heading towards Philip and Lizzie's place. She's walking fast and keeps looking over her shoulder. It looks like something's wrong.

'That it?' says Hawk.

Rick wants to end the call and see if Moira's okay, but he needs Hawk's help on something else. Fighting the urge to get out of the jeep and go to Moira, he says, 'Well, there is one other thing . . .'

'Okay, shoot,' says Hawk, working his gum hard. 'But you're buying next time we meet.'

'Deal,' says Rick. 'So there's this pain-in-the-ass local cop, Officer Schofield, that caught the case we're working. What can you tell me about him?'

◆ ◆ ◆

The four of them gather in the backyard at Lizzie and Philip's, sitting on the white patio furniture, as Moira and Rick debrief

49

on what happened earlier with Olivia Hamilton Ziegler and the unimpressive interaction they'd had with the local cops. Philip is writing notes on the glass patio doors that serve as their makeshift case board. It's not a murder board yet, although it might become one if Olivia's fears are correct.

'So from what you've said, the police aren't taking Olivia Hamilton Ziegler's concerns seriously?' says Lizzie.

'I think Officer Rodriguez wanted to,' says Moira. 'But her partner was, quite frankly, an arse.'

'Yeah, about that,' says Rick. 'I asked my law enforcement contact about Officer Schofield and the guy has a bad track record. My contact hasn't had any direct experience of the man, but he's heard plenty. Seems the guy is a real chauvinist asshole. He's had complaints made against him by two female co-workers in the past year and has had a couple of warnings for disrespectful conduct with female civilians. Rodriguez, his latest partner, has only worked alongside him for the past month, but the word in the locker room is she's putting the feelers out for a new partner already.'

'Sounds like the guy's got a big problem,' says Lizzie.

Moira nods. 'And that's even more reason why we need to stay on this case.'

'For sure,' says Rick. He looks at Lizzie and Philip. 'So are you in?'

Philip nods. 'Of course.'

'Definitely,' says Lizzie. 'Someone has to help Olivia Hamilton Ziegler.'

'Right, let's go through this.' Rick looks at the notes Philip's captured on the glass doors. 'Cody Ziegler has been missing for just over twenty-four hours. He isn't answering his calls or reading messages from his wife. His cell phone appears to be switched off as it's not appearing on the Find My Cellphone app. His wife and the people at his business haven't seen him and his car – a Lexus – is also missing.'

'And there were no signs of a disturbance?' says Lizzie, looking thoughtful.

'Olivia said nothing looked out of place to her,' says Moira. 'And we didn't see anything obvious, but we didn't have your CSI experience.'

Lizzie nods. 'Could be worth me going over there and doing a search for blood splatter.'

'Good idea,' says Rick. He glances at Philip, who's taking notes on the glass but seems awful quiet. 'What do you think, Philip?'

'Yes, yes,' says Philip, not turning round as he continues to write. 'I agree.'

'Okay, cool.' Rick frowns, puzzled. It's kind of odd. Philip usually loves to feel like he's the one in charge, directing their moves. Rick's happy enough taking the lead on the debrief but it doesn't seem right Philip not joining in with the discussion and just taking notes. It makes Rick think something's up.

He glances at Moira. At least she seems to be her usual self now, even if she looks a little pale beneath her tan. Leaning closer to her, he lowers his voice and says, 'You doing okay?'

Her eyes widen a moment, then she smiles. 'I'm fine. I got caught in the tropical downpour while I was walking the dogs earlier – but I'm all dried out now.'

Rick nods. 'Yeah, you have to watch out for them, I'm always getting caught.'

'So what else do we have?' asks Lizzie, looking pointedly at Rick and Moira.

'Well, I spoke with the manufacturer of the Zieglers' CCTV system – EQS Alarms. The model they have, the EQ1000, does reset itself to factory settings if the power is out for thirty seconds or longer, and the factory setting is live play rather than auto record.'

51

'That matches what she told us then,' says Moira.

'Exactly,' says Rick. 'They said you could get around the issue by purchasing a separate battery pack to act as an emergency supply to the system in the event of a power outage, but we don't know if the Zieglers have that.'

'I'll add it on the list to follow up on,' says Philip, his voice unusually subdued.

'I've also asked my contact to do a search on Cody Ziegler's licence plate over the last forty-eight hours so we can try and get a fix on where he went, or the car went, after Olivia left their home yesterday, and also see if the vehicle has been driven anywhere more recently today.' Rick looks at Philip. 'I was thinking we could ask around the community watch patrollers and see if any of them have seen Cody in the past twenty-four hours?'

'Yes, yes, good idea,' says Philip. 'I'll set up a meeting.'

'Good thinking,' says Moira, nodding. 'So what's our plan? Wait for the intel from your law enforcement contact, Rick. Philip will set up the community watch meeting. And Lizzie, you're going to head over to the Ziegler house to see if forensics can turn up any unusual blood patches or splatter. I think either Rick or myself should tag along as we've met Olivia already – so she feels comfortable. Trust is a big deal for her.'

'I'm happy to head over there with you, Lizzie,' says Rick, thinking he'd like the opportunity to observe Olivia a little more. It's true that she seems genuinely upset and worried for her husband, but Rick's been in the game a long time and he knows better than to take everything at face value. He's just about to say this when his cell phone, which is sitting on the glass-topped patio table beside his iced tea, buzzes as a call comes in.

Beside him, Moira flinches. Her expression looks real fearful.

Glancing at her, Rick wonders why she's so jumpy all of a sudden. Usually Moira is the coolest of them all. She's got real grit.

Reaching forward, he picks up his cell and answers the call. 'This is Denver.'

All he can hear is sobbing.

'Hello?' says Rick. He looks at the phone screen and recognises the number. 'Olivia, is that you?'

The sobbing continues. Then the woman on the other end of the line inhales sharply and says tearfully, 'They've got him.'

10

MOIRA

The situation has changed. A new scenario is in play. Moira knows she has to concentrate, she can't allow her thoughts to wander; she has to put the phone message she received earlier out of her mind.

It's thirty minutes after Rick took Olivia Hamilton Ziegler's call. Since then, they've rushed to her home and are now gathered in the retired actor's kitchen. Olivia's eyes are watery and bloodshot, the skin around them red. She looks much older, and far more fragile, than just a few hours earlier – the reality of what's happening is taking its toll.

They've gathered around the island unit. Lizzie's CSI field kit is on the counter next to her, Philip has a small spiral-bound notebook in his hand, and Moira is watching Olivia. Every action and reaction she makes could be a clue towards what's going on here. Because in the world of policing there's the story that is told to you, and there's the story that people's behaviour, speech and the environment around them tells. And here, for Moira, there seems to be a disconnect between the two types of story. Moira's gut instinct is telling her things don't entirely ring true.

Once Rick has snapped on his nitrile gloves, Olivia passes him the envelope. Moira moves closer to him so that she can see what's inside. The envelope has Olivia Hamilton Ziegler's address typed on the front and is postmarked yesterday.

Slowly, Rick removes the contents – a single sheet of paper with a photo printed on it. In the picture, Cody Ziegler is sitting on a chair in what appears to be a basement or garage. The lighting is poor but it's clear that he's bound to the chair with duct tape. There's more tape across his mouth and from the blood on his face it's obvious he's been beaten. Propped on his lap, with the front page facing the camera, is yesterday's newspaper.

Rick turns over the page. Moira reads the message typed on the back.

WE HAVE YOUR HUSBAND. AWAIT INSTRUCTIONS. NO COPS OR HE DIES.

'I called you as soon as I received it,' says Olivia, her voice thin and shaky. 'I didn't know what else to do. I can't believe this is happening. He's been kidnapped. They've taken him . . .'

'You did the right thing, ma'am,' says Rick, holding the paper out to Philip and Lizzie so they can see what's on it. 'We said earlier that we'd help you and we will.'

Olivia clasps her hands together and looks anxiously from Rick to Moira. 'So what do we do? They said no cops or they'll . . . they'll kill him. Oh Jeez. They can't hurt him. They can't . . . I just can't believe someone would do this. Cody never hurt anyone.'

Moira doesn't answer. Although Olivia had obviously suspected Cody had been taken, now her fears are confirmed it's clear she's having a really hard time holding herself together. Moira keeps her tone gentle as she asks, 'Do you know of anyone who'd want to hurt your husband?'

'No, I . . .' Olivia lets out a sob. She shakes her head vigorously. 'This can't be happening . . . it can't. Everyone loves Cody.

Whenever I pop by, his team at the office always tell me he's the best boss they've ever had, and he does so much for charity – he's always running marathons for pet welfare, or hosting a fundraiser for the local children's hospital. He's one of those people you just can't help but like, you know? I can't think of anyone . . .' She gestures to the picture in Rick's hand. 'Who would do this?'

'I know this is hard,' says Rick, his voice kind, sympathetic. 'But if there's anything, no matter how small or trivial it might seem, it could help us.'

Olivia nods. She bites her lip, staying silent. But Moira notices as she starts twisting her wedding band around her finger, slow at first and then faster. It's a new behaviour, not something she's seen Olivia do previously.

Reaching out, Moira puts her hand on Olivia's arm. 'Olivia, what is it?'

Olivia flinches. She looks towards Moira, her expression sheepish. 'I'm sorry, but I . . . haven't been entirely honest with you.' She turns to Rick. 'There *is* something that might be relevant. Cody didn't tell me much, but I knew he was worried even though he told me not to be.'

'What was it?' says Rick.

'There was a problem, with the business. In the last few months, he's been working longer and longer hours. Every night after dinner he'd lock himself in his study and work into the early hours.'

'Do you know what he was working on?' says Moira.

'Whenever I asked him what was going on he'd tell me that he had it under control and he didn't want to worry me.' Olivia pinches the bridge of her nose with her thumb and forefinger. 'Let me think . . .'

Moira glances at Rick. She knows he'll be thinking the same as her – that this information is a game changer. Whatever the issues with Cody's business were, they could very likely be connected to his disappearance.

She looks at Philip and Lizzie. Philip is head down, taking notes. Sitting beside him, Lizzie is listening closely but doesn't ask any questions. Both of them look tense, and Philip doesn't have his usual air of pompousness. Moira's glad they're leaving her and Rick to lead the discussion with Olivia as they've already built up some rapport and trust with her. If all four of them were asking questions, it would feel too much like an interrogation. But still, she wonders what's happened between the couple.

'Did you see any papers he was working on?' asks Rick, jogging Olivia from her thoughts.

'No, I'm sorry, I didn't,' says Olivia, twisting her wedding band around her finger again. 'But I know there were letters sent here, to the house, that upset him. I walked into the kitchen a couple of weeks back and he was opening one. When he pulled it from the envelope and read it, the blood seemed to drain clear from his face.'

'Did you ask him what it was?' says Moira, trying to push thoughts of the text message she'd received earlier from her mind – the message that had had a similar impact on her as the one Cody had received had on him.

Olivia nods. 'I asked what the matter was, but he just shook his head and hurried off to his study. I didn't see him for the rest of the day.'

Moira glances at Rick. The letters have to be connected. She can tell by the expression on his face that he's thinking the same. Looking back at Olivia, she asks, 'You said there was more than one letter? Do you remember when they arrived and how many?'

'Two or three, I think,' says Olivia, frowning. 'Two for sure. I recognised the envelope in the mail pile, after seeing his reaction that first time. The envelope was a deeper cream colour than a usual envelope, and the print a touch duller.'

Moira nods, forcing herself to focus hard on Olivia and Cody's situation. She files the information from Olivia in her mind; if the abductors are using a rare or unusual brand of stationery, it could be helpful. She glances towards the envelope on the kitchen counter, and the sheet of paper in Rick's gloved hand.

'How did the envelope and type compare to the one you received today?'

Olivia swallows hard. Her eyes become more watery. 'I think they're the same.'

11

LIZZIE

She's alone in Olivia Hamilton Ziegler's kitchen. To gather intelligence faster they've made the decision to split up, each following a different line of enquiry. She and Rick have stayed at Olivia's, Rick to search Cody's study for the letters and Lizzie to use her CSI field kit on the envelope and picture received by Olivia this morning. Moira is taking a trip to Cody's office on the outskirts of Orlando, and Philip is holding a special meeting of the Ocean Mist community patrollers.

On the countertop in front of her is the envelope and picture received by Olivia in this morning's post. Lizzie releases the clips either side of her CSI field kit case and opens the lid. Inside, neat and orderly, is her equipment. She needs to dust both items for fingerprints and, if there's opportunity, she'll also try to get a saliva swab, although that's a long shot as the envelope, from first glance, looks to be self-seal.

She'll need more light to work if she's going to get things done properly. Standing, she heads over to the row of light switches on the far wall and puts the overhead recessed ceiling lights on. Turning, she's about to return to the kitchen island when her gaze stops on the double fridge and the hundreds of magnets stuck on it – each from a different country or city across the world. She steps closer, looking at the magnets: an icy volcano from Iceland, a clog and tulip from Holland, the Sydney Opera House from Australia, and a multicoloured mask from New Orleans.

Lizzie feels a pang of regret. She'd always wanted to travel. She loves discovering new places and experiencing different cultures, but once they'd moved here to Florida Philip hadn't wanted to take any trips. They'd done a few short cruises around the Caribbean, but that's it, nothing further afield. A couple of years ago she'd tried to persuade him it'd be fun to visit their youngest daughter, Jennifer, out in Australia, but he'd said the flight was too long. After a while she'd given up mentioning it.

She shakes her head, annoyed with herself for letting him influence her. After what he's done, she's not having it for a moment more. Once they've helped Olivia Hamilton Ziegler get her husband back, she's going to book a trip to Australia to see Jennifer. And she's going to be very happy travelling there alone.

Her mind made up, Lizzie returns to the kitchen island and jumps back on to the stool. She turns her attention to her CSI field kit. One by one, she lifts the pieces of kit she'll need from the case and sets them down on the countertop: two iodine capsules with pre-connected plastic tubing, some iodine enhancer, a couple of clear plastic zip bags, a credit-card-sized magnifying glass, a marker pen, and a pair of nitrile gloves. It's been ten years since she was a full-time CSI but the preparation process helps her centre herself, the familiarity returning through muscle memory and repetition.

After putting on the nitrile gloves, she takes a breath and picks up the iodine capsule and plastic tubing. Pressing hard on the capsule to activate the iodine crystals, she clenches her fist around the capsule so that her body heat warms the iodine inside. She'd use different chemicals if she was in a lab, but out in the field she's always found iodine to be safest and most effective.

Once the iodine has had time to warm up, she blows into the short tubing mouthpiece on one side of the capsule, blowing the iodine fumes down the longer open-ended section of tubing on the other side of the capsule and on to the picture. As she blows, she sees the pale-yellow stain of the iodine spread across the paper, but she doesn't see what she's looking for. Undeterred, she continues blowing until she's covered the whole surface of the paper with the fumes. Lifting the paper up to the light, she inspects it closely, even though she's pretty sure of the situation.

She exhales hard, disappointed. There are no fingerprints on the paper. Whoever sent the picture of Cody must have been wearing gloves when they handled it.

Taking the second iodine capsule, Lizzie repeats the process with the envelope. This time, as she blows the fumes across the envelope, darker patches appear. These are fingerprints – the ridges clearly visible in the iodine. The problem here is the opposite of that with the paper. On the envelope there are too many fingerprints. Still, they could be useful, so she needs to act fast to preserve them.

One of the limitations with using iodine is that the prints will start to disappear again as the fuming dissipates. To stop this she needs to fully develop the prints, and then use the iodine enhancer.

Working quickly, Lizzie doses the envelope a second time with the iodine fumes and then activates the iodine enhancer and gently rubs the swab of enhancer liquid across each of the prints on the envelope. The enhancer fixes the iodine on the prints, stopping them disappearing as the fumes wear off, so she can compare them later against other fingerprints.

There are nine full prints and four partials. Lizzie doesn't hold out much hope of finding who they belong to, though. Having been through the mail, the envelope will have been handled by numerous people who are unconnected to its contents.

Lizzie thinks about her next move. If Rick is able to find the letter Olivia told them Cody received a few weeks ago, Lizzie can repeat the process on that and then assess the prints to identify duplicates. She also needs to take Olivia's prints so she can exclude her.

She flinches as she hears a knock on the back door. She ignores it. After all, this isn't her house and it's potentially a crime scene. She can't go letting in random people.

After about a half minute there's another knock, followed by the door being opened a few inches, and a man's voice calls out, 'Hi? Mrs Hamilton Ziegler?'

Sliding off her stool, Lizzie hurries to the back door. 'Who is this?'

'Miss Olivia?'

Lizzie opens the door wider to reveal a well-built, round-faced man wearing a Miami Dolphins ball cap, a black vest and khaki cargo shorts. He's holding a bucket filled with flowering plants in one hand, and a shovel in the other.

She smiles. 'Hello. I'm . . . I'm a friend of Olivia's.'

'Alrighty then, friend of Miss Olivia's,' says the man, smiling. He looks past Lizzie into the kitchen. 'Is Miss Olivia about? I need to speak with her or Mr Cody.'

Lizzie doesn't know if Olivia has told this man about Cody being missing so it's safer to say nothing. She shakes her head. 'No, sorry.'

The man's smile slips and he frowns. 'Is that right? Didn't I see her car parked out—'

'She's here, but she's not available. She has a visitor.' Lizzie wonders if she should ask to take the man's fingerprints, but decides against it. If he's the gardener, chances are he doesn't handle the mail at all. She'll speak to Olivia first.

'Ah alrighty then, no problem. Can you tell her I'll get started on the south border, but I'll need her input on the rock garden before I start moving stuff around?'

'I'll do that,' says Lizzie.

As the gardener heads off across the lawn, Lizzie closes the door and returns to her seat at the kitchen island. She looks down at the envelope on the countertop in front of her. She's done all she can to get it to reveal the fingerprints of the people who've handled it, but there's one more thing she can do.

A stationery brand name could be helpful. They should be able to cross-reference stores that sell the brand within the vicinity of where the envelope was posted, and they could visit those stores and see if the store assistants remember anyone purchasing the stationery within the time window they're looking at. It's a long shot, but it's something.

Picking up the magnifying glass, she inspects the envelope. She finds what she's looking for inside, below the crease of the flap. It's faint, but definitely there. A watermarked logo: *CALDARO*.

12

MOIRA

The drive takes Moira forty-three minutes. Cody Ziegler's office is situated on the outskirts of Orlando in a purpose-built business park. Turning off the highway, she pulls into a large car park that runs the length of the long beige-stucco building with dark-tinted windows. The area around the building is highly manicured, with miniature hedges and ornamental flower planting.

As she drives closer, Moira sees that the building is divided into office units. Glancing down at the Post-it note on the dashboard, she reads the address again – Unit 14, Woodland Springs Business Campus – and checks the numbers on the front of the building. Indicating left, she makes the turn and drives along the side of the building, looking for Unit 14. As she counts off the units, she realises Cody Ziegler's office is right at the end. Finding a space nearby, she parks.

Moira doesn't get out straight away. Instead, she pulls her phone from her pocket and checks the screen, feeling her heart rate accelerating as she does. But it's okay. There are no new messages or calls from the unknown number. There's been nothing since they sent the message a couple of hours ago telling her that they know who she is. But the lack of further contact doesn't mean that she's not in trouble, she knows that.

Taking a breath, Moira tries to get herself focused back on the case. She needs to decide what to do about the unknown caller, but she needs more information from them – to know for sure who they are, and what their intentions are – before she makes the decision on whether she's going to have to run again. Until then, she's got a job to do.

Opening the car door, Moira steps out into the afternoon heat. The sun is high overhead and the humidity makes the air taste damp on her tongue and heavy in her lungs. Walking quickly, she heads towards Unit 14.

The offices are ultra-modern. There's dark wooden flooring paired with white walls, and a white curved reception desk with DVIZION emblazoned in foot-high orange lettering across it. Behind the desk, an orange, blue and green canvas of modern art squiggles dominates the wall. Over on Moira's left is a cluster of bright green armchairs with white side tables and matching reading lamps, and beyond them is a corridor leading to what looks like a row of glass-walled meeting rooms. At first glance, the place seems deserted.

Moira loiters by the reception desk. Peering over the raised top, she sees there's an Apple laptop, a notepad and a half-drunk green smoothie on the counter below. She looks around for a bell to ring, but can't see anything, and so she walks past the armchairs and along the corridor.

In the glass-walled meeting room furthest from the entrance, she spots five people standing around a large whiteboard as a colleague draws out some kind of flow chart. Their backs are to her, and they don't turn around as she walks past, so Moira pushes open the door at the end of the corridor and finds herself in a large open-plan space that seems to be divided into different zones. There's a kitchen area with turquoise cabinets and a white sparkly countertop, an orange-walled cubby with a high bar-type table and six blue stools, and a lounging space with orange, green and blue beanbags and whiteboard walls with writing all over them. Over on the far side of the space, there are three doors, each with a large orange nameplate. Squinting, Moira reads them: *Cody Ziegler, Donna Neale, Bradley R George.*

Donna Neale: she recognises the name. Olivia had mentioned that Donna Neale is Cody's personal assistant and also the person who she'd spoken to earlier. She's the one who'd told her Cody hadn't arrived yesterday and that his Lexus wasn't in the car park.

Moira waits for someone to ask her who she is and what she's doing here. Unlike the entrance, this space has people in it, but none of them come over to her, or even glance in her direction. It seems odd; surely they'd be aware of a stranger in their midst? But the people sitting at the high bar desk stay focused on their laptop screens, and the group lounging on the beanbags continue their conversation. She's just about to walk over to the beanbag group when a young woman with her brown hair slicked back into a high ponytail and a stressed expression on her face scurries out of the kitchen area and almost crashes into her.

'Whoa,' says Moira, stepping back to avoid getting slammed in the stomach by the tray the woman's carrying. Coffee slops over the edge of the mugs on the tray, spilling on to the woman's short black dress.

'Sorry, I didn't . . .' The stressed-looking woman stops mid-sentence and cocks her head to one side. 'Excuse me, but who the hell are you?'

Moira gestures back towards the corridor. 'There was no one on reception so I—'

'You can't be back here.' The young woman looks even more stressed. Her face flushes red. 'It's office policy, no visitors in the inner sanctum. Come with me.'

'Okay, no problem.' Moira follows the woman across the open-plan space and out into the corridor. Given how stressed she seems, there's no point asking her any questions. Moira figures she'll wait until the woman has delivered her coffees and then try to get her to talk.

'Take a seat over there,' says the woman, nodding towards the reception armchairs as she stops beside the glass-walled meeting room, where the people are still gathered around their whiteboard. 'I'll be with you in a moment.'

Moira does as she asks. She picks an armchair facing the corridor and meeting rooms and sits down. A couple of minutes pass, and the woman doesn't reappear. Stifling a sigh, Moira checks her phone. There are no new messages from the unknown number. Right now she's not sure if that's a good or bad thing, but she's pretty sure there'll be another message soon. Her stomach swirls with nerves at the thought and she swallows hard.

Hearing the click of a door shutting, Moira looks up and sees the woman has left the tray of coffee in the meeting room and is now walking along the corridor towards her. She shoves her phone back into her pocket and gets her head back in the game.

The woman stops in front of her. 'So how can I help you?'

'Who's Bradley George?' says Moira, remembering the names she'd seen on the plates attached to the three closed office doors.

'Mr George is our Vice President, but he isn't in the office today – he's taking a well-earned vacation day.'

'Okay, no problem,' says Moira, even though the woman's manner is starting to grate on her. 'I'd like to speak to Donna Neale then.'

'Mr Ziegler's personal assistant?' From the woman's tone Moira guesses there's more than a little rivalry between the two women, at least from this one's perspective. 'What's your reason for calling on her?'

Moira ignores the question. 'Can you let her know I'm here and would like to speak with her?'

The woman raises her eyebrows. Shrugs. 'Well, I guess. I'll buzz her for you.'

As the woman goes around to the far side of the reception desk and makes the call, Moira fights the urge to check her mobile phone again. *It's ridiculous*, she thinks, clenching her hands together. She can't keep checking the damn thing. She must concentrate on the case.

A moment later the door at the far end of the corridor opens and a tall woman with bobbed black hair, a grey trouser suit with a green blouse, and a kind face walks towards her.

Moira stands as the woman approaches.

'I'm Donna Neale. I hear you'd like to speak with me,' says the woman. She glances towards the young woman sitting behind the reception desk. 'Unfortunately, I didn't catch your name or what it's regarding?'

'I'm Moira Flynn. I'm here on behalf of Olivia Hamilton Ziegler. I understand you spoke with her this morning.'

Donna's body language stiffens. Her expression turns to one of concern. 'Yes I did. Please come through to my office, it's a little more . . .' She glances towards the receptionist, who's pretending not to eavesdrop. 'Private.'

'What about the "no visitors in the inner sanctum" rule?' says Moira as they start walking along the corridor towards the door into the main office space. 'Your receptionist said visitors were prohibited from going through the double doors.'

'That girl,' says Donna, giving her a tight smile. 'Please don't believe a word that Ashley says.'

Donna's office is small and neat. There's a big window with a view of the car park, a modern wooden desk and a row of filing cabinets.

'This is so dreadful. I mean, I have no idea where Cody is. When Olivia called this morning and said she hadn't seen him since yesterday morning, I was simply beside myself. He's such a great man, I don't know where he would have gone, it would be just so awful if he . . .' She takes a breath.

Moira seizes the opportunity to get a word in. 'I understand you told Olivia earlier that Cody hadn't come into the office yesterday or today?'

Donna swallows hard. Nods. 'That's right. I wanted to be helpful. I wanted to do whatever I can to help Cody. Anything.'

Moira wonders how much Donna knows about the situation. Olivia didn't say how much she'd told Cody's PA, and Moira doesn't want to reveal anything that Olivia hadn't shared, so she says, 'Olivia asked myself and my colleagues to look into Cody's whereabouts. She's worried that him not returning home, or attending here at the office, is out of character.'

Donna nods vigorously. 'It is, it really is. I'm so worried.' She grasps Moira's hands. 'Like I said, I'll do anything to help.'

Moira gives Donna's hands a brief squeeze then lets go and takes a step back. The woman is clearly in a bit of a state about her missing boss. 'Olivia said you'd checked whether Cody's car was here?'

'Yes, that's right.' Donna gestures to an empty parking space on the corner of the building. 'He always parks right in that spot, regular as clockwork. And he always shows if he's got a meeting booked. He's very punctual, Cody, and very reliable.'

'Did he have any meetings arranged for yesterday?' asks Moira, knowing Olivia had told them he had one in the morning, but wanting to see if that matches with his PA's perspective.

'He sure did.' Donna taps her keyboard and the computer screen illuminates. She brings up a diary screen. 'This is yesterday's schedule. He had a meeting here in the office at 11.30 a.m. with BrightStar Media, then a lunch appointment at Brannigan's Steak House with Don Berkley and Richie Yarwood about the Skyline project, followed by an afternoon of spec pitches over at Melrose Talent.'

As Moira looks up from the screen, she notices there's a connecting door into the office on the left. Gesturing towards it, she says, 'Is that Cody's office through there?'

'Yes, when we were both in we'd usually leave the door open unless there was a meeting.'

Moira notes Donna's use of the past tense. She tilts her head to the side. 'Usually?'

Donna looks down, upset. 'More recently, Cody kept the door closed. He seemed . . . distracted and he was working such long hours. I worried, you know, that I'd done something to upset him, but when I mentioned it he said no it was just that he had a lot on but still . . .' She sniffs loudly. 'I worried, you know?'

'Do you have a key for the door?' says Moira, noting that Cody's behaviour of working longer and being less social with Olivia seems to have played out here at the office and with his PA too.

'I do, but Cody doesn't like people going into his office without him being present.'

Moira puts her hand on Donna's arm and gives it a reassuring squeeze. 'I think under the circumstances it'd be okay, don't you think?'

Donna holds her gaze for a long moment, before nodding. 'I reckon it'll be okay.'

'Great. So first it would be useful to talk to the staff here and find out when they last saw Cody. I'd also like to speak with Bradley George, your Vice President – I'm guessing he and Cody worked closely together as President and Vice President of the company. And then I'd like to take a look inside Cody's office.'

'I can gather everyone together for you, no problem, but Brad, well . . .' Donna pulls a face. 'He's on a vacation day today and last I heard he was heading off to the beach with his family. So you'll have to wait until tomorrow to speak with him.'

'You don't like him?' says Moira, thinking that, given Donna's reaction to his name, she definitely wants to speak to Bradley – or Brad, as he seems to be known – as soon as he's back.

'He's a good man, don't get me wrong, but he's not a creative person. He doesn't have the drive or dynamism of Cody. He's great at the numbers, though, and handles all the financial and corporate aspects, which is why he's a good number two for Cody.' Donna looks wistful. 'You see, Cody is a genius. He's a great producer, and such a visionary.'

Moira notes the PA's expression. It could be hero worship, a crush, or there could be more substance to it, like an affair. 'Did Cody have any problems with staff or clients? Any fallings-out?'

'No, like I said, everyone loves him and . . .' Donna frowns, thinking. 'Actually, now you come to mention it, there was this one production company he had an issue with.' She scrolls back through the diary on the computer screen. 'Ah yes, here it is. In late November, Marty Hannier, the CEO of Oak Whistle Productions, approached Cody. He presented a pitch for investing in a movie called *Breakout*. Well, Cody didn't think the script was up to much, and said the story had been done to death already. He also thought the figures seemed tight for the type of movie, even though Brad actually said he thought they were okay. Cody wasn't convinced, so he passed on the opportunity.'

'And it didn't go down well?' says Moira.

'Not one bit. Oak Whistle Productions declared bankruptcy a few weeks later, and Marty Hannier told any media who'd listen that it was Cody Ziegler who'd hammered the final nail into their financial coffin.'

Pulling out her phone, Moira taps out a few notes about Marty Hannier and Oak Whistle Productions – the incident definitely sounds like something to look into further. 'Thanks, that's really useful. I'd like to talk to the staff now.'

Donna lowers her voice. 'You don't think any of them have something to do with Cody going missing, do you?'

'I hope not,' says Moira. 'But at this stage we can't rule anything out.'

'I . . . okay. I understand, of course.' Donna bites her lip. She looks concerned. 'I'll go gather the troops for you right now.'

13

RICK

In an abduction case, the longer the clock ticks, the more likely things are to end badly. Leaving Lizzie in the kitchen to work her CSI magic, Rick has followed Olivia back along the hallway to her husband's minimalist study. As they step inside, Rick clears his throat, remembering the question he wanted to ask her about the CCTV system.

'Do you know if you bought the separate battery pack when you bought your CCTV and alarm system?'

'I'm sorry, I haven't a clue,' says Olivia. 'Cody handled all that.'

'Okay, no problem,' says Rick, deciding he'll google what the battery add-on looks like and how it attaches to the system so he can check it for himself.

He watches Olivia walk into the room in front of him. She's still as poised as she was earlier this morning, but she seems more vulnerable now. She's clearly real shaken up by the picture the abductors sent of her husband, but what Rick just doesn't get is why she wasn't fully honest with them when she called them over to see her first thing. The stuff about the letters Cody had been receiving these past few weeks, the business troubles and the increasingly long working days are important to the picture they're building of Cody. Rick's pretty damn sure they're key to working out who has taken him. He hopes that Olivia's told them everything now. And he hopes she's telling the truth. He doesn't want any more surprises.

As they stop just inside the study, he glances at Olivia and says, 'Do you know where the letters are?'

She shakes her head. 'I never saw where he put them. I don't come in here usually.'

Rick walks across the spotlessly clean, clutter-free room to the glass-topped desk in the middle of the study. There are no drawers, or places to hide anything, in the body of the desk. Bending down, he pushes the grey mesh chair out of the way and runs his fingers over the desk legs, feeling for concealed compartments. He finds nothing.

Straightening up, Rick looks across at Olivia, who's still standing in the doorway. 'Is there a trash can around here someplace? Or any closets or cabinets that your husband keeps locked?'

'I'm sorry, I don't know.'

'No problem, I'll check.'

The wall to his right is made up of bifold glass doors that lead out on to the neatly mown lawn and swimming pool beyond. There's a sturdy-looking man in a Miami Dolphins ball cap digging in one of the flowerbeds, a bucket of red flowering plants on the lawn beside him.

'Who's that?' asks Rick, gesturing out through the doors.

Olivia takes a few steps closer and squints towards the garden. 'Oh, that's just our gardener, Earl.'

Rick nods and continues his scan of the room. On the back wall there's a row of floor-to-ceiling closet doors from some built-ins. Rick moves over to them, opening each in turn. They all open easily; nothing is locked. He checks through the contents. One contains business journals and books, displayed in alphabetical order.

The next closet holds stationery and postage packets, but all are new; none are the used envelopes Olivia described Cody receiving recently. The third holds box files. From the labels on the side of the files – *The Three Lives of Alice Montague*, *LAST*, *Autumn Love Story*, *Burning Dust in November* – Rick assumes these hold the details of the independent movie projects that Cody's firm has invested in and worked with over the years.

He takes a few off the shelves at random, opens up the file and flicks through the contents. They contain shooting plans, meeting notes, decision logs, risk registers and budget reports. Nothing appears out of place.

'Did you find anything?' says Olivia, with hope in her voice.

'No, ma'am, not as yet.'

Rick puts the box files back where they came from. There must be forty files here at least. His gut tells him he's not going to find what he's looking for in them, but if the rest of this search is unfruitful he'll revisit these files and search through every piece of paper in every one of them, just to be sure.

Moving on from the closets, he scans the remaining two walls. Both have white-painted wainscoting to waist height, with the plastered wall above painted the same colour as the wood. On the left wall, there's a vast fireplace with a black glossy mantel contrasting against the stark white of the wall, and two huge modern art paintings. Reaching up, he lifts the large canvases off the wall, checking for a hidden cubbyhole or storage locker behind each. But there's nothing.

He moves over to the last wall. Other than the doorway leading out to the hall, and an oversized clock on the top section of the wall, there's nothing here.

This can't be right, thinks Rick. There has to be a place where Cody Ziegler would lock away important business papers and other sensitive material, like the letters Olivia had witnessed him receiving recently.

Starting from the left, he moves methodically along the wall, knocking on the plasterwork and listening for changes in how the wall sounds that could suggest a hollow compartment.

There's no change in sound. It doesn't make sense. Where is Cody Ziegler hiding the threatening letters he received? They have to be here someplace.

Stooping down and moving back in the opposite direction, Rick presses his hands against the painted wood wainscoting, feeling for any variations in the panels. Again, he finds nothing out of the ordinary.

He frowns. Thinking. The letters have to be here somewhere.

He looks down, and that's when he notices it. There's a subtle difference in the creasing in one corner of the large area rug covering the centre of the room. Moving across to it, he bends down to lift the corner of the rug and peels it back a few feet.

Olivia steps closer. Surprise in her voice. 'Is that . . . ?'

'Sure looks like it.' Kneeling down, Rick pulls a handle to open the hatch. The door, clad in wooden boards that match the rest of the flooring, swings up to reveal a hidden floor compartment. The secret space is a floor safe. He looks up at Olivia. 'You know about this?'

'We have a safe in the panic room, that's where all our valuables are,' says Olivia, shaking her head. 'I thought it was the only one.'

Her answer seems honest enough but then she's an actress, and he knows she's a good one. 'Any idea of the combination?'

'I don't . . .' She stops, thinking. 'Try 08-22. That's our wedding anniversary.'

Nodding, Rick presses the buttons on the keypad. It's got to be worth a shot. As he presses UNLOCK there's a loud clunk and the door releases. Opening it fully, Rick takes a look inside the safe. There's a small stack of papers, and on top of the bundle are some dark cream envelopes.

Rick turns again to look at Olivia. As he does, movement outside the bifold doors catches his eye. He looks towards it and sees Earl the gardener walking away from the patio. He's not carrying anything, and there's something different to the man's posture now compared to when Rick saw him earlier. Rick frowns. Was the gardener watching them?

'Are you okay?' asks Olivia.

Rick turns back towards her. Nods. 'Yes, I'm fine. Are you happy for me to take these papers out?'

'Sure,' says Olivia. She bites her lip.

Reaching inside, Rick lifts out the contents of the safe. With Olivia beside him, he carries the stack across to Cody's desk. 'Okay then, let's see what we have here.'

The papers all seem to be legal documents – contracts, amendments and addendums. On top are three cream envelopes, each typed and addressed to Cody Ziegler at his home address. Rick glances at Olivia. 'Do these look familiar?'

Olivia nods. 'They all look like the envelope I saw him opening a few weeks ago.'

'Okay. Then let's take a look at what's inside.' Pulling a pair of nitrile gloves from his pocket, Rick snaps them on and then picks up the envelope on the top of the stack. 'You ready?'

Olivia swallows hard. Clasps her hands together, twisting her wedding band around her finger. 'Yes, do it.'

Rick opens the envelope and takes out the paper inside. It's a letter, and is typed rather than handwritten. His pulse accelerates as he reads. His mouth goes dry. 'What the hell is . . . ?'

Olivia moves closer so she can read the letter. She inhales quickly. Lets out a sob.

Rick rereads the letter. Murmurs under his breath, 'Oh Jeez.'

Whoever sent this has made one thing explicitly clear.

Cody Ziegler is in extreme danger.

14

MOIRA

Out in the open-plan area, Donna claps her hands together, her voice wavering slightly as she speaks. 'Gather round, folks. There's some . . . Cody is . . .' She clears her throat. 'I need you all to meet someone.'

Her colleagues slowly stop what they're doing, get up from the beanbags and the stools at the high bar desk and congregate in front of Donna. Ashley the receptionist comes through from the front, presumably having been called by one of her co-workers, and the group who were in the meeting room earlier follow behind her. As Cody's PA, Donna seems to have a big influence on what happens here.

Moira looks around the ensemble. There are sixteen of them – nine men and seven women. Aside from Donna, most of them appear to be under thirty. Just looking at them makes Moira feel old.

Donna gestures towards her. 'This is Moira Flynn. She's here on behalf of Cody's wife and she needs to speak with us all.'

Moira nods her thanks to Donna and turns to address the group. She's no stranger to briefing large groups of people from back in her DCI days. She keeps her tone friendly but professional as she explains the situation.

'Cody Ziegler is believed missing. I'm an investigator working on behalf of Mrs Hamilton Ziegler, and I'm trying to establish a timeline of his movements before his disappearance.' She pauses, letting the people gathered around her process the information. 'Our last sighting of him was yesterday morning around nine thirty at his home. I need to know if any of you had contact with him before or after that.'

There are murmurs between the co-workers and expressions of surprise on some of their faces. Others are shaking their heads, looking unconvinced.

'What do you mean, he's believed missing?' says a flame-haired woman dressed in a green trouser suit. 'I was just emailing with him yesterday.'

'Why would he go off somewhere? He has important meetings today, and he never misses meetings,' says a tall willowy-looking guy with a receding hairline. 'Makes no sense to me.'

There are nods from his colleagues. Moira scans the group, reading the mood. Their expressions suggest a mix of emotions are in play, ranging from shock to suspicion. In her experience, that's pretty normal in these types of circumstances.

'He's a great boss. Super reliable,' says a curvy blonde. 'Maybe he just got double booked.'

'If he did, it wasn't in his diary,' says Donna, her tone defensive.

'Maybe it was a personal thing,' says the blonde, flicking her hair behind her shoulders. 'It could have been something he kept private.'

The guy in a check shirt and jeans standing beside her is nodding. 'Yeah, surely it's some kind of misunderstanding.'

'And it might be,' says Moira, injecting the firmness she used to use in her team meetings at the Met Police into her voice. 'But so far he's been missing for over twenty-four hours, his phone is switched off, and his car isn't at his house or here at the office. And therefore, as a precaution, I'm looking into the situation for Mrs Hamilton Ziegler. Because if he isn't okay, and if something bad has happened to him, it's better that we start the search now rather than delaying further. I'm sure, as you've all said he's such a great boss, that you'll be keen to help.'

There are more murmurs from the group and more nodding than before. She has their attention now. No one wants to look like they aren't willing to help the boss if he's in trouble.

'So, as I said before, it would be helpful for me to know when you last saw Cody Ziegler,' says Moira. 'Especially if you saw or spoke with him anytime after nine thirty yesterday morning.'

'The last time I saw Cody was when I left the office on Tuesday evening,' says Donna. 'It was a little after 8 p.m. He was in a meeting with Brad and Tim.'

A blond guy wearing a pale blue shirt, striped tie and black suit trousers raises his hand. 'I'm Tim. Tim Samson. We were doing our weekly progress update meeting. It finished just before 9 p.m. Brad left straight afterwards, Cody must have left about a half hour later. I stayed here until ten, writing up some actions. I was the last person to leave and I locked up and switched on the alarm.'

'Great, thanks,' says Moira. 'Anyone have contact with Cody between nine thirty Tuesday and now?'

A nervous-looking woman with long brown hair and a blue-patterned shift dress clears her throat. 'I didn't *see* him, but I spoke to him on a conference call yesterday morning from eight until around nine fifteen. Fernando, Brad and me – I'm Jenna – were on the call. We were discussing the Skyline project, briefing Cody on the budget and project milestone situation as he was due to have lunch with the guys from the production company.'

'Was there a problem with it?' says Moira.

'No, totally the opposite, they're under budget and ahead of schedule.'

An attractive-looking guy with unruly black hair and a well-cut suit nods. 'Fernando – I was on the call too – and I second that, was a good meeting. Cody seemed in good spirits.'

Moira makes a note in her phone. 'Did Cody say what he was going to do after the meeting ended?'

'Yes,' says the brown-haired woman. 'He said he was going to finish up a couple of emails and head into the office.'

'Said he'd be in by eleven latest,' says Fernando.

So he hadn't intended to miss his eleven thirty appointment, thinks Moira. Or if he had intended to, he wasn't letting on to anyone around him.

'That's really helpful, thank you.' She glances at Donna, and then looks back at the wider group. 'That's all for now, but if any of you think of anything that could be useful, I'll leave my contact details with Donna and feel free to give me a call.'

There are nods and okays from the group as they go back to their work. Moira can see some of them are worried about their boss, but most seem to think it's a misunderstanding or he's just running late – the fact that Cody is so well liked making it seem impossible in their minds that he could have been in an accident or worse. Moira wishes she could have told them he's been abducted and is being held against his will, but she can't because for all she knows there could be someone here in the office right now who had something to do with it. In this situation, everyone is a suspect until proven otherwise.

'Shall I show you Cody's office now?' asks Donna.

'That'd be great,' says Moira, following Cody's PA across the open-plan space and into her office.

She watches as Donna removes a long chain from around her neck and uses the key hanging from it to unlock the connecting door between her office and Cody's. It strikes Moira as rather odd that a personal assistant would keep an office key on a chain around her neck, but then if, as she'd previously wondered, there was something more between Donna and Cody, perhaps it would make a little more sense.

'Please come through,' says Donna, beckoning Moira through the connecting door.

Her first impression is that the office here is as neat and clutter-free as Cody's study at the home he shares with Olivia. The waste bin in the corner is empty, and there are no obviously locked cabinets – everything is displayed on open shelving, and the large white desk against the back wall doesn't have any drawers beneath it. The only thing on the desk is a docking station for a laptop.

Glancing over at Donna, Moira asks, 'Does Cody have a safe or lockable files?'

'No, not that I'm aware of,' says Donna. 'Anything super confidential he'd take home with him in his briefcase.'

'What sort of briefcase?'

'Chocolate brown, and a bit battered, vintage Gaultier, I think.'

Moira nods. She doesn't remember seeing a briefcase in Cody's study earlier this morning, but maybe Rick will find it when he's doing a more thorough search. 'Okay, thanks. I think I've seen enough.'

As Donna escorts her out of Cody's office and back through the open-plan space, Moira gets the distinct feeling that the woman is relieved she's leaving. She wonders what that's about. Donna's been helpful, and Moira hasn't detected her lying or being obstructive. But nonetheless, something feels slightly off.

'Thanks for your help,' says Moira, handing Donna a Post-it note with her mobile number written on it. 'I'll be in touch if I need to ask you any further questions, and you can call me anytime if you think of anything that could be important.'

Donna takes the Post-it and nods. 'Of course, that's no problem, anything to help Cody and Olivia. Obviously, anything.'

Moira holds her gaze a moment. Again, Donna seems genuine enough, but her smile looks slightly forced, and it doesn't reach all the way to her eyes. 'I appreciate that.'

'You will make sure he's okay, won't you?' says Donna, her lower lip quivering. 'He's very important to me. I couldn't bear it if something untoward were to have happened . . .'

'We're doing all we can,' says Moira, feeling a tad sorry for the woman. From Donna's behaviour, Moira's pretty sure she has a big crush on her boss even though she hasn't admitted it. Holding that secret is most likely the source of the tension Moira's picking up on.

Leaving the open-plan area through the door into the corridor, Moira heads back to reception. She spots Ashley sitting behind the desk, nods goodbye, and keeps walking towards the door.

Leaping up from behind the desk, Ashley hurries to block Moira's exit. 'I need to talk to you,' she says in a stage whisper.

Moira sidesteps her, hands up. 'You need to . . . ?'

'Quick, in here,' says Ashley, opening a door to the right of the reception desk and ushering Moira inside what seems to be a storeroom. Closing the door behind them, Ashley turns to face Moira. 'Look, you need to know the truth, for Cody's sake. Even if things might get a little heated. It's true we all think Cody's great, you know, especially Donna.' She gives a little shake of her head. 'And he's the best boss most of us have ever had, and that's the truth, but that doesn't mean the man's an angel, and it sure as shit doesn't mean this place suits everyone who works here, you know?'

Moira nods. Interested that Ashley's disinterest of earlier seems to be a thing of the past. There's passion and urgency in her voice now, rather than indifference.

'So listen, there was this one guy, Dirk Baldwin.' She shakes her head. 'And let's just say, things didn't work out so well.'

'What happened?' asks Moira, blinking as her eyes try to adjust to the gloomy, windowless storeroom.

'Well, at first things were okay. Dirk was learning the ropes and he messed up a couple of times, but when you're new that's okay, you need to learn and make sure you don't do it again, you know?'

'Sure.' Moira listens to Ashley but she also runs her gaze over the shelves in the storeroom. Her eyes have become accustomed to the low light and she's able to identify the different stationery supplies. Everything is in white – envelopes, paper, notebooks, compliment slips. She can't see anything in the same dark cream as the envelope used by the abductor.

'So Dirk didn't learn. He kept messing up. Project milestones went untracked, financial payments were made late or for the wrong amount. So he got fired.'

'And how did he react?'

Ashley lets out a long whistle. 'Real bad. He had to get escorted from the building by security, and then he slapped a lawsuit on Cody and Brad for wrongful dismissal and victimisation. He claimed he'd been the scapegoat for dodgy practices, and he'd turn up here and march up and down all day waving a placard and yelling.'

Moira jots down what Ashley's said into the Notes app on her phone. 'What sort of practices?'

Ashley shrugs. 'I don't know, but a week later the lawsuit got withdrawn. We didn't hear anything from Dirk after that. I guess he either got bored or got paid.'

Moira figures it's far more likely Cody and Brad paid Dirk Baldwin off. She makes a note of the key points along with a reminder to find out why the lawsuit was withdrawn. She looks back at Ashley. 'I'm going to need to talk to Brad as soon as possible.' Taking a notepad and pen from the shelves, Moira scribbles her mobile number on to the top sheet of paper and hands it to Ashley. 'Call me as soon as Brad George shows up here tomorrow.'

'Okay,' says Ashley, frowning. 'But I'd have thought you'd already have Cody's little lapdog primed to do that.'

'You mean Donna?'

'Yeah. Who else?' says Ashley with a laugh.

'Tell me more about Donna and Cody, what's going on there?'

Ashley rolls her eyes. 'Going on? Ha! There's nothing to tell, although she'd sure like there to be, obviously. She's been in love with him for years but all he wants from her is her organisation and scheduling skills. So, of course, she totally hates me.'

So Donna has a crush then, that's unrequited. According to Ashley, anyway. Moira remembers what Donna said earlier – not to believe a word Ashley says – and wonders if jealousy is the real cause of it or whether there's something more. She keeps her eyes on Ashley's, watching her expression closely as she asks her next question. 'Why does Donna hate you?'

Ashley gives her a smug little smile. 'Because Cody only wants me.'

Moira holds Ashley's gaze. 'You're dating him?'

Ashley bats her lashes. 'Maybe.'

'Maybe or actually?' says Moira, her tone no-nonsense firm. 'This is important, Ashley. If we're going to find Cody, we need to know everything about him. Anything, no matter how unrelated it might seem, could be important.'

Ashley wrinkles up her nose then looks away, her bravado fading. She gives a little shrug. 'He likes me, I know he does, but he hasn't made a move. We haven't *done* anything.' She meets Moira's gaze again and pouts. 'Well, not yet, anyways.'

15

PHILIP

Every seat around the table in the back room of the Roadhouse is full. From his position at the head of the table, Philip looks around the patrollers of the Ocean Mist community watch. They're an interesting bunch, from golf fanatics Rory and Melly Kempler to the feisty octogenarian Dorothy and her friend the serial worrier Maeve, through to all-year-round Christmas decoration maker Clint, and all kinds of people in between. Philip's proud that the community watch attracts people into its ranks from all walks of life. It's even more the case now, of course, after the patrollers helped solve the mystery of the young woman found dead in Manatee Park pool. Now it seems everyone in the community wants to be an amateur sleuth.

Tapping his spoon against the side of his water glass, Philip calls the meeting to order. 'Let's make a start then. Thank you all for coming at short notice. As I said in my message, I'm investigating a missing person case, and I need all your help.'

There are excited whispers around the group. Melly nudges Rory with her elbow. Maeve drops her knitting on to the table and says something to the grey-haired woman sitting beside her, who Philip doesn't recognise. The hippy-looking twin brothers Rick got to know during the course of the last investigation turn to each other and start talking.

It might be barely afternoon but the lighting inside the Roadhouse is turned down low, making it seem as if it's already evening. It's for ambience, apparently – that's what the buxom landlady told Philip the one time he asked her to turn up the dimmer switch. He supposes it's to fit in with the way the place has been designed; it's a faux-historic building, all weatherboard, exposed brickwork, small windows and heavy dark wood furniture. It gives the place an ancient feel, even though it's little more than ten years old. It's not to Philip's taste but Rick likes it and the landlady, Sandi, gives them discounted rates and the first drink on the house, so Philip supposes he can't really complain.

As he looks around the table, Philip realises he only recognises about half the people here. It's not surprising, he thinks; there have been a lot of new members in the past couple of months and with all these newbies it's hard to keep up to date. Unfortunately, it also means many of them have no experience of a serious investigation. He needs to instil some discipline. It's time to get these rookies whipped into shape.

'Now look, this isn't a game like your pickleball or golf, it's serious,' says Philip, looking sternly at the gathered patrollers over the top of his glasses. It's a look that he feels gives him an added air of authority. He doesn't want these amateurs getting carried away with the drama. They need to get into line, shipshape, and fast. 'A man is missing. His life could be in danger. We need to find him.'

All eyes are on him now, just as they should be. This is his room. His meeting.

'Who's missing?' asks Dorothy, her left hand clutching at the pearls around her neck. 'Tell us now, we can take it, and don't go trying to protect us from what's happening in our own community, we get enough of that from the management here. I've not seen a thing on the community news about anybody going missing. Is he from around here?'

There are nods from the other patrollers. More murmurs, now echoing Dorothy's question and expressing dissatisfaction with the way things are or aren't reported at The Homestead.

'Ain't that the truth,' says Clint, taking off his Dodgers baseball cap and rubbing his forehead. 'Ever since Miss Moira said she suspected bad news stories weren't being reported around here, I've noticed that the management only ever tell us good things. It's like they're editing out anything they don't think fits in with the happily-ever-after image of The Homestead.' He shakes his head. 'It just ain't right. We have a right to know stuff going on in the place we live.'

'Yes, yes. It isn't right, absolutely, and Moira, my colleague, has an ongoing investigation into the bad news blackout and will report back here as soon as she has her findings ready,' says Philip, trying to get their attention focused back on him. He takes a breath. 'As for the missing man, yes, he is one of our own. He's a resident living here at The Homestead.'

Maeve gasps. Grabbing her wool and work in progress from the table, she starts to knit furiously, while under her breath she's whispering over and over, 'One of us? Oh no.'

'Where does he live?' asks Melly. Her expression has remained unchanged, but that's due to the Botox. There's fear in her eyes as she speaks. 'Does he live in Ocean Mist?'

Philip shakes his head. 'His name is Cody Ziegler and he lives over in Paradise Palms district.'

'The husband of that movie star?' says Melly, her hands going to her chest. The fear in her eyes giving way to interest. 'How exciting. Don't they live up on Millionaires' Row?'

'It's not exciting,' says Philip, even more sternly than before. 'It's very serious. And yes, that is where they live.'

'Oh, for sure, it's real awful,' says Melly. But there's excitement in her eyes now too as she looks across the table at Krista and Wendy-Mae and raises her eyebrows a fraction as she whispers, 'Millionaires' Row.'

Wendy-Mae wraps her arms tighter around her handbag. It's only then Philip sees that she has a dog inside her bag – some sort of doodle or poo, no doubt. It's small, ginger and fluffy. He clenches his jaw. Dogs aren't allowed here in the back function room of the Roadhouse. The blasted thing had better not start yapping.

'So they're not from Ocean Mist? Well, at least it's something they didn't get taken from right in our backyard, so soon after that poor young woman getting murdered,' says Dorothy, still clutching at her pearls. 'But poor Olivia Hamilton Ziegler, she must be going through hell. I must reach out to her.'

Philip nods. 'It's a very difficult time as you can imagine. That's why she's asked for our help.'

'But if we help, will we become targets?' asks Maeve, the anxiety clear in her voice, and she continues to speed-knit.

'I don't think so,' says Philip. He can't give them details, but he needs to tell them enough to reassure them so that they're willing to help. Puffing out his chest, he uses the confident tone he always used at press conferences and giving evidence in court hearings. 'Early clues indicate that Mr Ziegler was very specifically targeted.'

Further along the table, the ever glamorous seventy-year-old ex-model Melissa Kouloa gives a worried gasp. 'Do you think they're targeting celebrities?'

Beside her, Melissa's husband, Larry, an ex-dancer, rubs her arm reassuringly.

Philip shakes his head. 'No, not celebrities more broadly, specifically Cody Ziegler.'

Mark and Jack, the hippy brothers, look relieved. The longer-haired of the two says, 'That's good to know, thanks, man. Still rough for Mrs Hamilton Ziegler.'

'Indeed,' says Philip. He looks around the table. There are a lot of anxious-looking patrollers, and they're all staring back at him. He needs to do more to get them onside and find out if they know anything important. Injecting a reassuring tone into his voice, Philip says, 'It's important we stay calm, yes? There's no reason to believe the people who abducted Mr Ziegler will take another victim. Especially if we find them before they can.'

At the other end of the table, Clint's nodding. 'So how can we help?'

'We're putting together a timeline of Mr Ziegler's movements before his abduction. We're especially interested in the last thirty-two hours.' Philip removes some photographs from his jacket pocket and passes them around the table. 'These are recent pictures of Mr Ziegler. I need to know if any of you have seen him in the past thirty-two or forty-eight hours. And if you have, I need to know where he was, and what he was doing.'

As the patrollers look at the pictures, Sandi the landlady and her staff refill their coffee cups and put fresh pitchers of juice at each end of the table. Luckily, Sandi doesn't take issue with Wendy-Mae's dog. Philip nods his thanks to them, and scans the room. Everyone's quiet now, concentrating. He's pleased he's managed to get them to knuckle down.

It feels good to be here, doing something of value, thinks Philip. There's no Lizzie tutting and looking at him disapprovingly. No feelings of not being good enough, of not making the grade in his wife's eyes. Of him wondering over and again why it's all gone wrong.

He tries to push away the negative thoughts. The case is what matters most right now and he has to stay focused on that. The whole issue with Lizzie began when he allowed things in his personal life to impact his work; he can't allow it to happen again.

'I saw him yesterday morning,' says Jayne Barratt, a snowbird turned permanent resident who relocated here a couple of years back from England with her husband after retiring from her job as a primary school teacher.

Philip snaps his head up, his thoughts of Lizzie gone. 'What time? Where?'

Jayne frowns, thinking. She taps the emerald-green nail of her index finger against Cody's photo. 'It must have been a little after ten o'clock. I'd just popped in on my parents for morning coffee and chocolate cake, and was over on Ocean Walk Boulevard, heading into Sandy's Salon for my manicure, when I saw this man coming out of Pete's Coffee N Go.'

Philip nods, hope flaring inside him. That's right, Jayne's parents had also moved to The Homestead at the same time she had, and her dad's baking skills had quickly reached legendary status among the residents. Licking his lips, Philip tries to put thoughts of the perfectly made and presented baked goods from his mind and says, 'Did anything strike you as odd? How did he seem?'

Jayne shrugs. 'He seemed like a regular guy. He was carrying one of those little cardboard trays with two takeaway cups of coffee, and I think a bag or a briefcase.' She frowns. 'He looked kind of like he was in a rush to get somewhere. He wasn't running, but definitely doing a fast walk.'

'Did you see his vehicle?' says Philip, taking out his notepad and making a few notes.

'Sorry, no.' Jayne shakes her head. 'It was literally a quick passing glance – I was late and needed to hurry. My beauty therapist, Crystal, is a real stickler for timekeeping and I knew she'd charge me extra for being five minutes late.'

'Yes, yes, of course,' says Philip. He doesn't need to know about the blasted beauty therapist. 'So this was ten o'clock?'

'Five past the hour,' says Jayne. 'Or maybe eight minutes past.'

'Okay, good, good.' Philip jots down the time in his notebook. 'Was Mr Ziegler alone or with others?'

'Alone, as far as I could tell,' says Jayne.

'But he was carrying two cups of coffee?' says Philip.

'Yes . . . I think so.'

Philip makes a note about the coffees and looks back at Jayne. She's a well-liked resident and a reliable witness – he's heard good things about the book group she runs, and about how she's always kind enough to spend time advising other residents on the best books to buy for their grandchildren. 'Anything else you can tell me, anything unusual?'

'No, like I said, he just looked kind of regular,' says Jayne, shaking her head. Then she stops. Frowns. 'Actually, now you mention it, as we passed, I heard his mobile phone start ringing and I think he swore. I can't be sure, because I literally went into the salon a couple of strides later, but I'm pretty sure it was his phone.'

'Did you hear him answer it?' asks Philip.

'No, sorry, I must have been in the salon by then. Like I said, Crystal is a real clock-watcher so—'

'Yes, yes,' says Philip, noting down what she's said while inwardly cursing that Jayne hadn't been just a little later for her appointment so she'd have heard the phone exchange. 'Thanks, Jayne, you've been very helpful.'

While Jayne smiles from the compliment, Philip scans the faces of the other patrollers around the table. 'Anyone else remember seeing Mr Ziegler?'

No one speaks. Most shake their heads. A couple study the photos a little longer and then shrug.

'Well, thanks for looking,' says Philip, sensing he's got as much as he can from them for the time being. 'As I said earlier, this is an active investigation, so stay vigilant, and if you see Mr Ziegler at any time, day or night, call me or Rick immediately.'

Biting back disappointment, Philip collects up the photos. He hopes the others have managed to get some more concrete leads. The information from Jayne Barratt about Cody Ziegler carrying two coffees is interesting but there's nothing he's learned from this meeting that'll help them track Cody's whereabouts or impress Lizzie. As he tucks the pictures and his notebook back into his jacket pocket and heads out to the car park, he tries not to feel too deflated.

16

MOIRA

They rendezvous back at Philip and Lizzie's place. Moira's pleased to be the last to arrive – things are so awkward between the married couple right now that it's easier to be around them when it's the four of them; at least then she and Rick can speak to each other if Philip and Lizzie are having a moment.

They're gathered outside on the patio. Philip's standing at the patio doors, marker pen in hand, ready to add what they've found from their afternoon enquiries to the makeshift investigation board written on the glass doors. He looks at the three of them, sitting on the patio chairs. 'Let's see what we've got, yes?'

'I'll go first,' says Rick, raising his hand. 'There was nothing obvious in Cody's study, but with Olivia's help I found a hidden compartment in the floor that held a small safe. Olivia hadn't been aware of its existence, saying they had a large safe in the panic room where all the valuables were kept. Her reaction seemed genuine – she looked pretty shocked.'

'Although she is an actress,' says Lizzie. 'Her reaction might not be genuine – it'd be hard to tell.'

'True that,' says Rick. 'Anyways, along with a bunch of legal papers and contracts, there were three dark cream envelopes in the safe. With Olivia's permission I opened them and . . .' Rick gives a long whistle. 'They weren't good.'

Philip narrows his eyes. 'In what way?'

Rick takes out his phone and taps the photos app. 'I took pictures of them. They all follow a single sentence convention. And they're cryptic for sure. The first said: *BE SAFE – CLOSE YOUR EYES AND YOUR MOUTH*. The second: *STAY SILENT – SAVE A LIFE*. And the third said: *NO MORE WARNINGS – YOUR 9 LIVES ARE UP – CURIOSITY KILLED THE CODY.*

'He knew they were coming for him,' says Moira. 'But did he know who they were?'

Rick shakes his head. 'There's no way to tell, but he hadn't told Olivia about the nature of the threats.'

Lizzie's eyes widen but she stays silent. Then she frowns, looking thoughtful.

Taking the phone from Rick, Moira flicks through the photos of the three letters. They're stark and to the point. Clearly written on the assumption that the recipient would know what they referred to. 'Can you forward these to me? I'll ask Brad George, the VP, if Cody confided in him about them.'

'Good call,' says Rick. Taking the phone from Moira, he taps the screen a couple of times and Moira's own phone vibrates in her pocket as the images come through.

Moira's about to speak when Philip clears his throat loudly and says, 'An important find, Rick. And this means it's all the more imperative that we find Mr Ziegler. I impressed that point on the community watch, I can tell you. They weren't taking it nearly seriously enough for my liking and—'

'Sure,' says Moira. Philip seems to have recovered some of his usual bossiness, but there's tightness around his eyes that makes her think he's faking some of his usual bluster. She can see that Rick's looking pretty irritated. If Philip's going to cut across them as they give their updates, maybe they should get his out of the way sooner rather than later. 'How did the meeting with the community watch go?'

'It went well,' says Philip, a touch defensively.

'I knew the patrollers would come through for us,' says Rick. 'Were there any sightings of Cody Ziegler in the past day or so?'

'In fact there was,' says Philip, the smugness clear in his voice. He glances at Lizzie, but she's looking at the board rather than her husband. For a moment his triumphant expression falters and he looks crestfallen, then he regains his composure. 'Your friend, Jayne Barratt, saw him yesterday morning, at eight minutes past ten, coming out of Pete's Coffee N Go on Ocean Walk Boulevard.'

'You should write that on the board,' says Lizzie, still not looking directly at Philip.

'Yes, yes, of course,' says Philip, looking flustered as he jots the facts on to the patio doors.

Moira knows why Lizzie is acting this way towards Philip, and she gets it after what's happened between them, she really does, but it's going to be tricky working together effectively if Lizzie can't even bring herself to look at her husband.

'Did you say Jayne spotted him?' asks Rick.

Philip stops writing and turns back towards them. 'Yes, yes, Jayne Barratt. She was late for a manicure appointment at Sandy's Salon, and clock-watching because of it, so she's pretty definite on the time. She said Cody had two cups of takeaway coffee in a cardboard holder and a briefcase with him. As he passed her, his phone started ringing.'

Rick nods. 'Jayne's one of our best. We can rely on her intel.'

'Precisely what I thought,' says Philip.

'Did she hear him answer the call?' says Moira. 'Did he say the name of the person calling out loud?'

'Sadly no, but she thought she heard him curse,' says Philip, adding the coffee and briefcase details to the board. 'She didn't see his car either.'

It's good to have a positive sighting of Cody away from the house, thinks Moira. 'It's confirmation he did leave home between nine thirty and ten thirty, as Olivia suggested. Potentially on the way to his office.'

'But he didn't make it there,' says Philip.

'Indeed.' Rick glances at Moira. 'What did you discover at his office?'

Lizzie holds up her hand. 'Wait – Philip, did you say Cody was carrying two cups of coffee?'

'Yes, yes, that's what I said,' says Philip, glancing at his notebook and then underlining *TWO COFFEES* where it's written on the patio door glass.

Lizzie looks at Moira. Moira nods. 'So who was the second coffee for?'

Rick runs his fingers across his jaw. 'Good question. Were there any clues at his office?'

Moira shakes her head. 'No, none, but everyone seems to have loved Cody. Most of them seemed shocked to the point of disbelief that he was missing, but . . .' Moira pulls out her phone and opens the Notes app. 'There are a few things that pinged on my radar.'

'What sort of things?' asks Lizzie. She's fully engaged in the conversation now, unlike when her husband was speaking.

'Firstly, although no one there had a bad word to say about Cody, I did find out about two people who are definitely not part of his fan club. The first is an ex-employee, Dirk Baldwin, who was fired for making too many mistakes. Apparently he took it badly and filed a lawsuit against Cody and Brad for wrongful dismissal and victimisation. According to Ashley, the receptionist, Dirk was claiming he'd been made a scapegoat for the dodgy practices he'd tried to blow the whistle on. However, the lawsuit got withdrawn after a week and Dirk didn't go back to the offices. I think it's likely Cody paid him off, but that's a guess. I'd say he's someone we need to look at closer as a person of interest.'

'I agree,' says Rick, nodding. 'We need to get a look-see at that lawsuit and the particulars of the claim.'

'Definitely,' says Lizzie. She looks at Moira. 'You said there were a few things?'

'There are,' says Moira, nodding. 'The second person of interest is a guy named Marty Hannier. He was CEO of Oak Whistle Productions. Back in November last year he approached Cody with a pitch for a movie but Cody passed on it even though his VP was keen on the deal.'

Lizzie frowns. 'That sort of thing must happen all the time in the business, though. What makes this guy stand out?'

'Oak Whistle Productions were declared bankrupt a few weeks after Cody turned them down, and apparently Marty Hannier told the media that it was Cody Ziegler who'd hammered the final nail into their financial coffin. He lost his company and he blames Cody.'

'Yeah,' says Rick. 'I can see that'd give this Marty Hannier a motive for revenge.'

'Yes, yes,' says Philip, bullet-pointing the key points on to the patio door. 'So we've two potential persons of interest. Good work.'

'Thanks,' says Moira, even though she really doesn't need Philip's approval – this is an equally weighted team; there's no leader despite what Philip might think. 'There are a few other things that could be of use.'

'Shoot,' says Rick.

'I checked the envelopes and paper in the storeroom and they're all white, nothing cream. I also had a look around Cody's office but didn't find anything useful. There's also something going on between Cody's personal assistant and the receptionist. It might be a personality clash or jealousy, but Donna, the more mature PA, has a very obvious crush on her boss, and Ashley, the younger receptionist, says that Donna hates her because Cody only had eyes for her.'

'So he was seeing Ashley?' says Lizzie.

'That's what she implied, but when I pressed her on it she admitted nothing was going on.' Moira shrugs. 'It sounds like a bit of light flirting if it's anything.'

Rick nods. 'Interesting. You think the PA could get so pissed about it that she'd help with an abduction to get revenge?'

Moira considers it. 'I don't know. People will do some messed-up things in the name of unrequited love, but Donna the PA seemed very loyal to Cody. I didn't sense any anger towards him.'

'Some women are good at hiding how they're really feeling,' says Philip under his breath.

Lizzie shoots him a killer stare. He turns back to the patio doors and writes the key points from the discussion on the glass.

Moira thinks about the two coffees Jayne Barratt saw Cody carrying. 'It's possible he was bringing a coffee for his PA. She said they worked very closely together.'

'But wouldn't it have gone cold on the drive?' says Lizzie.

'Yeah, I guess so. It's a good forty minutes.' Moira exhales hard. 'The only other thing was that Donna said I shouldn't believe a word Ashley said. It wasn't directly in the context of Cody and her, but if she is involved in anything it would have made a good pre-emptive strike against Ashley's credibility.'

'Do you think that's why she did it?' asks Philip, looking at her over the top of his glasses.

'I don't know. It's something we need to bear in mind, though.' Moira consults her notes on the phone app. 'Other stuff of interest: in terms of the timeline, one of Cody's colleagues said he'd been in the office the evening before – so that's Tuesday night – and Cody left at around nine thirty. Yesterday – Wednesday – morning, two of Cody's colleagues confirmed they'd been on a conference call with him between eight and nine fifteen discussing the Skyline project. They said he seemed in good spirits and had told them he'd be in the office no later than eleven that morning. I checked his schedule with his PA and it all ties together. The only person I didn't get to speak to was his Vice President, who was on a vacation day, but I'll go back tomorrow morning to speak to him. Brad George is Cody's second in command and was in the late-night meeting on Tuesday and the Wednesday morning conference call, so it may be he can add more insight to what I've got so far.'

Philip adds the details to the timeline. 'Okay, so follow-up actions? Moira, I have you returning to the offices tomorrow to interview Brad George, yes?'

'Yep,' says Moira. Surely she'd been clear on that already?

'And we need someone to follow up on the lawsuit filed by Dirk Baldwin,' says Philip, tapping the marker against the glass. He looks at Lizzie. 'Can you do that?'

'Fine.' Lizzie doesn't meet his gaze.

'And I'll see if I can get a current address for him from one of my contacts,' says Rick. 'I'll do the same for Marty Hannier too.'

'Good, good,' says Philip. He stares at Lizzie. 'How did the CSI work go?'

'Nothing immediately usable,' says Lizzie curtly. She looks away from her husband, towards Moira and Rick. 'There were no prints on the letters Cody was sent over the past few weeks, or the picture sent to Olivia today. The envelopes have a lot of prints on them, but without being able to take the fingerprints of every mail worker who handled them it's impossible to narrow them down to viable persons of interest. I did take Olivia's prints, and excluded hers from the mix, but after discounting hers and those too smudged to read, I'm still left with seven unique prints.'

'If they wore gloves for the letters, the chances are they handled the envelope using them too,' says Moira.

'Exactly,' says Lizzie, her tone hardening as she glances at Philip. 'So, as I said, no useful information from the CSI work, okay?'

Philip doesn't say anything, instead turning and writing the information Lizzie's given on the glass of the patio door.

'There's something that might be helpful, though,' says Lizzie, looking back at Moira and Rick. 'I found a tiny watermark on the inside of the envelope. It was a logo for *CALDARO*. I googled it, and it seems that it's a popular stationery brand here in the US. The letters have all been posted from somewhere in Orlando – that's the mail stamp on them. I know it's a big area, but we could cross-reference places that sell the envelopes with Orlando zip codes and see if we can get a more precise location. Could be someone in the store would remember the person who bought them.'

Moira doesn't like to rain on Lizzie's parade, but she thinks the chances of a store assistant remembering a person who bought envelopes a few weeks or more back are slim to none. The envelopes have nothing to make them stand out as memorable, and with the thousands of people they must see every day in a place like Orlando, them remembering one customer would be an incredibly long shot. She's about to say something but Rick beats her to it.

'Don't think that'll fly,' he says, running his hand across the stubble on his jaw. 'Orlando is too big a place. I doubt any store assistant is going to remember a person who bought envelopes a while back.'

'Fine.' Lizzie crosses her arms. 'That's all I've got, sorry it's no use.'

'It's cool,' says Rick, his voice kind. 'The CSI angle was always a long shot.'

Pursing her lips, Lizzie says nothing.

Moira can tell her friend's taking what Rick said to heart, but it isn't personal. She reaches out and gives Lizzie's arm a squeeze. 'What you discovered *is* useful. We know the person or people involved wore gloves when they sent those letters – this tells us they're smart and were most likely planning on escalating the situation even back when the first letter was sent. That's valuable intel.'

'Sure is,' says Rick, nodding.

Lizzie pushes a loose strand of hair off her forehead and gives a half smile. 'Thanks.'

After he finishes writing up what Lizzie's told them on the board, Philip turns back towards them. 'Are you finished?'

'No,' snaps Lizzie without looking at him. 'What I don't get is why the kidnappers didn't issue a ransom demand at the same time as giving proof of life?'

It's a good question. Moira nods. 'Every abduction case is different. There's no set pattern. The proof of life establishes their credibility but doesn't reveal their hand too soon.'

'Yep, true,' says Rick, nodding. 'And by extending the timescale, they're increasing the fear and anxiety Olivia feels for her husband. It's a technique often used to make spouses or parents more compliant.'

'Yes, yes, I agree. Every case is different,' says Philip, looking over his shoulder from where he's writing on the patio doors.

Lizzie glares at her husband but doesn't say anything. Philip swallows hard and looks away.

Rick clears his throat. 'Anyways, the only other thing I have to add is that while I was at Olivia's I took another look at the CCTV system. As I reported this morning, the EQ1000 model the Zieglers have needs an external backup battery pack to be bought separately in order to keep the system running in the event of a power outage. Olivia said she didn't know if they had one. When I checked the system myself there wasn't a battery pack attached, but it was clear that the area around where it should have been had recently been accessed – the dust had been disturbed. I'd say it's highly likely the system was tampered with deliberately and the pack removed prior to the outage.'

'You suspect Olivia has something to do with Cody's disappearance?' asks Philip.

Rick looks thoughtful. 'She's not giving me any indication she's involved, but I've learned over the years not to rule anything out at too early a stage. We need to keep an eye on her, and not get too friendly.'

'She wouldn't be the first wife to want to get rid of her husband,' mutters Lizzie under her breath.

Philip's face flushes red. Saying nothing, he turns to the patio doors and rubs off the action for Rick on looking into the alarm, and then starts adding the new information about the CCTV.

'Look guys,' says Rick, trying to calm the situation between Philip and Lizzie. 'Whether Olivia's in on it or not, it's real important we find Cody Ziegler. That last letter he received was a clear threat against his life and the fact he's gone missing makes me think it's not a joke.'

'Agreed,' says Moira, nodding. 'We need to find him before it's too late.'

'So our avenues for investigation tomorrow are . . . ?' says Philip, starting a new column with the heading 'Friday Actions'.

'I'll go back to the offices and interview Brad George, the VP. Could be Cody confided in him about the threats,' says Moira. 'We also need to find a subtle way of asking around about anyone Cody might have been sharing a ride with yesterday – they could be in on the kidnapping, or be held captive themselves.'

Lizzie nods. 'And I'll see what I can find out about the lawsuit ex-employee Dirk Baldwin filed against the company.'

'I'll speak with my law enforcement contact and see if he's managed to turn up any sightings of Cody's Lexus through the traffic cameras,' says Rick. 'I'll also ask him to run an address search on Dirk Baldwin and Marty Hannier.' Rick looks at Philip. 'Once we've got their whereabouts, we can pay them a visit.'

Philip finishes jotting down the actions and turns to face the rest of them. His face flushes red again as he looks at Lizzie. 'Good work, team. Looks like we've got ourselves a plan.'

Dammit, thinks Moira. *This isn't Philip's team, no matter how much he'd like that to be true.* But as she watches his face fall – eyes sad, brow creased and mouth downturned – as he turns away to put the marker pen down by the patio doors, she grits her teeth, stifling the irritated retort she wants to make. Much as his pomposity grates on her, she can't kick a man when he's down.

17

LIZZIE

As she closes the door behind Moira and Rick, Lizzie's smile dies on her face. Philip is standing so close beside her she feels crowded, boxed in; claustrophobic. She shudders. Doesn't he understand she doesn't like being around him right now? She can hardly bear to look at him.

'That dig about wives wanting to kill their husbands was pretty low,' says Philip. There's a hurt expression on his face. Puppy-dog eyes looking at her like she's the bad guy in all this.

It makes her cross, him looking at her that way. He has no right, not after lying to her all these years. She's entitled to be angry. Shaking her head, she holds her hand up, her palm towards his face. 'And lying to your wife is a hell of a lot lower.'

He doesn't reply. Instead, he stands there staring at her; his mouth hangs partway open, and his puppy-dog eyes are getting more mournful.

I refuse to feel sorry for him, thinks Lizzie. *I just won't.* Trying to ignore her husband's pained expression, she says, 'Look, I'm getting a sandwich for myself tonight so you can sort out your own dinner.'

'Okay,' says Philip, his voice small, strained.

'Good.' Lizzie turns and walks along the hallway to the kitchen. She breathes easier, and feels less claustrophobic, with every step she takes away from him.

In the kitchen she takes a couple of slices of bread from the bread bin and butters them. Then she chooses a banana from the fruit bowl and slices it, placing it on one piece of bread, then spreads peanut butter on the other slice, and puts them together. Banana and peanut butter sandwiches are her go-to comfort food guilty pleasure, and after the experience at couples counselling and the stress of being around Philip she feels she deserves it.

Lizzie just wishes she'd been able to add more to the investigation in terms of leads. The forensics hadn't turned up anything of great value, and the envelopes and paper were too commonly stocked in stores and supermarkets to make an in-person search of stockists in Orlando viable. Right now, she feels like she's failing at everything: the investigation, and her marriage.

At least she's got an angle to focus on tomorrow. This Dirk Baldwin character sounds like he could have a grudge against Cody and his company. She's intrigued to get a look at the lawsuit he filed.

Lizzie flinches as she hears footsteps coming along the tiled hallway floor towards her. As Philip joins her in the kitchen, she tenses. She wishes he'd let her get her food in peace instead of invading her space yet again. She doesn't look at him, instead focusing on cutting her sandwich into squares and then making a cup of tea, but she can hear him blustering about, getting things out of the fridge behind her.

Philip clears his throat. 'Lizzie, sweetheart, what happened earlier – what you said about the therapy not being good – don't you think we should talk about it?'

'I told you what I think. There's nothing more to discuss,' says Lizzie, fishing out her teabag and adding some milk to her mug. 'I'm not going back there.'

Philip blows out hard.

'Look, don't try and pressure or guilt me into it,' says Lizzie, turning to look at him. 'I'm not going to change my mind on this.'

'Yes, yes. Okay.' Philip rubs his hand across his bald pate. His voice is quieter as he says, 'But I might go for another session.'

'Do what you like.' Lizzie picks up her sandwich and stomps out to the hallway. Pausing at the bottom of the stairs, she turns back to Philip, who is still standing in the kitchen. She's not sure how long she can do this; maybe she should look into getting a place of her own. 'I don't know why I bothered saying that – you always do exactly what the hell you want anyway. That's the bloody problem.'

18

MOIRA

Her mobile phone vibrating on the bedside table wakes her. Groping for it in the dark, she taps the screen and sees it's 04.06 a.m. Then her pulse accelerates as she sees who sent the message. It's from the unknown number.

YOU WON'T GET AWAY WITH IT

Moira tightens her grip on the handset. On the bed around her the dogs are still asleep, but she's wide awake. Fear forcing her heart rate higher still.

She scrolls through the two messages from the unknown number.

I KNOW WHO YOU ARE

YOU WON'T GET AWAY WITH IT

The number itself doesn't give any clue as to who is sending the messages. It's shorter than a regular number. It looks fake, made-up, if she's honest: 999666. But there's nothing pretend about the threats being made. Moira looks at the times the calls were made to her yesterday and when the messages were sent – morning yesterday, and very early morning today – and does the calculation in her head. She bites her lip as she realises that, even with the time difference, the calls and messages were sent during waking hours in England.

Even though she isn't cold, Moira shivers. Reaching across the bed, she strokes the silken head of Pip, the elderly sausage dog, who is happily snoring on the duvet nearby. She wishes she could sleep so peacefully.

But Moira isn't your average retiree. And the story she told Rick about the last job she led as an undercover police officer in London was only half of the truth. She'd told him how, using aliases, they'd set up a meet with the kingpin of a vicious and prolific criminal gang – Bobbie Porter. The meet had taken place on the twenty-fourth floor of a fancy riverside apartment building. She'd taken McCord and Riley with her – both young, talented officers she was mentoring to help get to the top of their game. The meet started okay, but it'd gone wrong fast. Things got tense. McCord turned on his colleague, Jennifer Riley, and shot her at point-blank range, allowing Porter and their heavies to get free and clear.

Moira takes a breath. Feels the panic catching in her chest.

Riley had bled out on the white sofa in seconds. Moira hadn't been able to save her. McCord had run to the balcony. It was dark. The rain was pouring, the wind whipping it hard against the building. McCord was crying. He'd pointed his gun at Moira's head. Screamed at her to keep back. His hand was shaking. His expression wretched. Then, as he started to lower his gun, he'd looked Moira direct in the eye and said something, but she couldn't make out all his words. All she heard was *don't trust* and *sorry* and *run*. Then McCord leaped over the railing and was gone.

There's no coming back from a twenty-four-storey dive.

With the rain pelting down on her, Moira had leaned out over the balcony rail and screamed McCord's name into the darkness. Back inside, a smoke grenade went off and the building alarm blared out as the armed response team stormed the penthouse. But they were too late; the subject had got away and Moira's team were gone.

Riley's blood was all over Moira's hands. McCord was dead after killing his colleague and telling Moira not to trust and to run. Smoke from the grenade was stinging her eyes and causing her throat to constrict. Everything had gone wrong.

Her breathing became laboured, impossible.

That was the moment she had her first panic attack.

At first she'd thought she'd be able to keep doing her job. Her boss, a good man who'd mentored her almost her entire career, wanted to support her and put her on extended sick leave, encouraging her to have regular sessions with the doc. But all that time without a case to focus on, it didn't do her any good.

She wanted answers to her questions: Why did McCord shoot Riley? What did he mean about not trusting? And why did he tell her to run? Why did he jump? And where was Bobbie Porter?

The questions swirled in her mind every minute of every day. But no one else wanted her to pursue them. Her boss told her she needed to stop obsessing; that she was on sick leave and needed to stay away from casework. The doc asked her how she could hope to get any answers when McCord was dead. No one in the force wanted to help, not really. Moira was alone.

So she'd told them she was going to find her own answers – at least about the whereabouts of Bobbie Porter. They had unfinished business – Moira was going to bring Porter in and get the truth.

That's when the incidents started.

At first it was small things – she'd see a muscle guy watching her from across the street, or a car tailing her; things that made her senses heighten and her fight-or-flight response kick in. The doc said it was her imagination. That post-traumatic stress did that to a person. But it felt very real to Moira.

Still, she didn't stop looking for answers about Bobbie Porter. She kept pushing and probing; reaching out to informants, looking for Porter in all the places their associates hung out, and asking her colleagues what they knew. She kept asking. Said she wouldn't let it drop.

They jumped her on her way home one dark evening after one of her sessions with the doc and beat her unconscious. She woke up in hospital after a kind citizen had seen her collapsed in an alleyway and called an ambulance.

When that didn't stop her, they set her apartment on fire and did something to the lock to jam the door closed. It was only because a passing dog walker saw the smoke and called the fire brigade so promptly that she wasn't killed. But the message was clear: *Shut up or die. Stop asking questions.*

She'd told her boss what happened. Couldn't figure out how the arsonist had got into her apartment building and targeted her specific apartment. Her boss had been sympathetic, but he told her she was making connections to the Porter operation that weren't there, that she needed to concentrate on getting well again and put all thoughts of the failed operation and the questions out of her mind. He said Porter was long gone – out of the country, no doubt. He told Moira she needed to focus on herself.

She'd tried, but the questions hadn't stopped, they'd multiplied. Swirling around in her mind, unanswered and taunting her: *When had McCord been turned by Porter? How could he kill his friend and colleague, Riley? Why tell her he was sorry? Who did he think couldn't be trusted? What or who should she be running from? Why did he betray her?*

There were no answers. There was only danger and death.

Knowing there's no hope of getting back to sleep right now, Moira pushes off the duvet and manages to get out of bed without disturbing the sleeping dogs. She pads across the carpet to the walk-in wardrobe. The lights come on automatically as she opens the door. On the lowest shelf at the back of the cupboard, hidden beneath a fake fur throw and a pile of old coats, is her metal lockbox. Using the smallest key on her keyring, she unlocks the box and opens the lid.

Lifting out the clear plastic folder at the top of the box, she opens it and takes out three envelopes. Opening the first, marked #1, she checks through the documents: a British passport, a UK driving licence and a birth certificate from Bletchley, Buckinghamshire. Opening the passport, Moira looks at the person in the picture staring back at her. She has a different hair colour and style – long and highlighted blonde, rather than short and black – and she's wearing brighter make-up, something Moira barely bothers with these days. But it's her, even though the name on the passport says Emily Jane Platt.

Moira shakes her head. Emily Jane Platt doesn't exist any more.

She opens envelope #2. It contains the same documents, this time in the name Moira Flynn. The picture is different – different hair and make-up, different clothes – but it's still her and the documents are good. Real.

The documents in envelope #3 are the odd ones out. They're fakes. Good, high-quality fakes that cost a lot of money, but fakes nonetheless. Moira tips out the passport and opens it up. Stares at the picture of the brunette with bobbed hair and dark eye make-up. Reads the name on the passport: Rachel Jean Baker.

Rachel Jean Baker is her backup plan. It's a new identity for if Moira Flynn doesn't work out. It's her second and last chance of making a new start, of switching to a different life; of creating another tabula rasa. But she really doesn't want to have to use it.

Putting the envelopes back into the plastic wallet and then setting it aside, she lifts out two thick buff folders, stuffed to the max with paperwork and held together by several thick elastic bands, and puts them on top of the plastic wallet with the envelopes. In the bottom of the lockbox is another metal box. Using the brass key on her keyring, she opens the box. Inside there's a Glock handgun, a couple of boxes of bullets, and a weapons-grade Taser.

Taking a breath, Moira lifts the gun out of the box and loads it. She's got a concealed carry firearms permit, so she can legally keep it with her. She'd purchased the gun, and applied for the permit, as a precaution. Now she's glad she did.

She learned the hard way you can't trust anyone.

It wasn't just McCord who'd betrayed her.

A few days after the fire, she'd gone to her boss's house. She hadn't called ahead to say she was on her way over. She'd wanted to speak off the record – to tell him her theories about the best way to catch Porter. Because although her boss had told her Porter had left the country, her sources were telling her that wasn't true.

But when she'd arrived, she'd glanced through the open curtains into the living room and seen her boss with another person. With her heart pounding against her ribs, Moira had crept closer to the window. Taken a closer look. Made sure her eyes weren't playing tricks on her. They weren't.

Bobbie Porter was in her boss's living room. They were laughing. Moira watched as Porter handed her boss – the man she'd trusted, who'd mentored her and been like a surrogate father to her – an envelope. She watched him open the flap and flick a finger across the bundles of notes. Saw him nod, and lip-read his words: *Leave it with me. I'll get DCI Platt out of the way.*

Moira – then Emily Platt – had retched, sour-tasting bile hitting the back of her throat. The implication was clear. Her boss wasn't the good man she believed him to be. He wasn't a friend and a mentor. He was a bad man, a liar – a dirty copper. And he'd taken blood money to get her killed.

She knew in that moment she'd never be safe. And she knew why.

Moira knows something dangerous. Bobbie Porter – criminal kingpin – isn't a man, as the police had always assumed. Bobbie Porter is a woman. And Moira had seen her face – she is the only one of the three officers who walked into the penthouse that night who is still alive. She can identify Porter. She was an eyewitness to the command Porter had given McCord to kill Riley – to murder a police officer. And the only person she'd told about this was her boss – he'd told her not to tell the other officers or to mention it in her statement, because if Porter had got to McCord there could be other police who'd been bought by Porter and her knowledge would make her a threat.

Then Moira had started asking questions and refused to stop. That had made her a target.

Moira places the chunky buff folders in the lockbox, and then picks up the plastic wallet with the passports and other documents inside and puts them on top.

An old friend of her father used to work in setting up new identities for people going into witness protection. He still had contacts. She'd asked him to do her a favour – two favours – and he did. And as soon as she had her new identities, she'd run.

She'd become Moira Flynn, and although it had taken a while to get used to, she's starting to enjoy living here at The Homestead. She doesn't want to have to run again. She doesn't want to give up this life.

Moira opens the messages from the unknown number on her mobile phone. Reads them again.

I KNOW WHO YOU ARE

She clenches her jaw. What the hell did they think she'd got away with? Her two closest colleagues – McCord and Riley – were dead, and she'd discovered her boss had been planning to kill her. She hadn't got away with anything. Instead, she'd lost everything.

Frowning, she taps out a reply.

WHO IS THIS??

She stares at the words for a long moment. Is it wise to reply – should she ignore and block the unknown number instead? Moira can't stand the not knowing, and if they've found her mobile number it wouldn't take too much more work to find her here at The Homestead. She needs to find out who is behind the messages. She needs to know if she has to run again.

Moira takes a deep breath and presses send.

Then she picks up the Glock and pads quietly back across the bedroom to the bed. Pip is still snoring softly. Marigold and Wolfie are stretched out together against one of the pillows. Slipping under the duvet, Moira places the gun on the bedside table beside her glass of water and recently started Michael Connelly paperback.

Lying back, she keeps her phone in her hand.

And waits for a reply.

19

RICK

The phone ringing startles him awake. Turning on the light, he picks up the handset and sees it's real early – 5.02 a.m. Then he sees it's Olivia Hamilton Ziegler calling him and he presses the green button to answer.

'Hello, this is Denver.'

It sounds like she's crying. 'Rick . . . is that you? I . . .'

'Yes, Miss Olivia, it's Rick Denver here. Are you okay, ma'am?'

'I . . . I'm . . . I . . .' She takes a loud, shaky breath in.

'What's the matter, ma'am? Are you in danger?'

'I . . .' There's a sob. 'I'm okay. It's Cody. They've sent another picture and a demand. I . . . I need your help, Rick. I don't know what to do.'

'You hold tight, ma'am. I'm on my way over right now.'

Hanging up, Rick calls Moira. She answers after one ring. He guesses she's not sleeping well again; he knows she's had issues with insomnia in the past. He tells her the situation and that he'll pick her up in ten minutes at the front of her house en route to Olivia Hamilton Ziegler's place. Then he hustles, getting dressed and ready in less than three minutes. This morning's workout will have to wait.

He's out front at Moira's place nine minutes later and she's already waiting on the porch. She hurries down the steps and along the path to the sidewalk as he draws up, jumping into the jeep as soon as he's stopped.

'Hey,' says Rick, his mood lifting as it always does when he sees Moira.

She gives him a tight smile. No pleasantries – straight to business. 'What did Olivia say on the phone?'

'Just that she'd gotten another picture and that this one has a demand with it. She was real upset, so I figured it'd be easier to talk to her in person and see the thing for ourselves.'

Moira nods. 'Good call.'

Rick glances at Moira as he puts the gear into drive and sets off towards Millionaires' Row. He knows it's early, but Moira seems tense and distracted, not her usual dynamic self. Even in the shadows of the jeep's interior, he can see she's frowning. 'You okay?'

'I'm fine,' says Moira. Her no-nonsense tone doesn't invite further questions.

He glances at her again as he takes a right turn. She definitely doesn't look fine to him. Her fists are clenched in her lap and there's a muscle pulsing in her forehead. But he knows what she's like; she holds her cards real close to her chest. There's no point pushing her for more answers about what's really going on with her. His best strategy is to keep things light and wait for when she's ready to talk. So he turns his thoughts to the job.

'I'm thinking we should try to persuade her to get the authorities involved. If she's gotten a ransom note, the cops can't ignore it. What do you think?'

Moira nods. 'I think bringing in the cops is the right call. It's a sensitive situation and none of us are professional hostage negotiators.'

'Okay, let's go with that recommendation and see what Olivia says.'

'Deal,' says Moira. She turns and stares out of the passenger window into the blackness. It'll be a couple of hours until the sun comes up. Most of the homes they pass are still in darkness, with only the external lights on their front porches on. Daily life in the retirement community doesn't start much before eight.

Rick wonders what Moira's thinking. He's not come across a woman who intrigues him as much as she does since he met his late wife, Alisha. It's been a little over five years since Alisha passed after her long battle with cancer, and Moira's the first woman who's made him think he might possibly be able to love again. Not that he's told her that, or acted on it in any way.

He makes the turn into Millionaires' Row and slows the jeep as they come up to the Ziegler mansion. Turning into the driveway, he doesn't need to press the buzzer to say they've arrived as the automatic gates start opening immediately. He glances up at the camera on the gatepost and guesses Olivia has been watching out for them.

He parks outside the house beside the fountain – the water jets are switched off now and the previously bubbling water is silent and still. He and Moira get out of the jeep and hurry up the steps to the front door. Olivia has the door open before they reach it.

Gone is the composed and stylish woman of yesterday. Olivia's wearing grey pyjamas, a pink towelling robe and slippers, no make-up, and her bobbed blonde hair is dishevelled and tufty. Her face is red and her eyes are bloodshot. She dabs at them with a tissue.

She looks past the two of them, scanning the driveway. Pulling her robe tighter around her, she beckons them inside. 'Thank God you're here. Quick, come in, please . . . hurry.'

Olivia closes the door behind them quickly, double-locking it with a deadlock and also sliding the metal door guard into place. Ushering them along the hallway, she says, 'I called you as soon as I found the note. Come through, it's in the kitchen.'

Rick frowns. She'd called him around 5 a.m. 'But the mail isn't delivered through the night so—'

'They didn't mail it,' says Olivia, stopping partway along the hallway and turning back to face them. 'They delivered it here.'

'When?' says Moira.

'It must have been sometime after midnight. It wasn't on the mat when I went up to bed, but it was lying there at four fifty this morning when I came downstairs for a glass of water.'

'On the doormat in this house?' says Rick. This is a worrying development.

'That's right.' Olivia takes a shaky breath. There's a tremble in her voice. 'They didn't leave it at the gate or put it in the mailbox, they brought it right up to the house and slipped it under the door.' Olivia shudders. Her eyes are wide, fearful. 'They got on to the property unseen and without activating the alarm.'

'You definitely set the alarm?' says Rick.

'I might be old, but I'm not an idiot,' says Olivia, folding her arms. 'I set the alarm and I checked that the CCTV was set to record. But when I found the letter and went to look at the CCTV feed, it'd switched back over to live only. Nothing after 4.30 a.m. was recorded.'

Rick glances at Moira. He knows she'll be thinking the same thing he is: that the signs are pointing to the perpetrator being someone who knows the house and the security systems in operation. It could be a friend or an employee, or a friend or acquaintance of one, but given this latest development it's less likely to be a totally unconnected stranger.

'So, what do you think?' asks Olivia, moving her weight from one foot to the other but not continuing on to the kitchen yet. 'What's our next step?'

'Look, we think you need to call the cops. Ransoms are highly volatile situations and we're not experts in hostage negotiation.' Rick looks at Moira and she nods reassuringly. 'The police could add value now.'

'No. I won't . . . I just . . . No,' says Olivia, her eyes widening as fresh tears cause them to water. 'I told you already, I don't trust the cops and you saw the way they were with me yesterday. I can't put Cody's life in those people's hands, I just can't.'

'We understand that,' says Moira, her tone reassuring. 'But they'll listen to you now. You have evidence your husband has been taken against his will and that his abductors are trying to extort money from you. It's the police's job to help you.'

'I said no, already.' Olivia's voice is getting louder, angrier. Her cheeks colour red. She looks from Moira to Rick. Stands in the middle of the hallway, blocking them going further towards the kitchen. 'If you won't help me then you can get out of my home right now and I'll do this alone.'

20

MOIRA

'That's not going to happen, ma'am,' says Rick, his tone calm, soothing. 'We'll help you for sure, but we want you to consider the options and what's best for your husband right now.'

'I've done that.' Olivia's tone is firm. She looks from Rick to Moira, her gaze steely, challenging. 'So are you going to help me or do I have to get him back on my own?'

Moira glances at Rick. She agrees that the police should be called in, but if Olivia is dead set against it they can't leave her to deal with the abductors herself. She can see from Rick's expression he's thinking the same. She looks back at Olivia. 'We're not going anywhere. We'll help you get your husband back.'

'Thank you.' Olivia exhales and to Moira it looks as if she's deflating in front of them. Turning, Olivia leads them through to the kitchen and walks across to the island unit. Removing a piece of paper from the countertop, she holds it out to Moira. 'This is what they sent.'

Taking it, Moira looks at the photo. Cody is holding yesterday's newspaper. Both his eyes are bloodshot with dark purple bruising underneath, and there's dried blood caked across his right cheekbone and down one side of his face. He looks beaten and dejected.

His gaze is unfocused. At the bottom of the page, typed in the same font as the previous communication, are the words:

> $1 MILLION. 4PM. BENCH AT START OF SHIMMERING LAKE TRAIL, MIDDLE LAKE NATURE RESERVE. WE'LL TEXT THE TRANSFER DETAILS WHEN YOU SIT ON THE BENCH. YOU'LL HAVE TEN MINUTES TO GET IT DONE. DO IT AND WE RELEASE HIM. DON'T DO IT AND HE DIES. CALL THE COPS – HE DIES.

'That's a hell of a lot of cash,' says Rick, reading the note over Moira's shoulder.

'It is,' says Moira, nodding. These abductors aren't messing about.

'I'll pay it. Anything to get Cody safe,' says Olivia. There's no hesitation, and no doubt in her voice. It makes Moira believe that she hasn't had anything to do with Cody's disappearance and that all of this is real.

Rick clears his throat. Looks awkward. 'Apologies for the direct question, ma'am, but do you have the money available?'

Olivia nods. 'I can get that amount together, yes.'

Moira can't imagine ever having one million dollars cash available just like that. The movie business pays well – she guesses that's obvious given Olivia and Cody live on Millionaires' Row – but Olivia must have been smart with her money too. It irritates Moira that Olivia is going to pay the abductors, but if she won't call the cops, and she and the others can't find Cody before 4 p.m., then paying up is their best chance of getting him out alive. She glances at her watch; it's almost six o'clock. They've got ten hours until the ransom exchange is due to take place.

'Can you transfer that much at once?' says Moira. 'Isn't there a daily limit?'

'With a standard US bank, yes, but if I use one of my offshore accounts and call them now to tell them I'll be making a large payment at around 4 p.m. today, I think I can make it happen. They usually let you do the validation questions and get the basic transfer set up in advance, and they're very discreet – that's what the high account fees pay for.'

Rick nods. 'We'll keep trying to locate Cody, ma'am, but I think it's best that you make that call, just in case.'

'Not a problem,' says Olivia. 'If you'll excuse me, I'll go and start the arrangements.'

'For sure,' says Rick. 'I'd like to take a look at the CCTV controls again. Can I get into the study?'

Olivia takes a set of keys off a hook over by a large chalkboard with the words 'milk', 'cheese', 'avocado' and 'hummus' listed on it, and hands them to Rick. 'This is a spare set. The key marked 6 is for the study. It's been locked since you and Lizzie left yesterday.'

◆ ◆ ◆

As Olivia goes upstairs to fetch her banking documents and start the process of getting the money ready for the exchange that afternoon, Rick and Moira head to Cody's study to look at the CCTV system.

Rick unlocks the door and Moira follows him across the neat, uncluttered study to the CCTV monitors and computer. As Rick checks the system, she looks around the room, again surprised by how spotless and impersonal it is, just like Cody's room at the office. It feels completely at odds with the warmth and homely personality of the rest of the house.

'Well, this is kind of strange,' says Rick.

Moira turns back towards him. He's squinting at the computer screen. 'What is it?'

Rick shakes his head. 'I don't get it. There's no sign this has been tampered with, or that the room has been broken into, and Olivia said it's been locked since Lizzie and me left yesterday. But the system was definitely in record mode when we left, I double-checked it.'

Moira frowns. 'You think Olivia did it herself? That she has something to do with the abduction?'

'Could be.' Rick looks thoughtful. 'She sure doesn't want us to call the cops. Doesn't that strike you as kind of odd given it's pretty clear the people holding Cody are real violent?'

Moira shakes her head. Olivia's reactions seem genuine enough to her, and she didn't hesitate in saying she'd pay the money. 'Honestly, I think she just hates cops. What would she gain from his kidnap and ransom if she's the one paying the money?'

Rick's expression darkens. 'Maybe paying the money isn't the endgame.'

Moira says nothing. She gets what Rick's implying – that the endgame for the abduction isn't payment of the ransom and return of Cody, it's Cody's death – but she can't see Olivia being involved. Still, Moira's worked in law enforcement long enough to know people aren't always what they seem. People lie. And actors are trained to pretend to be someone they're not. Personally, she thinks Olivia's genuine, but it's probably wise to still exercise caution.

Looking over at the CCTV system, Moira thinks for a moment. 'Don't a lot of these systems stream video direct to your phone or tablet? I know Cody has this fancy set-up here in the study, but what if he can also access and control it remotely? Did you ask them that when you called the company yesterday?'

'I did not,' says Rick, thankful that EQS Alarms operate a 24/7 advice line. 'But I will now.'

As Rick dials, Moira feels her own mobile vibrate in the pocket of her jeans. Pulling it out, she reads the message. Her heart rate accelerates. Her mouth goes dry. It's the unknown number again. They've ignored her question asking who they are. Instead, they've messaged:

YOU HAVE TO STOP

Moira takes a couple of deep breaths as she tries to steady her heart rate. She frowns. The message makes no sense. Yes, she brought the files with all her research – including the covert copies she'd made of the failed operation file and all the information on Bobbie Porter and her known associates – with her to Florida, but she hasn't done anything with them. She's resigned her job, fled her life in London and even changed her identity. There's nothing left *to* stop.

'Well, that sure was interesting.'

Moira flinches at the sudden sound of Rick's voice.

'Hey, you okay?' He's looking at her all concerned and kindly, and she wishes she could confide in him. But she can't; it wouldn't be fair. And if she has to run again, it's best he knows nothing. If they come looking for her, it'll be safer for him that way.

She shoves the phone back into her pocket. 'Yeah, sorry, I was miles away. Thinking about the case, the letter and how they delivered it by hand, you know?'

'Sure,' says Rick, but his expression tells her he's not buying her story.

Moira fakes a light-hearted tone and tries to move the conversation on, anxious to focus on something other than herself. 'So what did the security company say?'

'You're right. The EQ1000 model that the Zieglers have can be watched and controlled by a desktop control programme and a synced app for cell phones and tablets. For the app you need a passcode and double authentication through a pre-arranged cell phone number, but then you're good to go.'

'So that could be how they deactivated the alarm and the cameras. If the app is on Cody's phone, they could have taken control of it.'

'If Olivia didn't do it, then it's the next most plausible explanation.'

Moira remembers Cody's badly beaten face in the picture. 'Yeah. And from the look of it, they kept on hitting him until he told them the codes for his phone and the app, and how to deactivate the system.'

'I should've thought about remote access sooner,' says Rick, frowning. 'But that still doesn't explain how it went offline the night before Cody disappeared. If they beat him for the codes to access it in the past twenty-four hours, it must have been taken offline a different way that first night.'

He's right and Moira hasn't got an answer. All they've got are assumptions and hypotheses right now. If they're going to have any chance of finding Cody Ziegler before the 4 p.m. ransom deadline, they're going to need a whole lot more.

21

MOIRA

Philip and Lizzie arrive at the Ziegler place just after eight o'clock. In the time between checking out the security system, searching the route the person delivering the ransom note would have taken from the street to the house, and their friends arriving, Moira and Rick have made a few calls to get further information and set up some meetings. There's a lot to do if they're going to have a chance of finding Cody Ziegler before 4 p.m. today. Moira frowns, wondering how it can have taken Philip and Lizzie so long to get here. It's frustrating. There's no time to waste and she's keen to get a move on.

As Philip and Lizzie join them in the kitchen, Rick slides off his stool at the island beside Moira and gestures their friends over to join them. Olivia follows behind. She's looking more composed now – the shock of discovering the note has receded a little. Her hair is sleek and styled, and the redness has faded from her face.

Rick turns towards Olivia. 'If it's okay with you, we'll debrief our team members and then get to work?'

'That's fine, go ahead,' says Olivia, leaning her hip against the kitchen countertop.

Rick doesn't speak for a moment, obviously waiting for Olivia to move into a different room. When she doesn't show any sign of leaving, he says, 'We can use another room for the debrief if you'd like to stay in here?'

'No, this is good. But this is my home, and my husband's the one at risk,' says Olivia, her tone determined. Straightening up, she puts her hands on her hips. 'So I'm staying for your debrief.'

'Yes, ma'am,' says Rick, obviously deciding it's easier and more conducive to collaboration to agree rather than argue, but looking uncomfortable about it.

It's not ideal. Although it seems increasingly unlikely to Moira, there's still the possibility Olivia has some involvement in the abduction, and Rick certainly doesn't seem convinced enough of her innocence to take her off the suspects list. Moira would much prefer the workings of their investigation and their theories to be kept between the four of them.

The tension between Philip and Lizzie seems worse this morning, and it's not great for Olivia to witness that either. Moira really wants to get Lizzie alone for a proper chat to see what's going on, but with the case occupying their time right now she doesn't see an opportunity for that to happen any time soon. Hopefully the married pair will be able to stay civil for the sake of Olivia at least, but looking at the way their bodies are angled away from each other, and their glum expressions, Moira isn't sure that'll be possible.

'Okay, gather round, folks. The situation has changed,' says Rick, sitting back down and handing the most recently delivered note to Lizzie for her and Philip to read. 'Olivia received this ransom demand in the early hours of this morning, just before 5 a.m. The note was hand-delivered and slipped under the front door here at the main house.'

'How did they get through the gate? Wasn't the security system on?' asks Lizzie, surprised.

'It had been,' says Moira. 'But it was switched off before the note was delivered. We think the gate was opened remotely using an app on Cody's mobile phone, but we're waiting for the security company to confirm that. When Olivia had a look at the Find My Cellphone app this morning, Cody's phone had been switched off again. Rick has asked Hawk to see if he can get a report from the phone company for where the phone last pinged from—'

'But Hawk's not sure he'll get any luck with them, given this isn't an active police investigation and the cell phone companies can be pretty tight with their data,' adds Rick.

Philip runs his hand over his bald pate. Looks serious. 'Isn't there any CCTV of the people who delivered the ransom note?'

'Not from the house's system,' says Rick. 'But Moira's been in touch with Hank at the CCTV office and he's checking out the footage from the street cameras in this area between midnight and four fifty this morning – that's the time window when we believe the note was delivered. After we're done here, can you go over and meet him, Philip, and review the footage he's found?'

'Happy to.' Philip smiles briefly, and glances across at Lizzie, who immediately rolls her eyes and looks away from him. His expression returns to a frown.

'Great,' says Rick. He glances at Moira and raises his eyebrows.

She gets why. They'd discussed who should do what before Lizzie and Philip arrived, and had agreed that having husband and wife working independently of each other was going to get the best results. The tension between the two seems to be rising by the minute, and that doesn't create a good environment for clear, quick thinking and focus.

They have to get focused and find Cody before the ransom exchange. And the fact that Philip is letting her and Rick lead the investigation and the reallocation of work means he's definitely not his usual self. Normally he tries to take control. Right now, he doesn't even seem bothered that she and Rick responded to Olivia's emergency call and he's been brought in later. Moira never thought for one moment that she'd miss Philip being bossy and condescending, but his current behaviour is worryingly unlike him.

Moira nods at Rick. 'I had a text from Ashley half an hour ago to say the VP, Brad George, had arrived at the DVIZION offices, and I've just spoken with Donna, Cody's PA, who has confirmed that Brad's happy to meet me. I'm going to head over there straight after we've finished here.' She looks at Lizzie. 'We thought it'd be good if you could stay here and keep Olivia company. We're not expecting any further communication from the abductors until the ransom exchange at 4 p.m. at Middle Lake Nature Reserve, but they might mix things up and we need to be ready.'

Lizzie frowns and pushes an imaginary strand of hair from her face. Her voice is flat when she says, 'Well, I suppose I can.'

She's obviously not excited by a babysitting job and Moira can understand that, but there isn't any forensics work for Lizzie to do right now. 'You should be able to follow up on the lawsuit Dirk Baldwin filed while you're here. If you can get the details of the suit, and how it was resolved, we can double-check that against Brad George's perspective on it. It could also help us determine whether Baldwin wanted to harm Cody.'

'Definitely,' says Lizzie, her expression and voice much brighter and more animated now. She pats her messenger bag. 'I've got my iPad, so I can research the lawsuit no problem.'

'Great,' says Moira, relieved.

Rick nods. 'Okay, so that's good news. I'm going to make a few more calls to try and track down the whereabouts of Dirk Baldwin and Marty Hannier – our two persons of interest. Then I'll drive over to Middle Lake Nature Reserve to get the lay of the land for the ransom exchange.' He glances at Olivia. 'Ma'am, I'd appreciate it if you stayed home today. Anything you need, we can assist with, but I think it's safer if you remain here.'

Olivia crosses her arms and lifts her chin defiantly. For a moment Moira thinks she's going to refuse, but then she exhales and nods. 'Okay, fine, I'll stay here, but we won't be alone. My housekeeper will arrive in around an hour, and the pool guy will be here this afternoon. Should I call them and cancel?'

'Thanks, ma'am, I appreciate that. And I think it's better to stick with your routine and let the housekeeper and pool guy do their work as usual. But don't let on there's anything wrong,' says Rick.

'I understand,' says Olivia.

'Great.' Rick looks around the assembled group. 'Any questions?'

'No,' says Philip, grim-faced. 'Time is of the essence, yes? Let's get on with it.'

Moira nods. 'We'll regroup here at 2 p.m. to get prepped for the ransom delivery. According to Google Maps, the drive to Middle Lake Nature Reserve is twenty-two minutes, but I've no idea how the traffic will be this afternoon, so we need to allow enough time to get there comfortably for 4 p.m.'

'If we haven't found Cody by then,' says Philip.

'For sure,' says Rick. He doesn't look too confident, though.

Moira doesn't blame him. She isn't feeling confident either. She checks the time on her watch. It's almost nine. They've got seven hours before Olivia has to be sitting on the bench at the start of the Shimmering Lake Trail in Middle Lake Nature Reserve.

Time is not their friend today.

The clock is ticking.

22

PHILIP

The CCTV office is over on the other side of the Ocean Mist community towards the end of a street of mainly Spanish-style houses. It's set back a little way from the road, and is nothing like as glamorous as its neighbours.

Manoeuvring the Toyota into the otherwise empty line of parking bays, Philip gets out and heads towards the building. Investigating cases has always given him an adrenaline rush in the past, but today, with everything that's happening between Lizzie and him, he just feels miserable. Still, he tells himself to buck up. There's an investigation to be done. Olivia Hamilton Ziegler and her husband are counting on them. It's his duty to get the job done well and find Cody Ziegler.

Putting a bit more vim into his step, Philip marches towards the entrance. As he approaches, he notices there's a new keypad access unit and the old door has been replaced with a reinforced security door. A couple of months back, while they'd been investigating the death of the young woman in one of the pools at Manatee Park, the security hut had been broken into and Hank, a resident who takes some part-time shifts overseeing the CCTV operations, was attacked while on duty. The CCTV footage from the night of the murder had been stolen. Luckily, Moira had found

Hank and administered CPR until the emergency services arrived. Philip's glad they've tightened up the security, for Hank's sake. After all, the bloke isn't getting any younger and there are only so many whacks to the head a person can take.

Philip presses the buzzer on the intercom section of the keypad.

'Yeah hello?' A slightly tinny version of Hank's voice comes over the intercom speaker.

'Hank? It's Philip Sweetman here. I'm outside.'

'Great. Come on in,' says Hank. There's a clunk as the door lock disengages. 'I've found something you need to see.'

Pushing the door open, Philip enters the building. Pausing a moment to make sure the door closes properly and the bolt has re-engaged, he then strides down the corridor, ignoring the black and yellow tape on the floor a few feet inside with the words 'DO NOT CROSS' and the sign saying 'No entry beyond this point unless accompanied by a member of the security team'. At the end of the corridor there's a door marked 'Surveillance Suite'. Philip heads towards it.

He's a couple of feet away when the door opens and Hank appears in the doorway, grinning. The bruising over his face has gone now, although there's still a patch towards the back of his salt-and-pepper hair that's shorter than the rest due to it having been shaved to stitch up the wounds from the attack. He opens his arms out wide. 'Big Phil, great to see you.'

Philip smiles as Hank claps him on the back, welcoming him like an old friend. It's nice to feel wanted for a change. He doesn't even correct him for using the abbreviated version of his name that he hates so much. 'Thanks for doing this. You said you'd found something?'

'I surely have,' says Hank, leading Philip over to a double-length desk with four computer monitors. He sits down on the nearest chair and gestures for Philip to take the seat alongside him.

Tapping a couple of keys on the keyboard, Hank points to the left-of-centre monitor. 'Got you something here. This is the feed from the Turtle Rise Boulevard camera at 03.59 this morning.'

Philip squints towards the screen. As Hank plays the recording in slow motion, a dark-coloured SUV moves frame by frame across the screen. 'Is this the first camera to pick this vehicle up?'

'Yep. We've got a couple blind spots as two of our cameras are out for maintenance on the roads into this end of the district, but this camera and the two on Millionaires' Row are working just fine.'

Philip tuts loudly. It's annoying some of the cameras are out. Residents pay a premium homeowners' association fee – any issues with the CCTV should be fixed immediately. That's not Hank's fault, though, so he tries to let it go for now. 'Do you know which gatehouse entrance they used to get on-site?'

Hank leans back on his chair and exhales hard. 'Well, you see, that's a bit of a sore point right here and now.' He lowers his voice to a whisper even though there's only the two of them in the security suite. 'The plate recognition software's been glitching since Thanksgiving, and the CCTV cameras at the Ocean Mist entrance are out, some electrical fault I'm told. Management haven't been exactly rushing to fix the problems.'

Philip clenches his fists. First he finds out there are cameras not working, and now he's discovering that there's dodgy software too? If there's one thing he can't abide, it's organisations not fulfilling their duties. He knows there's a question over the way the management at The Homestead controls public-facing communications, but this slapdash approach to security surveillance is something else. The zero crime rate and high-tech security are both cornerstones of the luxury retirement community's marketing campaigns. Have the recent issues with burglaries and murder made them rethink their security investments? Philip shakes his head. 'We need to launch a campaign. Residents think they have CCTV security and secure entrances – if that's not the case, we need the management to rectify it immediately. Our monthly fees are high enough to cover the maintenance ten times over.'

'I hear you. Let's do that,' says Hank. 'But don't worry, because we've got some good images of the SUV here and that'll help you with your investigation.'

'I certainly hope so. Let's look at the other two camera feeds, yes?' says Philip, relaxing his fists a little. The blood is starting to pump stronger through his veins. Even though some of the cameras not working is highly frustrating, what Hank's discovered is good. The SUV could be a lead.

'Sure. I got them queued up for you right here,' says Hank, pointing to the two monitors on the right side of the desk. He taps the keyboard again, and the footage on one of the monitors starts playing in slow motion. 'This picks up the SUV from the point that the Turtle Rise camera loses them.'

Nodding, Philip keeps his gaze on the slow-motion video replay. The SUV makes the turn into Millionaires' Row, passes the camera and continues on along the street. The motion-activated camera continues to record the vehicle until the brake lights flare and a couple of seconds later it disappears around a bend in the road.

'And this one,' says Hank, moving the mouse and clicking it a couple of times. 'This here shows the feed from the second Millionaires' Row camera. It's maybe thirty feet from the Ziegler place.'

Philip watches as the SUV drives past the camera and stops at the side of the road. The lights are turned off but he's pretty sure the engine is still running. Moments later, a figure dressed in dark clothes and a balaclava gets out of the passenger side and jogs along the pavement towards the Ziegler house. They're holding an envelope in their hand.

As the figure disappears around the turn into the Ziegler driveway, Philip checks the timestamp on the bottom right of the camera footage: 04.01.32.

'This must be the point they delivered the note,' says Hank.

'Indeed,' says Philip. The SUV remains parked. He assumes there's someone in the driver's seat but it's hard to tell from this angle. There's no movement anywhere else on the street.

'Here they are, coming back,' says Hank, tapping the computer screen with his finger.

He's right; the figure is jogging back along the pavement to the SUV. Philip checks the timestamp: 04.04.59. That's a total of three and a half minutes to get through the security gates and on to the property, down the driveway to slip the envelope with the ransom demand under the front door, and then get back down the driveway to the SUV parked on the street.

'Slick operation,' says Hank, shaking his head.

'Indeed.' The speed adds weight to Rick and Moira's hypothesis that the abductors are using Cody Ziegler's mobile phone to access the house's security systems via an app. There's one thing about this that's jarring with Philip, though. If the abductors have access to Cody's phone, why didn't they text or call Olivia Hamilton Ziegler with the ransom demand? Philip frowns. 'But it's risky – some might say foolish – to come here and hand-deliver the note. Can you get a close-up on the plate?'

'I surely can,' says Hank, toggling the mouse to enlarge the licence plate. 'There you go.'

Philip squints closer at the screen. The licence plate is easy to read – it hasn't been covered or defaced. Pulling out his notepad, he jots down the type of plate and the licence number. He shakes his head. It seems too easy.

'You got something eating at you there, Big Phil?' says Hank. 'What's going on?'

'They stopped the CCTV and alarm at the Ziegler residence, probably via the victim's remote control, before they came on to the property,' says Philip. 'It seems strange to me that they'd do that, but they weren't bothered about the community CCTV.'

'Good point.' Hank pushes his wire-framed glasses back up on to the bridge of his nose. 'That would make me say these folks didn't know about our street cameras. We've gotten a fair few of them switched out recently – changing the more obvious traditional-style cameras for smaller, more covert equipment. Makes them a hell of a lot harder to spot and therefore much harder to vandalise.'

Philip nods, thinking. Even if the cameras are more covert, all the residents of The Homestead know about the street CCTV and it's a big part of the marketing for the community. That the people in the SUV weren't aware indicates to him that they're unfamiliar with the finer details of The Homestead and the cameras around the Ziegler property. Moira and Rick seem to think the person might be a friend or acquaintance of Cody Ziegler. This new information could help narrow down the field.

'This is great, Hank, thank you,' says Philip, getting up from his seat. 'You've been a massive help.'

'Not a problem, anything for a friend of Moira.'

Philip shakes Hank's hand. 'I'd be grateful if you didn't mention any of the details to anyone else for now. We don't want to risk our perpetrators hearing what we know.'

Hank taps the side of his nose. 'No worries, I'm like a vault.'

'Good man,' says Philip.

As he turns and hurries out of the surveillance suite, Philip dials Rick's number. He needs Rick to get his law enforcement contact to run the plate. The SUV could be a real break. If they can trace the owner, they should be able to find Cody Ziegler's abductors.

It's a solid lead, and he found it.

Philip punches the air in triumph.

23

MOIRA

Brad George is not what she'd been expecting. In her mind, those who work in the corporate world, especially those who handle the finances, are suited, serious-faced people. With an open-neck orange shirt under his slim-fit black suit jacket, his striped socks just visible between his trousers and black shoes, and his deep tan and perfectly styled blond hair, Brad George is the polar opposite.

Moira is sitting on one of the stylish yellow armchairs in his office, waiting for him to come and sit down. She takes a sip of the coffee Donna made her and she's thankful it's on the strong side because, despite the urgency of the job in hand, Moira is finding it hard to concentrate. The worry from the early morning phone message is still hovering over her like a pendulous cloud.

Trying to push away the thoughts of the threatening texts, Moira looks around Brad's office. It's nothing like Cody Ziegler's, even though it's the same basic layout. But whereas Cody's space was clutter-free and neat, Brad's is filled with personal items – photos of him playing sport, and others of him shaking the hand of movie stars – and his desk is piled high with files and paperwork.

Finally, Brad finishes searching on his desk, picks up a file and comes over to join her. He flashes her a charming smile. 'Sorry about that.'

'No problem,' says Moira. 'I appreciate you speaking to me this morning.'

'Of course, anything to help Cody, you know. I was totally choked up when Donna called and told me about the whole thing. I mean, I was just talking to him Wednesday and now he's missing . . .' Brad shakes his head. 'You hear about things like this happening, but you never think it's going to happen to you or someone you know.'

'I understand it must be upsetting,' says Moira. She needs to get Brad focused. 'Can you tell me when you last spoke with Cody Ziegler?'

'Sure, yeah, it was Wednesday morning, first thing, we had a briefing on the Skyline project.' Brad holds up the file. The word 'SKYLINE' is written in capital letters on the front. 'We needed to get him all set for the lunch he had scheduled with the guys from the production company.'

Moira makes a note on her phone for appearances, but what he's saying is consistent with what she was told yesterday by Donna and some of Cody's other colleagues. 'And how did he seem to you?'

'Fine, really great actually.' Brad smiles. His teeth are very white and even. 'I mean, he was Cody, right? So he was serious, focused on the project and asking a lot of pointy questions as usual. But it was a good meeting and at the end of the call he said he'd be in soon, before eleven anyways.'

'But he wasn't?' asks Moira.

Brad's smile droops. 'No.'

'Were you aware of whether Cody was planning on giving someone a lift that morning?'

'A lift?' Brad looks confused. 'Like a ride share? No, I . . . I don't think so anyways, but this whole thing's gotten me kind of turned around so I don't . . .'

'I understand,' says Moira. 'So you finished the call and then expected to see him in the office late morning?'

He shakes his head sadly. 'I never thought that'd be the last I'd hear from him.'

Moira keeps her expression neutral, but the fact that Brad is talking as if Cody is already dead hasn't escaped her notice. 'And how were things between the two of you?'

'Great. Brilliant.' His smile widens. 'We were colleagues, friends, for a long while, you know? So we're like brothers – different personalities but there's a lot of love between us.'

There's something off here, Moira's sure of it. Although Brad's enthusing about Cody, his smile seems fake and it doesn't reach his eyes. 'And the evening before he disappeared? I understand you were in a meeting with Cody. How did that go?'

'The meeting was fine,' says Brad, but his eyes aren't meeting her gaze any more.

Moira wonders if he was feeling as fine as he claims. Tim Samson had told her that he and Brad had been in a weekly progress update meeting until around nine the previous evening. He'd said Brad had gone straight home afterwards, but perhaps that wasn't the case. She goes with a hunch that something made them fall out. 'And the conversation you and Cody had straight after the meeting?'

Brad shakes his head. 'Look, one of our projects is over budget and I hadn't alerted Cody to it until Tuesday night. I've been liaising with the project team for a month on the situation and we were confident the finances would come back in line in a couple of weeks, so I hadn't flagged it. But Cody was really pissed. As soon as we were out of the meeting with Tim, he hauled me into his office and bawled me out. I didn't appreciate the no-confidence vote in my assessment of the situation and I told him as much, then I left for the night.'

'It must have been frustrating, upsetting even,' says Moira.

Brad shrugs. He flips the corner of the Skyline file back and forth with his index finger as he speaks. 'Yes and no. It happens from time to time. Cody is a control freak and he's tightly wound. Sometimes all that tension has to come out and it's usually vented at me. He'd never shout at the more junior staff or a client. So over the years I've gotten used to getting yelled at.' He gives a rueful smile. 'The thing is, Cody wants to know anything and everything all of the time. But the company's been growing – we're doing forty per cent more projects this year than last year. At the rate we're growing, he can't be hands on with everything any more, but he hasn't accepted it yet.'

Moira continues to make notes of the conversation on her phone. It's all useful background information. And this perspective of Cody as someone highly stressed, with a temper, is new. None of his other colleagues mentioned it yesterday. 'And how were things between the two of you the next morning?'

'Like I said, they were fine,' says Brad, putting the Skyline file on the table beside him. 'It was a good meeting. Cody blows hot every so often, but he cools down quick afterwards.'

Moira nods. 'Have you noticed him being more volatile recently?'

Brad leans back in his seat and crosses his arms. 'Why?'

'Olivia, his wife, said she thought he'd been concerned about something for a while, but he wouldn't tell her what was bothering him.'

Brad exhales hard. 'Running a business is stressful, and as I said, Cody takes on more than his fair share of the pressure.' He pauses, then continues more hesitantly. 'There is something that could have been adding to it . . .'

'Yes?'

Brad looks unsure. 'I don't want to get him into any trouble, though.'

'Given he's been missing for over forty-eight hours, I'd say he's already in trouble,' says Moira matter-of-factly. 'Anything you know that could help find him is important.'

'Well, like I said, we're doing far more projects this year than we've done before. The thing is, around five months ago we were heading into financial trouble. Covid had a big impact on our business and a lot of projects were grounded or delayed.' Brad shakes his head. 'We'd been talking about reducing costs and the number of projects we took on, and had gotten a plan drawn up to reduce our overheads. But just days before we pressed the button, Cody secured a new investor. This investor put a hell of a lot of money into the company – we're talking eight figures here – and so instead of a cost-reduction programme, we launched a massive expansion.'

There's something in Brad's tone that makes Moira believe he's not fully on board with the change. 'And you had concerns about that?'

He looks pained. Runs his hand through his hair. 'Look, I'm the Vice President. I'm responsible for monitoring and accounting for the money that comes in and out of DVIZION. But this new investor, Cody played that deal really close to his chest. He didn't let me meet them. He didn't even tell me who they were.'

'Isn't that unusual?'

'Very.' Brad shakes his head. He seems conflicted. 'He said they were a shy investor and wanted to stay a shadow partner rather than go public, but I just . . .'

'What is it?' says Moira. 'Anything you know could help us find Cody.'

He meets her gaze. 'It didn't add up right to me. We had a few heated debates, but Cody wouldn't budge; just wouldn't tell me who they were. I did a bit of digging – looked into the shell company the money was transferred from, tried to validate them as a legitimate investor, but I couldn't.' He shakes his head again. 'With the way Cody's gotten increasingly tense, and the freak-out the other day about the project going over budget, it makes me worry that he's got us into bed with some bad people.'

'Like who?'

Brad shifts his weight on the seat. Looks even more uncomfortable. 'I don't know for sure, but I worry it's something to do with the Mob.'

The Mob? Damn. That could put a whole new perspective on Cody's disappearance. While Moira doubts the Mob themselves would abduct Cody in order to ransom him – from what she knows of their MO, they'd be more likely to disappear him without trace – his association with them could have made him a target for their enemies.

Either way, she needs to know the identity of the mystery investor.

And she needs to know fast.

24

LIZZIE

Hunched over her laptop, sitting at the island unit in Olivia's kitchen, Lizzie is feeling frustrated. She hasn't got very far looking into the lawsuit that Dirk Baldwin brought against Cody Ziegler and DVIZION. She's found a brief mention online of it being filed and registered with the Florida Department of Labor, but there's no detail. She hasn't even discovered which legal firm was representing Dirk Baldwin. Also, when she looks at the Department's web page listings, as of today there's no mention of Dirk Baldwin or DVIZION.

She has limited knowledge about how employment lawsuits work here in the States, but from what she's found she guesses that once a complaint is withdrawn, the lawsuit details are expunged from the records. Sighing, she exits the Department of Labor website and opens a new search window to google Dirk Baldwin and see if he's on any social media.

Just as she's typing his name into the search field, Lizzie feels as if she's being watched. Looking towards the window, she sees the round, tanned face of Olivia's gardener peering in at her through the glass. When he sees she's spotted him, he quickly ducks out of view. 'What the . . . ?' Lizzie mutters, getting up and hurrying across to the window.

'You okay?' says Olivia, coming into the kitchen.

'Your gardener was just spying on me through the window,' says Lizzie, shuddering.

'What, Earl?' says Olivia. 'He's harmless, just a little overly familiar and protective sometimes.'

Lizzie frowns. Spying on people is more than a little over-familiar in her view. 'I thought he only worked Tuesdays and Thursdays?'

'Usually yes, but he said the flowerbeds needed some extra attention so he'd do an extra few days this week.'

'Has he done that before?' says Lizzie, thinking it's rather suspicious that the gardener has suddenly changed his working pattern the same week Cody has gone missing.

'Yes, a few times before, whenever the garden gets a little out of control.' Olivia gives a tight smile. 'Really, Earl is perfectly harmless.'

'Okay.' Lizzie's not one hundred per cent convinced, but she supposes Olivia knows Earl best.

'Good,' says Olivia. She looks deflated; nothing like the glamorous movie star Philip had shown Lizzie images of on IMDb earlier. *Stress does that to people*, Lizzie supposes, thinking of the dark circles under her own eyes that morning. Fear too. Olivia moves around to the other side of the island. 'I'm sorry, with everything going on I've forgotten my manners. I haven't asked you yet if you'd like a drink.'

'It's okay,' says Lizzie, moving away from the window and back to her seat at the island. 'I can only imagine what you're going through. How are you bearing up?'

Olivia doesn't answer right away. Instead, she moves over to the coffee maker, takes two mugs from the cabinet above it and pours coffee into them. She looks back at Lizzie. 'As is or milk?'

'A touch of milk, please,' says Lizzie, closing the lid of her laptop. She gets the sense Olivia wants to talk and as she's pretty much hit a wall on the lawsuit, she can make herself more useful by listening and supporting her.

Olivia adds milk to Lizzie's coffee and brings it over to the island. Setting the mugs down on the countertop, she climbs on to the stool opposite Lizzie. 'Sorry again.'

'It's fine, really,' says Lizzie, picking up the mug and taking a sip. It's good coffee – freshly ground, not instant. 'So how are you?'

Olivia looks down at her mug. 'I'm hanging in there, you know?'

Lizzie nods, even though she doesn't really know. 'It must be tough.'

'I just want him back home and safe.' Olivia shakes her head. 'What those assholes have done to him . . . his poor face . . .' She takes a shaky breath. 'Cody wouldn't hurt anyone. There isn't a violent bone in his body. That someone would do this to him is just unthinkable.'

'We'll get him back,' says Lizzie, hoping that they will.

'You asked yesterday if there was anyone I could think of who'd want to hurt Cody,' says Olivia hesitantly. 'I can't think of anyone who'd want to do him harm, but there's someone who might want to hurt me.'

Lizzie leans closer to Olivia. 'Who?'

'It's probably nothing,' says Olivia, looking conflicted. 'But after Tamsin died, there was a bunch of unpleasantness about her will. She'd left a few pieces of jewellery and some sentimental items to me, and a small amount of money to her brother, Bryce, but the rest was donated as a legacy gift to the Helping Hearts Foundation – a local animal rescue where I'm the patron.'

Lizzie nods along as Olivia speaks. 'So what was the problem?'

Olivia lets out a long sigh. 'Tamsin's brother didn't want the money going to the foundation. Bryce said that I'd poisoned Tamsin against him and forced her to give the money to the charity rather than to him.' She shakes her head. 'It wasn't true, of course. Tamsin had given Bryce many handouts over the years and he'd never attempted to pay her back. She knew he'd often gamble away the money, and she wanted the money she'd earned to do some good, that's why she gifted it to the foundation.'

'So what happened?' says Lizzie.

'Bryce contested the will through every court that he could. His last appeal was rejected a few months ago, and the will was executed. He called me a couple of times, screaming cuss words and threatening he'd get revenge.' Olivia shudders. 'I never thought he'd actually do anything violent, but now Cody's been taken . . . maybe he's hurting Cody to get back at me?'

'It's a possibility,' says Lizzie cautiously. This might be important. Tamsin's brother could be a person of interest – they need to speak to him. 'Do you have a telephone number and address for Bryce?'

'I do. I blocked his numbers after the last time he screamed at me, but I still have his landline and cell phone jotted down.' Olivia goes over to the far side of the kitchen cabinets and opens a drawer. Taking out a small blue notebook, she flicks through the pages and then reads out the numbers.

Lizzie jots them down. 'And his address?'

'Sure, I have that too.' Olivia meets Lizzie's gaze. 'But he lives over in San Diego.'

After Lizzie has written down the address, and Olivia has put her notebook back in the drawer, they sit for a moment in uneasy silence. Lizzie looks at the phone number for Tamsin's brother. She's itching to call Bryce, but she forces herself to wait until Olivia is out of the room. Given the behaviour Olivia has described, who knows how the man might react.

Olivia clears her throat. 'You must think it weird, the set-up between Cody and me?'

'I understand why you did what you did. The media can be heartless and the way they hound people is awful.' Lizzie shrugs. 'I can understand you'd want to avoid that.'

Olivia holds her gaze a long moment, as if deciding whether to say more. Then she nods. 'Some people might say our marriage is a sham, but it's real in every way aside from the sex. He's my best friend. We tell each other everything.'

'He didn't tell you about the trouble he was in, though, or what was in those letters – those threats. He lied by omission – doesn't that bother you?' The words are out of Lizzie's mouth before she can think better of it. She hadn't meant to be so direct.

Olivia frowns. 'He didn't lie. And knowing Cody, he didn't tell me because he wanted to protect me.'

'But he *should* have told you,' says Lizzie, clutching her mug tighter. 'You're his wife, you have a right to know.'

Olivia cocks her head to one side. 'Something tells me we're not talking about Cody and me any longer, am I right?'

Lizzie bites her lip. She takes a sip of coffee, then lets go of her mug, twisting her three rings around her wedding finger. 'My husband didn't tell me about a health problem he had until the worst happened.'

'But surely, as he's still alive, it means the worst hasn't happened,' says Olivia, taking a sip of coffee.

Lizzie nods. She doesn't tell Olivia about the little girl who lost her life after being abducted because Philip was too busy having secret medical tests in hospital to pass along a priority tip-off that could have enabled her to be found before she died. 'He lied by omission.'

Olivia looks thoughtful. 'Maybe he did, but that doesn't mean he was wrong to do it.'

Lizzie says nothing. Philip *was* wrong. He was very wrong.

'Look, Tamsin didn't tell me when the cancer returned a third time. We'd fought it together twice before, but that third time, when the doctors found it had spread and told her there was nothing more they could do, she decided to keep it from me. I only knew three weeks before she died, and she only told me then because I was on at her to go see her doctor as she wasn't feeling good.' Olivia tears up. She takes a breath, steadying herself, and has another mouthful of coffee. 'My Tam lived alone with the secret that she was dying for almost six months.'

'But why didn't she tell you?' asks Lizzie, her tone sympathetic.

'Because she wanted our last few months together to be happy. She said that once I knew about the cancer returning it would've always been there, like a dark shadow in the background, blighting everything we did.' Olivia exhales hard. 'And she knew that I'd want her to fight it, to find other treatments, try something, anything, that might give us more time. She didn't want that and she didn't want our last few months together spent arguing.'

'But when you found out she'd kept it from you, weren't you angry?' says Lizzie.

'Angry at the cancer, yes, and at how unfair life can be sometimes, for sure, but at Tam – never.' Olivia looks down at her almost empty coffee mug. Moves it from side to side with her fingers. Her voice is quieter when she continues. 'Knowing she shouldered the burden of the illness alone for all those months broke my heart. I wish I could have supported her more. But it was her cancer and her choice. I have to respect that.'

Lizzie nods. She supposes there are some parallels between Tamsin and Philip's health situations. But Philip didn't hide the truth from his family and employer because he didn't want to spoil the time he had left with them. He did it for his own selfish reasons – because his ego couldn't have stood not being able to continue in his job, and as a result he put other people's lives in jeopardy.

149

She looks back at Olivia and gives her a sad smile. 'I'm so sorry for your loss.'

'Thanks.'

Lizzie doesn't know what more to say. No words seem enough.

'When Tam died, I fell apart. Cody was my rock – without him I doubt I'd have got through it.' Olivia shivers. 'If anything happens to him, I'll never forgive myself.'

Lizzie frowns. 'But you didn't cause this.'

'I know, but the ransom delivery depends on me. If I mess it up . . .'

Reaching across the island, Lizzie puts her hand on Olivia's arm and gives it a squeeze. 'You won't.'

'I hope not.' Olivia looks serious. 'Don't waste your time on anger. Cherish the people you love, Lizzie. You never know when they won't be around any more.'

Lizzie holds Olivia's gaze for a long moment as she thinks about Philip and the way he hid the truth for so long about his health and why he'd really had to retire so suddenly. 'Surely a real relationship, when someone really loves you, means sharing everything. Telling you the truth, no matter how bad it is?'

'Not always.' Olivia puts her hand over Lizzie's and gives it a squeeze. 'In my experience, sometimes it's better not to know.'

25

RICK

He meets Philip half a block from the address Hawk messaged him for Dirk Baldwin. As he scans the on-street parking bays that flank the row of stores, looking for a spot, Rick sees Philip's Toyota tucked into a bay outside the Pampered Pooch dog salon. He's not surprised; Philip's the most punctual guy he knows.

Steering the jeep into a bay a few spots along, Rick kills the engine. Dirk Baldwin's place is about a half hour by car from the DVIZION offices, and according to Hawk, the date he moved here coincided with him starting work for Cody Ziegler. Rick glances along the storefronts – alongside the grooming parlour there's a Subway sandwich shop, a beauty salon and a mini mart. It seems a nice enough part of town.

He walks over to Philip's car. Philip doesn't notice him at first. He's staring into space and looks deep in thought. Rick raps his knuckles on the passenger window and waves at his friend.

Philip flinches and turns to the window. He smiles when he sees who it is, raising his hand in greeting before getting out of the vehicle. 'Sorry, Rick. Didn't see you there.'

'No worries. You all set to check this guy out?'

'Yes, yes,' says Philip, keeping pace with Rick as they head along the sidewalk towards the apartment building where Dirk Baldwin lives. 'Do we have any more intel on the lawsuit?'

Rick tries not to act surprised that Philip hasn't heard from his wife on this already. He shakes his head. 'Lizzie messaged me. She said there's no details online other than the date of the original filing.'

'Right,' says Philip with a nod. His tone's businesslike. 'Better see what we can get out of this fellow then.'

'For sure, although Lizzie says Olivia told her about another potential person of interest – Tamsin's brother. Apparently he was angry about the amount Tamsin left him in her will and blames Olivia. I've said for Lizzie to make contact with him,' says Rick.

'Good, good,' says Philip.

Rick waits for him to say more but he doesn't. He exhales, relieved that Philip is putting the issue between him and Lizzie to the back of his mind and concentrating on the case. If he's honest, Rick's doubly relieved that Philip doesn't want to talk about the issue with Lizzie. Advice on family bliss isn't something he feels qualified to give.

◆ ◆ ◆

Dirk Baldwin's apartment block is pretty nice. It's a five-storey, relatively new construction building with a large, clean foyer and working elevators. They gain access by grabbing the door before it closes after a young couple exit and slipping inside – better to get up to the apartment before letting Dirk know they're there, so that there's less chance of him managing to dodge them.

Dirk's place is on the fourth floor, and although Rick would've been happy to take the stairs for the added cardio workout, he doubts Philip would have been thrilled.

As they step out of the elevator, Philip glances at Rick. 'You okay to take the lead on this?'

Rick tries not to show his surprise, even though it's unlike Philip to want to play second in a person-of-interest interview. 'Sure.'

They find Dirk's apartment at the far end of the corridor, adjacent to the door to the fire escape. Rick's pleased they didn't have to forewarn Dirk they were coming. It would've been easy for him to slip out the fire exit to avoid them.

Rick glances at Philip and raises an eyebrow. He nods, so Rick gives the door three firm raps and takes a step back to wait.

After a few seconds, the door opens a couple inches. A slider bar is visible through the gap. Rick can't see the person inside and they don't say anything. He glances at Philip, who raises his eyebrows.

'Dirk Baldwin?' says Rick.

A male voice says, 'Who wants to know?'

Rick considers how to respond. It's a tricky one. If he says he's a friend of Cody Ziegler then chances are the door will get slammed in his face, but if he tells this guy that they're investigating Cody's disappearance it could be fatal for Cody if Dirk is connected to his disappearance. Playing it safe, Rick decides to dodge the question entirely. 'I understand you filed a lawsuit against DVIZION – your ex-employers? We'd like to speak with you about it.'

'What are you, journos?' asks the man, his tone nervous. 'I dropped the lawsuit. I've got nothing to say.'

'We'd just like a few minutes of your time, sir,' says Rick, his voice calm, soothing.

'I . . . can't.'

'They pay you off, son?' says Philip.

'How many of you are out there?' There's real fear in the man's voice now. 'I said I'm not talking, yeah?'

Rick moves along to the far side of the door so he can get a better look through the gap. From what he can see, the guy on the other side of the door is mid-twenties, super slim, dressed in a T-shirt and jeans. He looks real agitated. Rick lowers his voice. 'So they paid you off, huh?'

'I can't say anything, okay?' The man sounds desperate. 'Please . . . just go.'

Rick nods at Philip. It's clear they're not going to get anything of use from Dirk Baldwin. At least not right now. But he hasn't closed the door, so maybe there's hope.

Taking an old receipt from his pocket, Rick borrows a pen from Philip and jots his cell phone number on to it. Leaning forward, he slips the paper through the gap in the door. 'We're going now. But if you change your mind and feel like talking, call me.'

The guy says nothing as he pulls the door closed.

It's not the outcome Rick was hoping for, but that's the way leads can go sometimes. Walking back along the corridor, he thinks about how agitated Dirk Baldwin had gotten, and the fear in his voice when he'd told them he wouldn't talk. It didn't add up right to Rick. A few weeks back this guy had apparently been parading outside the DVIZION offices, yelling and making a real scene. Now he wanted to fade into the background, seemingly afraid to talk. Something had happened to cause that switch-a-roo and Rick's pretty darn sure it wasn't just a gagging order. A gagging order wouldn't cause the guy to be that afraid, and man, he looked terrified.

As they enter the elevator, Philip shakes his head. 'Well, that was a waste of bloody time.'

'Maybe,' says Rick, still convinced there's more than the obvious going on here. 'He might call.'

'Unlikely,' says Philip. 'If they paid him off and slapped a gagging order on him then he can't talk unless he wants to hand back the money.'

Rick knows Philip's right, but he had a real sense that beneath the fear, and the demands for them to leave, Dirk actually wanted to tell them something. He's been in law enforcement long enough to know that oftentimes when he has a hunch like this, it turns out to be right.

As he presses the button for the lobby and the elevator slowly descends, Rick realises something else that was off with Dirk Baldwin's behaviour: he didn't seem angry with Cody Ziegler. From what Moira had been told by his colleagues at DVIZION, Dirk had been furious and real loud about letting everyone know it. If that's changed, Rick wants to know why. In his experience, even when folks get paid off, it doesn't make them any less mad about the injustice they'd experienced.

'Do you think Olivia's telling the truth about everything?' says Philip, cutting into Rick's thoughts.

'Maybe. She seems on the level but—'

'She's an actress?' says Philip.

'Yep, exactly.' Rick frowns. 'I think we need to treat her with caution, especially if she's in the room when we're talking about our investigation.'

Philip nods. 'It doesn't feel right or professional her being with us when we discuss the case, but we could use it to our advantage. If we reveal things – true or not – when she's listening, we could watch to see how she reacts.'

Rick thinks for a moment. It's a good call. Oftentimes, a person's behaviour – the tells and involuntary expressions they make – show you more about what they're thinking than their words. 'Yeah, let's try that.'

'Good, good. So what's our next move?' asks Philip as they step out of the elevator and cross the foyer to the exit.

Again, Rick finds it strange that Philip is asking for direction – usually he's trying to assert his authority and call the shots. It can be tiring, working with him when he's being like that, but weirdly Rick finds he kind of misses the usual bossy, opinionated Philip. 'We need to . . .'

Feeling his cell phone buzz in his pocket, Rick stops mid-sentence and pulls it out, hopeful Dirk Baldwin has changed his mind already. But when he looks at the screen, Rick sees it isn't Dirk. He presses answer. 'Hey, buddy. What've you got for me?'

'I've got an address for that Marty Hannier dude you asked about and a read on that plate,' says Hawk, his gum-chewing clearly audible between words.

'Appreciate that,' says Rick, pulling an old parking lot ticket from his wallet and gesturing at Philip to borrow his pen again. 'Hit me with it.'

'Right, so the address I've gotten for Hannier is over at a modular home community in Kissimmee Village, Kissimmee. It's a rental and it looks like he's moved there recently – last week or so.'

Rick writes down the address as Hawk says it. 'Okay, cool. I'll check that out. What about the licence plate, did you find the SUV?'

'Well, kinda,' says Hawk, his jaws working the gum double time. 'Except it ain't an SUV registered on that plate, it's a green Toyota Prius.'

'A Prius?' says Rick, looking at Philip, who raises an eyebrow. 'You sure?'

'Totally,' says Hawk. 'I had my contact run it twice. The vehicle with that plate isn't an SUV, no doubt.'

Rick frowns. 'Is the Prius reported stolen?'

'Nah, not yet anyways,' says Hawk. 'You want the address where it's registered?'

'For sure,' says Rick. He draws a line under Marty Hannier's address and notes down the address that the licence plate is registered to. 'You got a name for the owner?'

'Yep,' says Hawk. There's a rustle of paper. 'It's a Mrs Melinda Grace. According to her DMV record, she's a seventy-six-year-old widow.'

'That's real helpful. Thanks, buddy.'

'No problem. Just remember that the way things are going, you'll be buying me a season ticket real soon.'

'I hear you,' says Rick, smiling. Hawk is a big baseball fan. 'Later.'

He turns to Philip as he ends the call. 'Looks like the SUV had a cloned plate – the licence number is from a green Prius.'

'I heard,' says Philip. He exhales hard, looking real deflated. 'I thought that licence plate would be the key to cracking this thing. Now we're right back at nothing again.'

It's not like Philip to have such a defeatist attitude. Obviously, whatever is going on between him and Lizzie is hitting him hard. Rick keeps his tone upbeat. 'Sure it's a setback, but we've gotten an address for Marty Hannier. That could be useful.'

'Yeah,' says Philip, but his tone is flat.

'Look, I think we should check out the Prius anyways. You never know, it could be relevant.'

'The "leave no stone unturned" approach?' says Philip, nodding. 'I suppose it's as good a strategy as any.'

'Exactly,' says Rick. He needs to give Philip a job to do, a focus. Hopefully, it'll help lift him out of his funk and spark the usual bull-by-the-horns Philip back into action. 'So how'd you want to do this? You want to check out Hannier or the Prius?'

Philip runs his hand over his bald pate. 'You take Hannier and I'll go see the Prius.'

'Deal,' says Rick. He rips the ticket in half, giving Philip the section with the address for Melinda Grace, the registered owner of the Prius. 'Let me know how it goes.'

Philip takes the ticket. 'Will do.'

'Great,' says Rick, watching as Philip walks slowly back to his own vehicle and climbs inside. He sure hopes Philip will push through whatever it is that's eating at him and concentrate on the case. Following up leads can be a dangerous business – you've got to have your eyes wide open and be on the alert.

If you're not focused, that's when things can go bad real fast.

26

MOIRA

Moira takes the scenic route from the DVIZION offices back to The Homestead. Unlike the main freeway, this road winds its way around the collection of seven lakes locally referred to as the Lucky Lagoons. Timewise it takes longer, but it's a much prettier drive.

As she steers around the snaking double bends and twists, Moira wonders which route is Cody Ziegler's preference, and makes a mental note to ask Olivia if she knows. The sun is high in the sky, its light shimmering off the reflection of the water, and there's not a single cloud. If she were a betting woman, she'd put money on Cody taking this route to work.

Thinking back to the interview with Brad George, she frowns. The information she's gathered over the last twenty-four hours has revealed conflicting sides to Cody's personality: the much loved, kind-hearted boss versus the angry, ranting colleague; the community-minded independent film champion versus the businessman in bed with the Mob. It doesn't tie together well and that bothers her.

She dials Rick's number.

He answers after three rings. There's interference down the line and it sounds as if he's driving too. 'Hey, you doing okay?'

'I'm fine, but I just finished interviewing Cody's VP, Brad George, and there's something he said that I think you need to know.'

'Okay. Shoot.'

As she continues to steer her way along the twisty-turny lakeside road, Moira summarises the key points from her discussion with Brad George. She ends with the financial difficulties and how Cody had kept him out of the loop on the new investor. 'Brad was worried about it – thought it wasn't right that, as the VP, he didn't know their identity. He said he worried that Cody had made a deal with some bad people. He feared it could be the Mob.'

'Is that right?' Rick's silent a moment. There's traffic noise – a horn blares, and the sound of engines revving. 'The way I see it, even if he is in bed with the Mob, this abduction just doesn't feel like the way they do business. I handled a good few organised-crime-related incidents back in the day, and in my experience they tend to disappear folks rather than ransom them. If the Mob was trying to exert pressure on Cody, by my reckoning their move would have been to abduct Olivia.'

Moira nods, even though she knows Rick can't see her. She presses the accelerator harder as the car climbs a short hill – central Florida is far more undulating than she'd imagined it before moving here. 'I was thinking the same. There are the threats sent to his house, this mysterious investor, and now a possible Mob link – it's possible all three are connected, or they could be totally unrelated and we're barking up the wrong tree.'

'Yeah, for sure,' says Rick, sounding thoughtful. 'Like I said, I'm not seeing the Mob link, but we should follow up on the investor and find out their identity for certain.'

'Yep, agreed.' Over to her left, a flock of turkey buzzards peck in the grass at the side of the road. They flap away as she gets close. 'I'm on my way back to—'

She stops talking as something catches her eye. Where the turkey buzzards had been pecking around at the side of the road, a car's-width section of the scrappy gorse bushes and undergrowth has been flattened. It looks as if a vehicle coming around the bend from the other direction didn't make the turn and continued straight ahead.

'Moira, you still there?' asks Rick.

'Yeah, I . . .' She pumps the brakes. 'I'm going to need to call you back.'

'What is it?' Rick sounds concerned.

'Not sure,' says Moira, indicating left and pulling across the road on to the edge of the asphalt a little way past the flattened vegetation. 'Let me check it out and I'll let you know.'

Disconnecting the call before Rick has the chance to ask her anything else, Moira undoes her seat belt and jumps out of the car. Hurrying around the car to the area of disturbed scrub, she sees tyre marks on the dirt at the edge of the road leading to the flattened gorse and weeds. Avoiding the area, she steps over the dirt on to the verge.

She feels her heart rate accelerate.

Beyond the scrub, the ground falls away steeply. The tyre tracks continue on – their indents clearly visible in the grass – all the way down the steep slope. They only end when they reach the water.

Scrambling over the edge, Moira hurries down the slope towards the lake. There's nothing in the water that she can see, but there's only one set of tracks, and no sign that the vehicle was driven back up the slope to the road. As she picks her way across the coarse tufty grass and uneven ground, her mind is whirring.

Cody's Lexus hasn't been spotted since he left home two mornings ago.

Rick's law enforcement colleague picked the car up on a few downtown cameras, the time coinciding with when Cody was spotted by

Jayne Barratt getting coffee to go at Pete's Coffee N Go. After that, there were no further sightings.

If Cody had used this route to go to the office, he'd have been driving the road in the opposite direction to her – the same direction as the car that made these tyre marks.

Could the photos of Cody with the newspaper have been faked? Is she wrong – are the Mob involved?

Is there something in the lake?

Moira breaks into a run. Her feet slide on the grass as she sprints down the steep slope. She fights to keep her balance, refusing to slow down.

She stops a few feet from the water's edge and catches her breath. Putting her hands above her eyes to shield her vision from the sun, Moira scans the water. It looks undisturbed – calm – but she knows looks can be deceiving. This lake is one of the largest of the Lucky Lagoons; there could be several double-decker buses hidden beneath the surface and it would be impossible to tell.

As she moves closer to the edge, Moira tries not to think about alligators, but fails. Every ripple or glint of sunshine on the water makes her flinch. This is Florida, after all, and in the Sunshine State they always say that where there's water there's gators.

She stops again, the toes of her trainers just a couple of inches from the water, noticing that the light reflection on a section of water about twenty yards across the lake looks strange; kind of mottled and dull rather than shimmering.

Moira squints towards it, but she can't get a proper look at this angle. It looks as if there could be something just beneath the surface that's causing the sun to reflect differently, but she can't be sure.

Moira takes a breath. There's only one way to find out for certain.

Pulling her phone out of her jeans' pocket, she puts it and her handbag on the ground. Yanking off her trainers and socks, she leaves them with the bag and steps into the lake. Her toes sink into soft mud and the water is far colder than she'd anticipated. Undeterred, she pushes on, wading out into the lake as fast as she can, her gaze fixed on the patch of water.

The lake bottom slopes away quickly and within five strides it's lapping around her waist. Another few steps and she's swimming.

Her water-soaked clothes pull her downwards and she grits her teeth, powering on as she front crawls towards the patch of water with the strange reflection. There's a splash across to the left, and a quick movement over on the far bank catches her eye, but when she takes a breath and looks over there, she sees the bank is empty. Pushing herself to swim fast, she tries not to think about gators.

Moira's almost at the spot where the strange reflection is happening when her foot hits something solid. *It's not a gator, but something metal or plastic*, she thinks. Stopping to tread water, Moira ducks her head under the surface. The water's murky, but she can just see the outline of a vehicle. A car.

Heart pounding, Moira dives down. The lower she goes, the colder the water.

The car windows are closed. Peering through the glass of the rear window, she tries to see if there's anyone inside, but the visibility is too hazy. She moves to the next window and cups her hands around her eyes as she looks again through the glass.

Moira lets out a cry. Air bubbles explode from her mouth.

Realisation jolts through her body like an electric shock.

There's someone inside the car.

Moira squints through the glass, but the water's too murky for her to be able to make out their features.

She yanks at the door handles – they're all locked. She thumps on the window, but the person remains motionless. Even though Moira knows it's futile, she whacks her fists against the glass, but she's not strong enough to break it.

Heart pounding, Moira moves quickly towards the front of the vehicle. The visibility is getting worse – the movement causing more silt to swirl around her. She reaches down until her hands hit a silver bonnet and she follows the curve of it down to the front grille.

Her eyes are stinging. Her lungs are starting to empty and she knows she'll need to go back to the surface for another breath and to call 911 for help, but she can't go yet. She needs to know. So she pushes herself lower into the depths of the lake until she can see the licence plate.

It's a Florida plate, with the limited-edition palm trees design. She reads the number: 100 CTZ.

Moira's heart rate thumps in her chest, echoing thunder-loud in her ears. She clamps her mouth shut, fighting the urge to take a breath. Pressing her palms against the bonnet of the car she pushes off, thrusting upwards, towards the surface, kicking hard.

She needs to get to her phone. She has to call 911. And she needs to call Rick.

She's found Cody Ziegler's car, and Cody might be inside.

27

PHILIP

Sitting in his car, Philip looks across the street at the address Rick gave him for Mrs Melinda Grace. The place looks decent. It's a two-storey cream-stucco home with a well-tended yard and a tidy porch. The green Prius – its licence plate matching the one seen on the SUV the abductors used to deliver the ransom note – is parked on the driveway. It's nearly ten years old but looks polished and well maintained.

Philip shakes his head. Reluctantly, he has to admit that Rick's law enforcement contact was right. He'd been half hoping that he'd come here and find the licence plate on the Prius was similar but not the same as the one he'd seen on the CCTV, and that Rick's contact had made a mistake. But that's not the case.

He feels despondency setting in as he ponders his next move. He'd been so pleased to get the plate from the CCTV – thought maybe Lizzie would be happy, impressed even, that he'd generated a new lead. Now he has nothing to show for his morning's work and that just won't do. He needs to impress Lizzie, has to show her that he's still good at his work – that he can add value to this investigation – even if he's made mistakes in the past.

After all, she fell in love with him while they were working together, their eyes meeting over a crime scene in the cricket club locker room back when she was a rookie CSI and he was a newly minted DI. She said she'd loved the way his mind worked almost as much as she loved his body. He looks down at his slight paunch. Perhaps if he can solve the case and show her that his mind is still just as smart, she'll love him again.

He looks back across the street at the Prius.

Think, man, think, he tells himself. What's the best plan of action?

Nothing comes to him. He looks away from the car and along the street at the other houses. It seems a nice neighbourhood. Lost for a next move, he decides to get out of his car and take a closer look at the Prius. He's not even sure why he's doing it, but he's driven all this way and he supposes it's a good excuse to delay telling the others he's not found anything useful for a bit longer.

Not wanting to look suspicious, Philip doesn't cross directly over to the house. Instead, he takes a stroll half a block along the street away from the property, then crosses over and walks back along the pavement towards the house owned by Mrs Melinda Grace. He was right about the neighbourhood. Each one of the homes is well looked after – neatly tended gardens, good paintwork and clean stucco. When he reaches the house where the Prius is parked, he stops at the end of the driveway, unsure how to proceed.

'Can I help you?' asks a stern-looking woman coming out of the front door and on to the porch. *Blast*, thinks Philip. This must be Melinda Grace. She's an older lady, barely five foot tall, he'd guess, with greying curls cut into a short style that frames her face. She's wearing sweatpants and a T-shirt, and holding a broom in front of her body like a weapon. 'I said, can I help you?'

Philip takes a step back. 'No, no, I'm fine, thanks very much.'

'You from England?'

He nods.

She puts one hand on her hip. Shakes the broom at him with the other. 'Well, I've been watching you these past few minutes sitting outside my house and now walking up and down on the sidewalk, and I'm thinking to myself, "That guy sure looks like he's up to no good." So what are you doing?'

'Okay, you've got me,' Philip says, forcing a smile. Playing into the tourist-and-not-from-around-here assumption, he holds his hands up. 'I'm completely lost.'

The lady frowns, still suspicious. 'Where are you trying to get to?'

Philip thinks fast. '844 Sugar Maple Drive? It should be around here someplace, according to my satnav.'

'Well, if it is I've not heard of it,' says the lady, her frown deepening.

Philip gets his notebook out of his pocket and flips it open, pretending to read an address. He shakes his head, and takes a few steps up the driveway towards the woman until he's close to the back end of the Prius. Pointing at his notebook, he says, 'Sugar Maple Drive – that's definitely what it says here.'

The woman narrows her eyes. She's still looking suspiciously at him but she leans the broom against the door frame and takes her hand off her hip, so he can tell that she's starting to think he could be genuine. 'Why are you going there?'

'The person who lives there has a car for sale – a Prius actually. That's why I thought this could be the place I'm looking for.' He gestures towards the green Prius, and that's when he notices the marks. Around the screws that keep the licence plate in place, there are red rusty marks. And the plate is hanging down on one side, like it hasn't been attached properly. As the lady starts talking, telling him about the streets nearby – none of which are Sugar Maple Drive – he nods along while he scans the rest of the plate.

There are scrape marks near the screws. And the dirt on the plate has been smudged in the precise places a person would position their fingers to hold the plate as they removed it. As the area beneath where the person's fingers were are clean white, it's likely the marks were made very recently. Philip thinks for a moment. Of course, it could be that Melinda Grace had some work done on the vehicle recently that required the plate to be removed, but given the SUV used to drop off the ransom note had the same licence number, Philip's willing to wager that it isn't a coincidence.

'I said, don't you agree?' The woman's voice is louder now, breaking into Philip's thoughts.

He looks back at her. 'Sorry, don't I agree with what?'

She gives an irritated shake of her head. 'That your navigator's playing tricks?'

Philip shrugs amiably. 'Perhaps it is. You never know with technology.'

'Well, I guess that's true,' says the woman, her tone becoming slightly friendlier. 'But anyways, like I said, you're in the wrong street.'

'Thanks for your help.'

'No problem.'

He takes a few steps and then turns back towards the woman. 'Just one last thing,' he says, gesturing to the Prius. 'Have you had work done on your car recently? Only your plate looks like it's come loose.'

'I have not,' says the woman, frowning as she comes along the driveway to inspect the car. Shaking her head, she mutters to herself, 'I don't know how that happened. I'll have to get Dwight at the garage to sort it out for me.'

'Well, I'll be getting on my way then,' says Philip.

Nodding, the woman picks up her broom and retreats into her house. Philip takes one last look at the marks on the plate, and heads back across the street to his own car. Yes, yes, if he's not mistaken, that plate has been removed recently, and that puts a very different slant on things.

It makes him think that perhaps the SUV plate wasn't a random cloning but rather that the people in the SUV took the actual plate from Melinda Grace's Prius, drove to The Homestead and did the ransom note drop at Olivia Hamilton Ziegler's place, and then hurriedly reattached the plate to the Prius on their return trip. That way, their SUV became untraceable.

But it also means they've left him a clue. Philip feels the fizz of adrenaline in his veins. He feels sharper, more invigorated. Maybe he *is* in with a shot at solving this.

He runs through what he knows. From what he's seen of Melinda Grace, she's unlikely to be mixed up in Cody Ziegler's abduction – her quick response to seeing Philip himself outside and challenging him on his intentions indicate a law-abiding rule stickler with a community-minded spirit. So, assuming the Prius was picked at random and convenience-based, the SUV must have passed Melinda Grace's property on the way to and from The Homestead. If the driver and passenger didn't want to have the vehicle identified easily through its real plate, Philip reckons they would swap the plate as soon as possible after leaving their own place, before they'd been picked up on any highway traffic cameras.

Philip nods to himself as he climbs back into his own Toyota. He's got an idea.

He dials Rick's number.

Ricks answers quickly. It sounds like he's driving. 'Philip? How's it going?'

'Good, good,' says Philip. 'I've been out to look at the Prius with the licence plate that I saw on the SUV in that CCTV footage. I got a good look at the vehicle and it looks to me like the plate was tampered with recently.'

'You think the owner is involved?' asks Rick.

'No, I don't, but I think the abductors took the plate last night and returned it on their way back. They must have been in a hurry as the plate was hanging off on one side. I asked the owner about it – she said the car hadn't had any work done recently and she was surprised about the plate not being on properly.'

Rick's silent a moment. 'That's kind of strange. Why return it?'

It's a good question. 'It's just a hypothesis, but I think the SUV came from nearby. They drove along this street and used the plate from the Prius in case they were picked up on any traffic cameras – that way the cops wouldn't be able to trace the SUV back to a registered address.'

'I guess it could be possible,' says Rick. He sounds sceptical. 'But why didn't they just keep the stolen plate or use a fake plate? Less hassle and less risk that way than returning it.'

'It's unconventional, I understand that,' says Philip. He knows this is a long shot, but he's convinced there's something in it. It's a reach, yes, but he doesn't think he's seeing things that aren't there. 'But look, this plate has been recently removed and reattached, and call it a hunch or whatever, but I think it could be connected. Can your law enforcement guy get me a list of the vehicles that fit the SUV's description and are registered within a five-mile radius of Melinda Grace's address?'

'I reckon so, but what then?' asks Rick, still sounding unconvinced.

'Well, unless you've got something else for me to follow up, I'd like to run with this. I'll do drive-bys of each local SUV and check for signs of their plates being recently removed.'

There's a sound of an indicator being put on, then Rick says, 'What if you can't tell? It might not be possible to—'

'Look, it's worth a try, isn't it?' says Philip, his tone getting firmer and his voice louder. 'It's a hunch, I know, but I've got a lot of experience from back in the day. If we don't have any viable leads, what's the harm in me looking into this?'

Rick doesn't answer immediately. He blows out. 'Okay, sure. I'll call my guy and then message the list over to you. Check out the SUVs and let me know.'

'Will do,' says Philip. He tries to ignore the lack of enthusiasm in Rick's tone and reminds himself that Rick isn't his boss, they're equals.

Ninety per cent of police work is following the evidence and chasing down solid leads, but ten per cent is about instinct – the feeling you get when something doesn't add up and you have a hunch to follow a route of enquiry that's less conventional. Although Philip knows he's generally a pretty conventional fellow, he's always had a good natural instinct. His hunches have paid off many times over the years and he has a strong feeling this is going to be another one of those times. The other three might all doubt him, but he's not going to let that deter him.

He'll show them all.

28

RICK

Marty Hannier's one-storey, double-wide trailer home sits on a corner lot on the edge of the Parkland Rise mobile home community. It's closest the road, opposite a commercial body shop, a bunch of industrial-looking buildings and a fried chicken takeout. It's a nice enough property, with beige cladding and large windows, and four wooden steps leading up to the door; but it's not the sort of place Rick had figured the CEO of a movie company would live.

Pulling the jeep on to the driveway, Rick parks behind a beat-up Honda and gets out of his vehicle. He hasn't called ahead, preferring instead to show up and hope Marty Hannier is at home. Given what he's heard, he doesn't know how Marty will react to being asked about Cody Ziegler. Better to have the element of surprise on his side, just as he had with Dirk Baldwin.

Making his way up the wooden steps, Rick raps on the door three times and waits. He can hear the faint sound of a TV playing inside – sounds like some kind of sports show – but no one comes to the door. Rick waits another minute, then knocks on the door again, harder. This time, Rick hears movement inside and through the frosted glass sees the silhouette of a person coming towards the door.

Moments later it's pulled back and a tall, unshaven guy wearing grubby candy-striped boxer shorts and mirrored shades stands, unsteadily, in the doorway. He looks Rick up and down. Curls his lip. 'Yeah?'

Rick can smell the alcohol fumes from three paces away. 'Are you Marty Hannier?'

'Who-wants-to-know?' says the guy, his words slurring into each other.

He decides to play it serious, as if he was still back on the job. 'Mr Hannier, my name is Rick Denver. I'd like to ask you a couple of questions.'

'What about?' says the man, frowning.

Rick doesn't answer, instead pushing to confirm the man's identity. 'Can you confirm you're Mr Marty Hannier of Oak Whistle Productions?'

'Oak Whistle Productions, well damn,' says the man, shaking his head. 'Yeah, I'm Marty. Now what do you want?'

Rick keeps his tone professional and hopes Marty Hannier is too drunk to think of asking him for any official ID. 'For the record, can you confirm when you last saw Cody Ziegler, sir?'

'Cody Ziegler? You've come here – to my home – to ask me about Cody Ziegler?' Marty's shouting now. He's pointing his beer bottle at Rick. Spittle flying from his lips as he says, 'That asshole screwed me over real good. You know what he said? He told me *Breakout* was the worst script he'd ever read – that it was derivative and immature. My script! The best thing I'd written, and he damn near laughed at it!'

'Well, I sure am sorry to—'

'*Breakout* would have been a sure-thing success. It was my best work – brilliant! But that bastard Ziegler, he insulted me and refused to get on board.' Marty blows out hard. 'I put everything I had into that script. I'd already laid down a load of money in retainers in preparation for going into production. That movie was going to be how I made my name in the business – how I transitioned from indies to mainstream and really made Oak Whistle Productions a force to be reckoned with. But Ziegler strung me along for months and then killed the project, and my dream. I lost all the money I'd paid in retainers and my company went bust. Then I lost my house, and pretty soon afterwards my wife ran off and left me.' He gestures towards the mobile home. 'Now I live here alone and only get to see my kids every third weekend. It's a real crock of shit, and it's all Ziegler's fault.'

From what Rick can see of the inside of Marty's home, it looks like the chores haven't been done for days. Every surface is covered in old fried-chicken cartons and empty beer bottles, and the man is clearly day drinking. He wonders if Marty has the ability to plan a kidnapping right now, unless his drunken appearance is an act – a way of giving himself a 'not capable' alibi. 'You working on anything now?'

'A script, yeah,' says Marty, a sick smile spreading across his face. 'It's a revenge thriller about a guy who loses everything and plots how to get payback from the man who was responsible. It's like a *Groundhog Day* kinda deal, except in my movie the guy gets retribution in a different way every day.'

Rick raises his eyebrows. 'Let me guess, the man responsible is modelled on Cody Ziegler?'

Marty guffaws. 'It's real satisfying coming up with different ways to get revenge.'

'You thinking of acting on any of them for real?' says Rick, his tone serious.

'Hey, man, why are you asking?' Marty holds his hands up, looking wary. 'Is Ziegler in some kind of trouble?'

Rick keeps his expression neutral. 'I'm afraid I can't answer that.'

'I bet your ass you can't.' Marty leans towards him. Looks over his shades. 'You're from the Police Department or the FBI or some such, ain't ya? I can tell just from looking at you, so I'm thinking you're here because Ziegler's either gotten into trouble or has caused trouble, am I right, Mr Lawman?'

Rick shakes his head. Doesn't correct Marty on the fact that he's not a lawman any more. 'Like I said, I—'

'Yeah, yeah, you can't confirm or deny.' Marty sniggers to himself and clinks the beer bottle against the door frame before draining it in one. He wipes his mouth on the back of his hand and grins. 'Well, maybe I can't confirm or deny anything either, but I'll tell you this, I hope that bastard *is* in trouble. And I hope that trouble hurts him and *his* finances real bad, just like he screwed me over.'

Marty stops talking for a moment as he loses his balance. He makes a grab for the door frame, just managing to stop himself from falling. When he looks back at Rick there's an expression of pure hatred on his face. 'You know what, Mr Lawman, I hope Ziegler has an agonising death and rots in hell. He damn well deserves it.'

Saying nothing, Rick looks into Marty's bloodshot eyes. The man is serious, that's for sure; Marty Hannier wishes Cody Ziegler dead.

The question is, how far would he go to make it happen?

29

LIZZIE

Lizzie has the Uber drop her off a little early and walks the rest of the way along the road on foot. Ducking under the police tape while the only uniform on guard duty is busy fending off questions from a handful of journalists and rubberneckers, Lizzie's able to sneak unseen past the cordon and down the slope towards the lake. It's naughty, she knows, but there's no way she'll get access via the cops and she wants to be there to support Moira.

As she hurries down the slope towards the water, she spots Moira over to the left. She's wrapped in a blue metallic space blanket and is talking with two uniformed police officers. Straight ahead, a large tow truck is reversing towards the edge of the lake. There are several police cars and an ambulance parked a little way from the water. No one shouts to say Lizzie shouldn't be there. They barely glance at her. That's the benefit of being in your sixties – you're seen as unthreatening and assumed to be doing what you're meant to where you're meant to be doing it. As she's recently started to discover, assumptions like that make it so much easier to break the rules.

As Lizzie gets closer to Moira, there's a shout from the tow truck and the two officers stop talking to Moira and hurry over to the water's edge. Moira turns towards her and Lizzie waves, hurrying the last few yards towards her friend. 'You okay?' she asks.

'A bit damp, but I'm fine,' says Moira. She puts her hand up to her brow, shielding her eyes from the sun as she looks at what's going on at the water's edge. She's putting on a good show but Lizzie doesn't think Moira looks at all fine. She looks pale and stressed, very different to her usual confident self.

There's a loud clanking noise as a heavy-duty winch with a massive hook is lowered down into the water. A wetsuited diver takes hold of the hook and, as the chain it's attached to starts to unravel, swims out into the lake and then dives beneath the surface.

'That's where the car is,' says Moira, her expression grim. 'They're going to pull it out. The body is still inside.'

Lizzie squints towards the lake. Shakes her head. 'But the car isn't visible at all. How on earth did you find it?'

Moira doesn't take her eyes off the lake. 'It was luck really. This location is about halfway between Cody's office and home. It's quiet here and the road isn't busy. When I saw the vegetation was crushed and the tyre tracks leading to the water's edge, I put two and two together. It's a good place to ambush a driver, and an easy place to hide a vehicle.'

Lizzie nods but she doubts it would have occurred to her to make that connection, especially not at the moment, with her mind half full of her own problems as well as the case. 'If they apprehended him and sank the car, does that mean Cody's . . . ?'

'I don't think it's Cody – we saw those photos of him with the daily newspaper, and given the Lexus has been missing a couple of days, I'd say it was sunk on the day he disappeared. But there is someone in there, I'm sure of it. I couldn't open the doors, so I swam around the car and peered into the windows as best I could, but it was too murky to see clearly.'

'So you might be mistaken?' says Lizzie hopefully.

Moira shakes her head. 'I don't think so.'

Over in the lake, the diver resurfaces and shouts towards the tow truck. They give the thumbs up. There's a toot of the truck's horn, and the winch slowly starts to wind in the chain. Lizzie watches as the slack is gathered up. Moments later the winch's motor roars louder, sounding more strained, the now taut chain clanking as it's gradually wound in.

The car emerges, back end first, from the lake. Water pours off it, leaving the Lexus's metallic silver paintwork dulled by a layer of mud and green pondweed and algae stuck around the wing mirrors and across the windscreen. Lizzie reads the licence plate. 'That's definitely Cody's car.'

'Yep,' says Moira, looking pensive as the Lexus is winched clear of the water and dragged a few metres higher up the bank before the winch motor is switched off and the truck's engine killed.

The cops approach the Lexus. Lizzie feels suddenly nauseous. What if Cody *is* in the vehicle? She shudders at the thought of what it'll do to Olivia.

Lizzie glances at Moira. From the intense way she's watching the officers approach the car, Lizzie can see her friend is just as nervous as she is. Feeling the need to break the tension, she says, 'Philip and I went to couples therapy yesterday.'

Moira turns to look at her. 'How did it go?'

Lizzie shakes her head. 'Disaster. I told him I won't go to another session.'

'Sorry,' says Moira, looking at her with a sympathetic expression.

Tears fill Lizzie's eyes and she wishes she hadn't said anything. She doesn't want to get upset – not here, not on a job.

'What do you want to do?' asks Moira, her tone gentle, kind.

'I want to find Cody Ziegler, and I want to go and see my youngest daughter in Australia.' Lizzie sighs. 'Other than that, I just don't know.'

Moira studies her face for a long moment. 'Are you sure about not knowing? In my experience, people usually do know what they want – it's acting on it that's complicated.'

Lizzie looks away. Moira's right, of course, but she really doesn't want to talk about this right now. She doesn't even want to admit it to herself. So she points towards the Lexus and the officers who are searching inside it. 'We should know soon.'

Moira grimaces. 'Yeah.'

They watch in silence as the police officers open the driver's side door. The tension's palpable. Lizzie's nausea intensifies.

A female officer with her ginger hair tied back in a long braid shouts across to the medics waiting a few yards from the vehicle and gestures for them to hurry over. She then looks up the hill towards the police cordon, where a new police car has just arrived, and waves vigorously. Lizzie watches as a petite female officer exits the car and rushes down the slope, with her stocky male partner following at a steadier pace.

Moira curses under her breath. 'Those are the officers who came out to Olivia's house after she'd reported Cody missing. Rodriguez and Schofield. Schofield is a real arsehole.'

They watch as the officers reach the Lexus. While the police photographer takes pictures inside the car, there's some discussion between the paramedics and the officers, but Lizzie is too far away to hear what's being said. She turns to Moira. 'What do you think's going on?'

'They're probably discussing next steps. They'll need to move the body.'

Moments later the paramedics head back to the ambulance and fetch a gurney. Lizzie swallows hard. She clasps her hands together. This means there's definitely a body.

It seems to take ages for the paramedics to prepare to move the body from the car to the gurney. Lizzie can feel the tension tightening like a knot in her stomach. What if it *is* Cody in the Lexus? How will they tell Olivia the bad news?

There's a shout from one of the paramedics, and they lift the body out of the car. The person has dark hair and is wearing a red skirt suit with black boots. As they place her on to the gurney, one arm falls limply from the stretcher bed and hangs over the side. Lifeless.

Lizzie feels a rush of relief that she won't have to tell Olivia her husband is dead, then immediately feels guilty. It's a tragedy that the woman has lost her life.

'Let's get closer,' says Moira, moving down the slope towards the Lexus. 'We need to know who she is, and see if we can get a look inside the vehicle.'

As they move towards the group huddled around the gurney, Lizzie watches as the recently arrived female officer reaches her gloved hands into the pockets of the victim's jacket. Removing a small wallet, the officer opens it and takes out what looks like a driver's licence. 'Pamela Blake, thirty-eight, lived over in Well Water gated community.'

'Well Water?' whispers Lizzie, turning towards Moira. 'That's less than half a mile from The Homestead.'

Moira nods. Taking a step back, she says under her breath, 'Incoming. We've got trouble.'

Lizzie glances back towards the gurney and sees a sturdy male officer marching towards them. His cheeks are flushed, and his shirt has big damp patches beneath the armpits.

As he gets closer, he points at Moira. 'You! I recognise you, you were with the old actress reporting her husband as a misper yesterday.'

Moira nods. She says nothing, her lips are pursed, and Lizzie can tell that her friend is trying not to say something she might regret later.

'Yeah? Am I right?' prompts Officer Schofield, obviously wanting an answer. 'Her husband is the man who owns this vehicle.'

'I was with Mrs Hamilton Ziegler yesterday morning, yes,' says Moira, her tone cold. 'When you told her that her husband had probably run off with a younger woman.'

'And I was right, wasn't I?' says Officer Schofield, with a slight smirk. 'He did have a younger woman with him. Too bad she's dead now.'

'Shame on you,' says Lizzie. 'A woman has lost her life, have some respect.'

'Yes she has,' says Officer Schofield. 'And I'm putting out an APB on your friend Cody Ziegler, because it sure looks to me like he meant for her to die in that vehicle.'

'What do you mean?' says Lizzie. She can't believe Schofield is jumping to assumptions rather than methodically examining the evidence. 'You think Cody killed her?'

'Well, the doors were locked, and there's no sign of the keys,' says Officer Schofield, his voice turning serious. 'That woman was trapped inside the vehicle as it sank. The medics have said the initial signs are that she drowned, although we'll need to wait for the coroner to have that confirmed. And seeing as Mr Ziegler owns the car, and has been missing a couple of days, I'd say we've got all the hallmarks of a killer on the run here.'

'Or the people that took Cody Ziegler didn't want the woman with him to ID them and so they killed her,' says Moira.

Officer Schofield shrugs. 'I prefer my idea. Aren't the Zieglers meant to have the happiest marriage in the movie world? Maybe his bit on the side was going to expose him as a cheater – I bet the papers would pay a lot for that story – and he decided to get rid of her. These rich people think they can get away with anything, even homicide, but I've got the measure of this Cody Ziegler. He's going to pay for what he's done.'

Lizzie clenches her fists. 'You're wrong, there's no—'

'Anyways, I was told you found the car,' says Schofield, ignoring Lizzie as he looks pointedly at Moira. 'How'd you do that?'

Moira shrugs, mimicking Schofield a moment earlier. 'Lucky guess.'

Schofield narrows his gaze, clearly trying to weigh up whether she's being serious or mocking him. 'You've given a statement?'

'Yes, and your co-workers have told me I'm free to go. So that's what I'm going to do,' says Moira, turning away from Schofield. She looks at Lizzie. 'We need to get back to Olivia and update her.'

Reaching out, Officer Schofield puts his hand on Moira's shoulder and turns her back around to face him. 'Now don't go getting in our way, lady. This is a police matter and we don't need your help. There's an experienced detective getting assigned to the case. He'll call you if we need any more information.'

'Get your hands off me,' says Moira, her tone granite hard and her expression furious. 'Right now.'

Schofield lets go. His cheeks flush redder.

Moira looks at him with disgust, then turns and strides up the bank towards the road. Lizzie has to almost run to keep up with her.

'What the hell is that man's problem?' says Lizzie as she catches up with Moira.

Moira exhales loudly. 'He's an arsehole, like I said. He doesn't care that a woman is dead, and he's obviously already made up his mind that Cody is behind it. I just hope this detective they're bringing in knows what they're doing.'

'Yeah,' says Lizzie, looking thoughtful. 'Cody's still being held against his will out there somewhere.'

Moira nods, her expression determined. 'And we're going to find him.'

30

PHILIP

He waits, parked up a couple of streets over from Melinda Grace's home. When the list comes through, there are forty-seven SUVs within a five-mile radius. Messaging Rick to let him know his plan, Philip orders the vehicles on the list from the closest to furthest distance from Melinda's home, and sets off to visit the first address.

Humming the tune of Wagner's 'Ride of the Valkyries' to himself as he drives, Philip feels purposeful again. He's on a mission. As he waits at a set of lights, he takes a glance at his mobile. There's no reply from Rick. No acknowledgement of what Philip's said he's doing.

Refusing to let it dampen his mood, Philip hums louder. He's right to do this and he's going to show Lizzie he's still got what it takes. Sod Rick and his doubts.

He hums faster – the classic piece nearing its climax – as he drives the Toyota another half block to the first address. He's on the hunt and it's a good feeling. It's making him feel better by the second. He feels back in charge – calling the shots and making decisions – just as he should be. The business with Lizzie has drained him of his energy. Following up on this hypothesis is invigorating.

Pulling up on the street outside the first address on the list, Philip keeps the engine running and surveys the property. It's a two-storey grey-stucco house with white trim and a white door on the attached double garage. The front garden looks neat, the grass is mown and the plants in the border look healthy. He glances along the street. It's a nice place – clean and tidy with well-maintained homes. It doesn't look like the sort of place you'd hold an abducted man hostage, but then he's learned over his career that appearances can be deceiving.

The SUV isn't on the driveway, so it could be that the owner is out using it, or it could be in the two-car garage. There's only one way to find out.

Undoing his seat belt, Philip climbs out of his car and strides up the drive to the garage door. He's not humming any more but the 'Ride of the Valkyries' is still playing in his mind. The garage door is one of those automatic types, with a line of small rectangular windows cut into the door towards the top. Standing on tiptoes, he peers through the window into the garage. The SUV is parked in the right-hand-side bay. He checks the plate against his list; it's a match. But the vehicle isn't the dark colour it says on his list; it must have been resprayed as it's now a pearlescent white.

Philip frowns. Of course, the respray could have been done to hide the SUV's identity, but he doesn't think so. There's some rusting around the wheel arches and the way the paint has corroded with the rust makes him think this is an old respray; six months at least.

Hurrying back to his Toyota before he's challenged about what he's doing, Philip jumps into his car and starts the engine. He looks at the next address on the list and taps the details into his satnav. It's an eight-minute drive.

He makes it in six minutes and pulls up a few yards short of the driveway. The neighbourhood is nice, and the house is a big one-storey that looks like it's been recently repainted. The SUV he's looking for is on the driveway, but he doubts it's a contender.

Philip glances back at the list. It details this SUV as black, and it is, but what isn't on the list is that the vehicle has advertising along the length of the body. In big, hot-pink block lettering are the words 'JESS WRIGHT FITNESS UR WAY' along with email, phone and web address. He shakes his head. The SUV on the CCTV footage was plain – no sign writing, no decals, not even a bumper sticker. Mentally crossing this vehicle off his list, Philip puts the next address into the satnav and sets off again.

The thirteen-minute drive takes him out of the nice neighbourhoods and on to a street that's pretty run-down. The houses are older ranch-style one-storeys here, and they don't look like they're ageing well. The paint is peeling from many of them, and he spots several car ports that are leaning at distinctly unsafe angles.

Up ahead he spots an SUV parked on a crumbling concrete driveway beside a shabby blue and white ranch home. The vehicle is a dark navy colour made matt from sun damage and lack of care. The rear licence plate is hanging down on one side, obviously being held on to the car by a single screw. Still, the number matches what he's got on his list. This is the vehicle. But it doesn't have any wheels; it's propped up on cinder blocks. Weeds have grown through the cracked driveway, up around the cinder blocks and into the car's wheel arches.

Philip runs his hand over his bald pate. He doesn't hold out much hope for this one. On the CCTV from outside Olivia Hamilton Ziegler's place, the SUV had looked in good condition; the paint was glossy and clean and the licence plate fully attached. But he needs to be thorough. After all, taking the wheels off could be a ruse to make anyone looking think the vehicle is out of commission. He needs to take a closer look to be certain.

Getting out of his car, Philip takes a few steps towards the SUV. There's a dog barking nearby, but it's difficult to place exactly where it is – could be in the back garden of the SUV's house, or one of the neighbours – still, it's pretty close. Philip shudders. He doesn't like big dogs, not since he got a nasty bite from one during a night raid when he was a young, wet-behind-the-ears uniform.

From here he can see that the driver's side rear window is missing the glass, and the plastic that's been duct-taped across the window frame looks old and perished, indicating the damage isn't recent. Philip stops and bends down, pretending to tie one of his laces, while he takes a better look at the licence plate. There are no scrape marks around the screw holes, and no fingerprints or smudges in the grime. Nothing obvious to suggest the plate has been removed or changed any time recently.

He straightens up. Convinced this SUV is a dead end just like the first two.

In his shirt pocket, his mobile phone pings. Taking it out, he reads the message on the Retired Detectives Club WhatsApp group.

> LIZZIE: Moira found Cody's Lexus submerged in one of the Lucky Lagoons. There was a woman's body inside. Police and Medical on scene. I'm here with Moira – she's wet but okay. Police divers searching for Cody – so far nothing. We've not mentioned ransom.

Philip wonders how Moira found the Lexus if it was submerged. Perhaps it was floating; that happens sometimes, he's heard. He taps out a reply.

> PHILIP: Hope Moira ok. I'm looking at SUVs that fit description and close in location to Prius that the plates the SUV had were taken or cloned from.

The message that Lizzie is typing comes on the screen. He gives a little smile, expecting that she's going to tell him what he's doing is a good idea and some words of encouragement. It's good they can message like this. It gives him hope.

> LIZZIE: There's damage to rear of Lexus. Moira thinks could have been shunted down slope into lake. Look for silver paint on SUV (Lexus is silver).

His smile drops. The hope dissolves like a bitter taste on his tongue. There are no words of encouragement. Lizzie hasn't even acknowledged that he's had a good idea. All she's done is issue an order – bossing him about like he's not capable of taking the information she's given him and using his initiative to check for silver paint on the SUVs.

He flinches as the dog starts barking again. Every few barks it adds a snarl. It sounds to Philip as if the creature is coming closer. Not wanting to see if it is, or to meet the owner, he turns and retreats swiftly to his own car.

Safely back in the Toyota, he locks the doors and starts the engine. He checks his phone again, but there are no new messages from Lizzie. Sighing, he puts it into his pocket.

As he looks back up at the street, his gaze is drawn to the front window of the one-storey ranch house. The curtain twitches, and he's sure there's a human-shaped shadow moving behind it. Not wanting to stick around, he quickly taps the address of the next SUV on the list into the satnav and puts the Toyota into drive.

Grim-faced, Philip accelerates away from the run-down neighbourhood and out on to the highway. Humming the 'Ride of the Valkyries' again as the miles per hour on the speedometer tick up, he tries not to let Lizzie's lack of support get to him.

She might not have acknowledged it, but he's a good detective and he's got a great nose for sniffing out clues. He's on to something, he's certain of it; this search could produce a solid lead. Puffing out his chest, Philip tells himself that he's doing the right thing. He's going to find the SUV that delivered the ransom note, and to hell with the others.

Yes, yes. That's right. *He's* right. And he's definitely going to bloody well show them.

31

RICK

He's broken the speed limit all along the route from Kissimmee to get here fast. Hasn't been able to shake the nauseous feeling he'd gotten as soon as he'd read Lizzie's message about Moira, the car and the lake. He has to see for himself that Moira's okay.

Ditching the jeep in front of the police cordon, Rick sprints up to the barrier and is about to tell the uniformed officer on duty that he needs to get through when his attention is caught by two people walking up the grass slope.

Relief surges through him and he raises his hand, waving, as he calls, 'Moira! Lizzie! Hey!'

Lizzie raises her hand. Moira gives him a half smile. They reach the top of the slope and step over the scrubby gorse and on to the blacktop, heading towards the barrier.

Rick ducks underneath, ignoring the cop telling him to stay put, and hurries towards them. 'Are you okay? Are you hurt?'

'I'm fine,' says Moira. 'A bit wet, but okay.'

He looks at her. She's pale, and her clothes are damp, but otherwise she seems uninjured. He exhales, relieved. Feels his heart rate start to slow. Staring past Moira and down the grassy slope towards the lake, he sees an algae- and mud-covered silver Lexus is being winched on to a tow trunk. He looks back at Moira. 'How the hell did you manage to find the car?'

She tells him how she spotted the flattened scrub when she'd been talking to him on the phone, and then, once she'd pulled over, she'd seen the tyre tracks leading to the lake. When she says about swimming into the lake and diving down to find the car, Rick can't help but be impressed. He's always admired Moira's grit, but searching the lake is a whole other level. He smiles at her. 'You did real good.'

Moira blows out hard. 'A woman lost her life. Her name was Pamela Blake and she lived in Well Water gated community, not far from The Homestead. She was only thirty-eight.'

Rick looks solemn. Thirty-eight years of age is nothing. 'How did it happen?'

'From what we've been told, she was locked inside the Lexus when it went into the water. The cops said she drowned.' Moira shakes her head. 'She must have been terrified. To be trapped with no way to get free as the car sank . . .'

'Real nasty,' says Rick.

'From what we could tell, there was no sign of the briefcase or bag that Jayne Barratt spotted Cody carrying when he was leaving the coffee place on his way to the office the morning he went missing,' says Lizzie. 'But the two takeaway coffee cups are still in the cup holders.'

Rick frowns. 'So whoever took Cody Ziegler also took the briefcase.'

'Looks that way,' says Moira. 'But the cops think Cody did this – that he killed Pamela deliberately and then went on the run. They've put an APB out on him, so he's basically now a fugitive.'

Rick frowns. 'Seriously?'

'Yeah. I said it was more likely whoever took Cody killed Pamela, because she'd seen their faces and they didn't want to risk her IDing them, but Schofield, the arsehole cop we met yesterday at Olivia's, wasn't having any of it.'

'Jesus, what's wrong with that guy?' says Rick. The cops are barking up the wrong tree, he's pretty sure of it. They should be exploring all avenues right now, not just fixating on Cody as the killer. He looks at Lizzie. 'In your message you said the car is damaged?'

'Yes, but it's minimal – some scraped-off paint and a slight dent,' says Lizzie. 'It doesn't look like impact at speed, more as if it happened from the Lexus getting shunted down the slope by another vehicle.'

'It was deliberate,' says Moira. 'There's no doubt. But I agree with Lizzie, I don't think an accident caused Cody to stop here.'

'Then what did?' says Rick, turning to look across the scrub at the side of the blacktop, and the grass leading down to the lake.

Moira closes her eyes a moment. 'Look, I've got some ideas but let's discuss it later. Right now, I need to head home. I could really do with some dry clothes.'

Rick nods, irritated with himself for keeping Moira talking rather than being sensitive to her needs. 'I hear you. Let's reconvene at the Ziegler house in an hour. I'll put a message on our WhatsApp group to let Philip know.'

'Sounds good,' says Moira. 'That'll give me time to take the dogs for a quick run.'

'And I'll try those numbers for Tamsin's brother, Bryce, again. I've had no luck so far,' says Lizzie.

Rick nods but his eyes are still on Moira. 'You know, Olivia could be involved in this. That poor woman dying inside the vehicle.' He shakes his head. 'Why kill her? Like I said before, maybe there's something we're not seeing, a reason Olivia would want her husband out of the way.'

Lizzie narrows her eyes. 'Like what? Why would she want him abducted?'

'What if the goal isn't the abduction and it's more lethal?' says Rick.

'But there's a ransom demand to pay so I don't—'

'He's saying the end result isn't Cody getting free, it's Cody dying,' says Moira, tiredness making her voice quieter than usual. 'The ransom money could be a pay-off for the kidnappers to finish the job.'

Lizzie says nothing. She looks from Moira to Rick. Shakes her head. 'No, no, I don't believe it. Olivia loves Cody, she'd never—'

'We need to be sure,' says Rick. 'I was talking with Philip and he had a good idea – that we feed her some intel, real or fabricated, to see how she reacts. It could—'

'You want to test her?' says Lizzie loudly. 'She's distraught, alone, and you want to test her? Jesus! What's the matter with you?'

'I . . .' Rick watches as Lizzie stomps away from him, muttering angrily to herself. He looks at Moira. 'That didn't go as I'd hoped.'

She shrugs and glances over towards the Lexus. 'It was bad timing, Rick. This whole thing is messed up. That poor woman.' Exhaling hard, she looks across at Lizzie, who's waiting outside Moira's car. 'Give her some time, she'll come around.'

'Okay,' says Rick, reaching out and giving Moira's arm a squeeze. 'See you back at Olivia's.'

As he walks towards the jeep, Rick blows out hard and rolls his shoulders a few times. Unclenching his fists, he feels the adrenaline that's pumped through his veins since he first found out that Moira had ended up in the lake slowly start to dissipate. The thought that she could have been hurt or drowned, and no one would have been around to help, had slammed him bam in the chest. And just now, despite what she's been through – the trauma of finding the young woman in the car and her exhaustion – she'd still tried to reassure him that things would be okay with Lizzie. She really is something.

He shakes his head. He'd had a couple of dates early last year, but none of them could hold a candle to his beloved wife, Alisha, and he'd made peace with the fact that he'd be alone, a single widower, for the rest of his days.

But Moira, with her smarts and her looks and her grit – well, hell, if he was going to fall in love for the second time in his life, Rick is pretty sure it's going to be with her.

32

PHILIP

The address the next SUV on the list is registered to lies on the outskirts of town. The properties here are spaced out wider and the land around them is far more generous than the more built-up areas he's just come from. The house at the address Philip's looking for is tucked back from the road, nestled in the shadow of a cluster of oak trees. He would have missed it if it wasn't for the large Stars and Stripes on the flagpole beside the mailbox.

Feeling it unwise to park directly outside the property, Philip continues on along the street. It seems that the house is the last on the road, as after the boundary fence the land turns to scrub and then a few hundred yards later a new fence begins, enclosing what looks like acres of neatly planted rows of orange trees. He finds a gateway about half a mile along and pulls into it to make a U-turn, then heads back towards the address.

There's nowhere good to park, so he stops fifty or so yards before the property and pulls the Toyota on to the verge as best he can. Climbing out of the car, he stands beside it for a moment, getting a sense of the place. The sun is beating down; the temperature must be well into the thirties. And it's quiet here. There's very little passing traffic and he can't hear anything from the houses. The birds in the trees overhead and the bugs in the scrub are the noisiest things around. Compared to The Homestead, and his own home in the Ocean Mist community, this place feels like the middle of nowhere.

Philip walks along the tarmac to the property, slowing his pace as he gets close. The main house is a dilapidated one-storey with a sagging roof and wooden cladding that looks like it's got termites, rot, or both. There are some brick outbuildings, and what seems to be an old shipping container, around the back of the property. There's no sign of the SUV.

There's also no driveway as such, just a car's-width strip of dirt that's been baked by the sun and pressed solid from vehicles bumping off the tarmac and on to the ground to the side of the house. From the look of the tyre tracks that continue along past the house and around to the right, it could be that the shipping container is being used as a makeshift garage. He squints towards it, fancying he can see the outline of a large dark-coloured vehicle inside. It could be the SUV, but it's hard to tell with only a partial view of the shipping container and the trees casting dark shadows across the property.

Philip looks around – there's no sight or sound of anyone nearby. If he were on official police business like back in the day, he'd be calling for backup right now. He knows he should probably message Rick or Lizzie and let them know where he is, but since they don't seem to care what he's doing he wonders why the hell should he? If this is the place where the SUV is stashed, then he wants all the glory of finding it for himself. They didn't believe in his idea, or in Lizzie's case support him in it, so they don't deserve to share in his success. *After all*, thinks Philip, *fortune favours the brave*. Yes, yes, he'll show them how brave he is.

Mind made up, Philip puffs out his chest and steps off the road on to the baked dirt. Doing this solo is risky. He needs to get a better look inside the shipping container and then leave. In and out fast – job done.

Walking briskly up the earth track, he tells himself to stay alert. There are no lights on in the run-down house, but that doesn't mean there's nobody home. He treads lightly, scanning his surroundings for danger and listening out for noises other than birds and bugs. The further he walks from the road, the more isolated the place feels. He passes an old fridge left with its door open by the side of the house, dark mould speckling its insides. There's a water bowl with faded letters spelling DOG and a long metal chain attached to a bracket on the wall of the house. He glances around but sees no other sign that there's a dog here. He quickens his steps, eager to get this done.

Passing the house, he follows the curve of the dirt track around to the right. The shipping container is maybe fifty feet away. There's a crack as a dried tree branch snaps beneath his foot. He flinches, and then laughs at himself. He has faced down many murderers and hardened criminals during his career, and now he's jumping out of his skin at a broken branch? Ridiculous.

Reaching the old shipping container, he sees it's in bad shape – rusting and largely overgrown with weeds and vegetation. The dirt has been sloped up to the metal floor of the container to make it smoother for vehicles to enter. The doors are hanging low on their rusting hinges and pinned back with cinder blocks. From the look of them, he doubts they've shut in years. Further inside the container he can see the outline of the vehicle. It certainly looks like an SUV, but he needs to get a closer look.

Philip does a final scan of the area, checking the coast is clear. It's turned eerily quiet – no birds are singing – but he tries not to let that put him off.

He steps inside. Even though the end doors are open, as soon as he's walked a few yards into the container and out of the sunlight the interior gets increasingly gloomy. The once white metal sides are riddled with flaking orange rust, and there's dirt and mouldy leaves scattered across the corrugated metal floor. On the left of the container there are tools propped up against the side: shovels, rakes and forks. There's a battered-looking dresser a little further along, piled high with what looks like car parts. Stacked alongside it are gas cans and water caddies. Philip wrinkles up his nose. It's cold in here, and it smells musty.

His footsteps clank on the metal floor and the sound echoes around the space. In the distance, beyond the SUV, he can see the solid metal end of the container and it makes him feel a bit claustrophobic. There's only one way in and out of here; he's like a fish in a barrel. But he can't let that put him off. He's got a job to do. Clenching his jaw, he keeps on walking.

And he's glad he does. The vehicle *is* an SUV. It's black and the plate matches the number on his list. Philip feels hope flare in his chest. This could be the vehicle from the CCTV.

Crouching down at the back end of the car, he inspects the licence plate and the screws attaching it to the vehicle. There are scrape marks around the screws and smudges around the edge of the plate, just as there had been on the Prius. His heart rate accelerates faster. He's done it. Found it. This has to be the SUV used for the ransom note drop.

Pride surges through him. He's still got it. He knew his hypothesis would pay off.

Now he needs to call Rick. Philip can't wait to tell his friend that he was right. And Lizzie needs to know it too. That'll show them. Taking his mobile from his shirt pocket, he taps Rick's name in his recent calls list and waits for the call to connect. And waits. Then the phone beeps and 'Call Failed' comes up on the screen.

Blast and dammit.

Philip tries again. And again the call doesn't connect. He looks at the screen and realises he's got no phone service. He exhales hard, supposing it's the walls of the metal shipping container blocking the signal. Never mind, there's something else he needs to check.

Moving along the side of the SUV, Philip leans down and peers at the front end of the vehicle. Lizzie had said in her message that there was rear-end damage to Cody Ziegler's Lexus and they suspected it had been shunted into the lake by another car; he needs to see if there's any indication the SUV was involved.

It's hard to tell in the gloom. He bends further, squinting at the bumper, but it's so dark at this end of the container he still can't see properly. Straightening up, he pushes his glasses back up on to the bridge of his nose and takes out his mobile phone. Switching on the torch function, he directs the beam at the front of the SUV and leans down again.

Slowly, he moves the torch beam across the bumper. Nothing, nothing . . . then yes, just off centre there's a streak of silver paint and a scratch of, maybe, seven inches. This is great news; further confirmation that he's found the SUV used to deliver the ransom note.

With the joy of being right pulsing through him, Philip switches off the torch and opens his phone's camera to take a few snaps of the damage to message the others as soon as he's back outside. There's no doubt now. This *is* the SUV. He is triumphant.

As he puts the phone back into his pocket, Philip hears a noise behind him. A dull thud, like a muffled footstep on metal. The hairs rise on the back of his neck and he looks around for something to protect himself with, but there's nothing – all the tools are on the opposite side of the container. Clenching his fists, he starts to turn back towards the door. Quickly thinking of a cover story. 'Hello there, I seem to have got myself all turned around and—'

Philip feels the blow before he registers the man looming over him. His vision blurs. Pain vibrates through his skull. He drops to his knees. His mouth opening as he tries to force his mind to think of something that'll get him out of this mess. 'I say—'

He doesn't get the chance to finish his sentence. The man's fist punches him hard. Philip feels something go pop in his nose and then excruciating pain. Blackness clouds his vision and he feels himself falling. He hits the corrugated metal floor with his shoulder first, then the side of his head. He tastes dirt and mouldy leaves on his tongue. Then there's a fast whoosh of air and a blow to his stomach has him doubled up and retching.

He gasps and stares up at his attacker, needing to see who they are – remember them. But his vision's too blurred to get a proper look. 'W . . . why are . . . ?'

The second blow crushes his ribs and makes his chest feel like fire.

Philip grunts. Gasps.

Then there's only darkness.

33

MOIRA

Moira, Rick and Lizzie are gathered in Olivia's kitchen, sitting around the island unit while they wait for Philip to join them. Just like before, Olivia has insisted on being present. The cops had called her before they'd arrived, telling her they'd found Cody's car, and that the body of a woman had been found inside. Olivia hadn't taken it well.

'They wouldn't even tell me the woman's name,' says Olivia as she busies herself with making sandwiches, thrusting the knife down hard into the bread as she cuts off the crusts. 'And they said they'd put out an APB for Cody. That he's being considered a fugitive. It's ridiculous.'

'You could tell them about the ransom demand,' says Rick. 'That would give them a different perspective and they'd be able to refocus their search accordingly.'

'No, that's not going to happen,' says Olivia, her voice rising in volume as she drops the knife on to the countertop with a clatter. 'They don't care a damn about Cody, and I could tell that man, Officer Schofield, was enjoying telling me that they think my husband is a cheating, murdering fugitive. There's no way I want to risk Cody's safety by showing them the ransom note. The kidnappers said no cops and I'm doing what they said.'

'Okay, we hear you,' says Moira, her voice soothing. She can tell there's no point in trying to persuade Olivia to bring in the police; there's just no way she's going to listen. 'No cops, as agreed.'

'Good,' says Olivia. 'So who was the woman in the car?'

'Her name was Pamela Blake,' says Moira, watching Olivia's expression for signs of recognition.

'Oh my word.' Olivia's hands fly up to her chest. 'Pammy? I know Pammy, she's a good friend of Cody.'

'Friend or girlfriend?' says Rick gruffly.

Olivia looks surprised by his tone. 'I mean, they're close, I guess. They carpool sometimes – Pammy works out of an office along the street from the DVIZION office, and she's come over here for dinner a few times, but she's never stayed over. So yes, I'd say they're just friends.'

Rick frowns. 'And you're sure about that?'

Olivia turns to look at him, her eyebrows raised. 'I don't think I care for your tone or what you're implying. Why don't you just come right out and ask me if I'm behind the poor girl's death and Cody's abduction? You obviously think that I am.'

Lizzie puts her hands out. 'No, Olivia, that's not at all what—'

'Well, are you?' says Rick, talking across Lizzie.

Lizzie glares at Rick. Moira wishes he'd stop. This isn't the right time to try and test Olivia, not when she's already riled up and they've got less than two hours before the ransom exchange is due to happen.

'No. I'm not. I don't want my husband dead, and I certainly didn't wish any harm to Pammy. Jeez!' Shaking her head, Olivia slaps her palms down on to the countertop. 'I liked that poor girl, and I love my husband. Platonically, yes, but it's still love. Why isn't that good enough for you?'

'It is,' says Lizzie quickly. 'We all—'

'You insist on being in the room every time we're discussing the case,' says Rick bluntly. 'You won't give us privacy to work, and you want to know everything. That's unusual. It makes me suspicious as to why.'

Olivia holds his gaze. 'I want to know what's going on because I just want my husband safe. Why don't you understand that?'

'We do,' says Moira, looking pointedly at Rick. He needs to stop. This antagonistic approach isn't helping and they're running out of time. A lot has happened this morning and they need to collate the intel they've each gathered and decide if they've got any chance of finding Cody before 4 p.m. If they haven't, they'll need to plan how to handle the ransom exchange.

'Okay, fine,' says Rick, holding his hands up as if in surrender. 'I believe you.'

Olivia keeps looking at him for a long moment, then nods. 'Okay.'

Neither of them looks happy, but Moira hopes at least they can move on now. She's pretty sure Olivia isn't hiding anything from them, and what matters is finding Cody. Especially now that they know the ransom note isn't an empty threat. These people have proven that they're willing to kill. Moira can't allow another person to die.

As Olivia thumps down a plate of sandwiches in front of each of them and sets a pitcher of lemonade and five glasses on the counter, Moira watches Lizzie glance at the sandwiches and the glass that Olivia has put in front of the empty stool beside her and then check her watch, frowning.

'Philip should be here by now,' says Lizzie. 'We agreed to meet at two o'clock even before you found the car.'

Moira glances up at the wall clock. It's seventeen minutes past two. Philip's nearly twenty minutes late – strange for a man who's a stickler for punctuality. 'We need to get started or we're going to run out of time.'

Lizzie glances at her watch again and scowls, irritated. She looks at Rick. 'Did he tell you he wasn't coming back for the ransom drop?'

'Nope,' says Rick, his tone affable, the antagonism of a few minutes ago seemingly over. 'I haven't heard anything from him since that last group message he sent.'

'Do you think he's okay?' asks Olivia, looking worried.

'Maybe he isn't coming back,' says Moira, thinking about the message Philip had sent earlier. 'He could have meant he was going to check out all the addresses with SUVs registered before he returns.'

'I bet you're right and he's on some mission to get through the whole list of vehicles today.' Lizzie looks really annoyed. 'I thought it was clear we needed him for the ransom drop, but he's so bloody selfish . . . we should start without him.'

'It's okay,' says Rick. 'Let's get started. I'll message Philip now to remind him to get back here. But if he doesn't make it back, we'll manage fine between us.'

Moira nods and gives Olivia, who's looking worried now, a reassuring smile.

'Fine,' says Lizzie, rummaging in her messenger bag. 'I don't have anything much to report – the search into Dirk Baldwin's legal claim was a dead end. But as we don't have our case board here, I'll take notes on my iPad and transfer them to the board once I'm home.'

'Great,' says Rick. 'So Philip and I visited with Dirk Baldwin first. He was real nervous about us talking with him and wouldn't open the door wider than a couple inches – keeping the security chain on the whole time.'

Moira has visited potential witnesses who have behaved the same way before. She tilts her head. 'Did he say if he'd been threatened?'

Olivia frowns and puts down the sandwich she'd been holding. 'Are you implying that Cody threatened him? He wouldn't do that. I don't believe—'

'I'm not saying Cody threatened him.' Moira holds her hands palms out towards Olivia, knowing she needs to keep the woman calm and onside. Frankly, it'd be a lot easier if she wasn't in the room, but Olivia's already made it clear that in her house they have to let her be part of the discussions; not even backing down under Rick's challenge. 'It's just that from the way Rick describes Dirk Baldwin acting, it sounds like he was afraid.'

'Yeah, he was real worried about something,' says Rick. 'Could be someone threatened him either physically or legally. He said he *wasn't allowed* to speak to us. So that sounds like he made a deal to drop the lawsuit and it came with a gagging order.'

Moira nods. It makes sense. She picks up one of the sandwiches – Monterey Jack cheese and salad – and takes a bite. It's been ages since she ate and suddenly she feels ravenous.

'So you got no new information from him?' says Lizzie, looking up from the iPad she's been typing notes on to and taking a sip of lemonade.

Rick shakes his head. 'Nope. Nothing new. I gave him my number and told him to call me if he wanted to talk, but he hasn't made contact yet.'

'Okay,' says Lizzie, jotting down what Rick's said.

'After Philip and me split up, I paid a visit to our other person of interest – Marty Hannier.' Rick lets out a long whistle. 'And boy is that guy mad at Cody. As we'd already learned, he's real pissed at DVIZION for not supporting his venture, and at Cody especially. He's bitter and angry, and said outright that he wished

Cody an agonising death. He was real drunk, and he thought I was a lawman, and that still didn't stop him. He's either stupid or beyond caring, and I'd put my money on the latter. Given his level of intoxication, I don't think he's capable of masterminding a kidnapping, but we should probably look into him more. The state he's in, I doubt it'd take much to persuade him to get mixed up in some kind of revenge.' Rick exhales. 'And that's all I got.'

Moira nods. Hannier sounds like an interesting character, and definitely someone to keep on their radar. She looks across at Olivia, who has been very quiet since the altercation with Rick. 'Did Cody mention Marty Hannier to you, or did Hannier ever try to contact him here at the house?'

Olivia thinks for a moment. 'No, I don't think so.' She frowns. 'Cody might have mentioned a company going bust and the head guy blaming him, but as far as I know Hannier never called here.'

'Okay, thanks,' says Moira. She finishes the last of her sandwich and glances at the wall clock. It's almost quarter to three. They need to speed this up and get to a decision about next steps fast. So far there's nothing of practical use in the search for Cody. 'Right, so we've already talked about how I found Cody's Lexus in a lake at the Lucky Lagoons. It had either been forced off the road or flagged down, most likely when Cody was en route to the office. The body of Pamela Blake was locked inside. Paramedics believe cause of death was drowning but the coroner will need to confirm. The cops are treating Cody as their prime suspect for her murder, but I think it's far more likely that she was killed because she'd seen the kidnappers' faces and they wanted to be sure that she couldn't ID them. Given the car was in the water for a while, there's unlikely to be much in terms of forensics.'

'True,' says Rick, nodding solemnly. 'But I've got my law enforcement contact on standby to get a copy of the autopsy and any forensic results as soon as they're in anyways.'

'Good,' says Moira, having a quick gulp of lemonade to give Lizzie more time to finish typing. 'Also, I met with Cody's VP, Brad George, at the DVIZION offices this morning. Brad's an interesting character. He was chatty and forthcoming about his and Cody's working relationship.'

'In what way?' says Rick, taking a bite of his sandwich.

'Well, they did have an argument the evening before Cody disappeared,' says Moira. 'Brad didn't try to hide the fact. He said he and Cody were like brothers – they had a lot of love for each other, but didn't always see eye to eye. When I pressed him on what happened specifically, he said that he'd not told Cody about a project that was going over budget. Cody found out and yelled at him. He said it wasn't an unusual occurrence and that Cody was a control freak.'

Olivia exhales loudly. She's shaking her head. Frowning. 'Cody's *not* a control freak, and if he raised his voice he must have been pushed to breaking point.'

'Yes, didn't you say the team seemed to love him?' says Lizzie, looking confused.

'Yeah, that's what I got from the rest of the team, and when I put that to Brad, he agreed – said they do – but it's him as second in command who tends to get bawled out.'

Rick nods. Lizzie types what Moira's said on to the iPad. Olivia crosses her arms and purses her lips tight.

Moira knows she's going to have to tread carefully with the next point. 'One thing of interest is that DVIZION was in financial trouble five months ago. Brad said it looked like they were going to have to scale back their projects, but then they secured more investment. As a result, they've ended up doing a rapid-expansion programme rather than a cost-cutting programme. There's something else, too.'

'What is it?' asks Lizzie.

Moira hesitates. Olivia's face and neck are flushed and her jaw is clenched. If Moira mentions that Cody kept the new investor's identity secret and Brad fears there's a Mob connection, then there's a real risk of alienating Olivia. Rick's questioning has already riled her up and Moira doesn't think it'll take much to upset her again. They can't afford that so close to the ransom exchange. Moira's already told Rick that Brad mentioned the Mob, and both her and Rick felt it seemed unlikely they're involved in Cody's abduction given it doesn't fit with their usual MO, so it doesn't seem worth risking talking about it right now.

Moira looks at the clock again. She isn't experienced in ransom exchanges, but it feels like they're cutting things ridiculously close. Operations like this are usually strategised for hours, if not days. They've got minutes. She shakes her head. 'It doesn't matter. Look, it's three o'clock. The ransom exchange is set for an hour. There's nothing in what we've found that's a sure-fire lead on where they're holding Cody. I think we need to pause our enquiries and get ready to do the exchange.'

Rick nods, looking thoughtful. 'You're right – we don't have anything that points to the location Cody is being held. A pre-emptive rescue isn't going to be possible.' He looks at Olivia. 'We need to plan our strategy for handling the ransom exchange. Are you okay with that?'

'Of course,' says Olivia, uncrossing her arms.

'Okay,' says Rick, putting the letter with the details of the ransom exchange on the island counter. 'Let's decide how we're going to do this and get Cody back safe.'

34

LIZZIE

Lizzie arrives at the Middle Lake Nature Reserve half an hour before the ransom exchange is due. With only one car shared between her and Philip, and Philip not having made it back in time to Olivia's for them to do this together, she's had to get another Uber.

The day is still unseasonably warm, but the sun's rays are starting to lose their power as it gradually sinks lower in the sky. Walking across the car park towards the start of the Shimmering Lake Trail, Lizzie scans her surroundings. The parking area is pretty small, with just fifteen spaces. At the moment there are only three cars here and none of them are occupied.

Taking out her phone, Lizzie's pleased to see she has a decent signal. Pressing her call list, she dials Tamsin's brother's landline again. It rings seven times and she's about to hang up when a woman's voice answers.

'Hello?'

'Hi, can I speak to Bryce, please?'

'Who is this?'

'My name is Lizzie Sweetman. I'm a friend of the Zieglers and I'd really like to—'

'You've got a damn nerve,' says the woman, her tone ice cold. 'My husband won't speak to you, not after what that woman did to him.'

'It's really important, could you ask him to—'

'No I cannot. He's not home at the moment, and even if he were I know for sure he'd not want to speak to you. Just leave us alone, you hear?'

'But I . . .' Lizzie stops talking as the call disconnects. The woman has hung up.

Lizzie curses under her breath. His wife had said Bryce wasn't at home. Lizzie needs to talk to Bryce and she needs to know where he is. She dials his mobile again, but it goes straight to voicemail. She's already left a message, so she doesn't bother with another.

The noise of gravel under wheels as the Uber pulls out of the car park, off to pick up the next fare, makes Lizzie flinch and she's suddenly struck by how isolated this place is. On The Homestead she's so used to being surrounded by other people she can't remember what it feels like to be the only person in a place. Shivering, she tries to ignore the uneasy feeling gnawing in her stomach. Right in this moment, she feels very alone.

Stop it, she tells herself. You can do this.

Clenching her fists, she strides out faster towards the start of the trail. Her cover story for being here when the ransom exchange is due to take place is that she's returning from a hike, so it's important she gets hiking or she won't be back in time. She'd hoped to be doing this with Philip, but with him a no-show she's had to come on her own. She sighs. It's so typical of Philip to put working on his own lead ahead of the already agreed plan.

As she leaves the car park and crosses a short stretch of grass with four benches positioned along it, she notes that this is the location where the ransom exchange will take place. Once she's returned from her hike, she needs to head to the bench at the furthest point from the one where Olivia will be sitting. The benches aren't far apart, so she'll still be close enough to help if needed.

Lizzie steps on to the trail. The footing is dry sandy dirt and there are a number of different-length hikes from this point. Consulting the map on the noticeboard, she picks the one-mile trail, which should enable her to look like a genuine hiker and still come back to this point in time for the ransom exchange.

Setting off, Lizzie follows the pink route markers. The nature reserve is beautiful. Palms and taller trees line the pathway and continue out as far as Lizzie can see. She stops to admire some delicate purple flowers, wondering what they are. It's so peaceful here with just the singing of the birds overhead and the sound of crickets in the bushes breaking the silence. She even spots a wild tortoise.

As she reaches the half-mile point at the far end of the trail, the pathway starts to loop around to the left and back towards the car park. Lizzie feels the hint of a breeze on her bare arms. Over to the right of the path she spots a pretty white orchid. Philip loves his orchids and he'd have been excited to see this one growing in the wild. For a moment she's sad he didn't get to see it.

Frowning, she thinks again about him not showing up to help with the ransom exchange. The last message she'd had from him said he was following up leads on the SUV, but he hadn't specifically said he wouldn't be coming back for the exchange. Maybe Moira is right and his message implied he was continuing with the SUV search. Maybe.

He can be selfish, yes, and he always has been tunnel visioned about following up leads and cracking a case. But it's odd that he didn't come back to help with the exchange; something like that is exactly the sort of important operation that Philip would usually want to lead. That he didn't even show up is unexpected.

Lizzie replays in her mind the last conversation she had with him – how she'd told him the couples counselling wasn't going to work and she refused to go back. He'd been hurt. She'd seen the pain in his eyes and the sadness in his deflated body language. She thinks about what Olivia said: how sometimes it's better not to know things about your partner. Lizzie shakes her head. She doesn't believe that.

Philip's always been a proud man. And he's always tried to play the lead in their little group of retired detectives, but for the last couple of days he's taken much more of a back seat – not challenging Moira for the lead as he has done before. Lizzie bites her lip. Maybe she's the reason he didn't come back – perhaps he can't face working with her.

She's not sure how she feels about it if that's true. They're both part of this team. It's only fair that they're both part of this operation. Still, he's a grown man and he can make his own choices. She clenches her fists. After all, he proved that well enough by lying to her all these years.

Following the path as it continues to curve around towards the car park, Lizzie checks her watch. It's ten to four. She's got ten minutes before the ransom exchange, and she needs to be in position before Olivia and Rick arrive. Picking up the pace, she strides faster.

It doesn't take her long. Slowing to a gentle stroll as the end of the trail comes into view, Lizzie takes a deep breath. It's important she looks casual, like a regular, everyday hiker. Beyond the trail and the benches she can see that there are a few more vehicles in the car park. She wonders if any of them belong to the abductors.

As she exits the trail, Lizzie heads towards the bench furthest from the path. Plonking herself down, she gets out her phone and checks her messages. There's still no further word from Philip. For a moment she's tempted to message him and ask where on earth he is, but she forces herself not to. If he's chosen not to help with the ransom exchange, she doesn't want him to think that they're missing him; that she's missing him. No. That'll only make his God complex even worse.

Focusing back on the job in hand, Lizzie tries to sit casually and not draw attention to herself. Having been a CSI rather than a detective, she's never done surveillance work. It might be a regular thing for the others, but she's nervous she'll muck things up by giving the game away.

A couple with a toddler with blonde pigtails and a small dog walk towards the start of the trail. The little girl runs across the grass with the man chasing after her. Picking her up, he swings her onto his shoulders and she squeals with delight. The woman hurries after them with the dog, laughing.

Lizzie smiles, thinking back to when her own kids were young. Home had been such a happy place back then, always filled with fun and laughter. She shakes her head. The kids are all grown up now, and in the last few months home has had a solemn, empty feel.

She watches the man put his arm around the woman and kiss her. She and Philip used to be like that once. Lizzie sighs. Feels tears prick at her eyes and quickly blinks them away.

It's no use getting upset, she tells herself. Things never stay the same.

As the display on her phone changes to four o'clock, she sees Olivia and Rick walking towards the bench furthest away. Although the kidnappers said Olivia should come alone, they're going with a plan that enables Rick to be there to support her. Rick's dressed in a black chauffeur's uniform with a peaked cap, and is holding Olivia's elbow, assisting her as she walks. Olivia is playing her part and pretending that she's too frail to walk unaided. It's a convincing act, even though the uniform that belonged to Olivia's old chauffeur, who recently retired, is more than a little on the tight side for Rick's man-mountain frame.

It's time.

Lizzie thinks of how scared Olivia was that she'd let Cody down and clenches her fingers tighter around her mobile phone. The ransom exchange has to go well. The kidnappers were very clear that they'd kill Cody if things didn't go to plan, and with Pamela Blake found dead in Cody's car, it's obvious they're capable of following through on the threat.

Lizzie watches Olivia and Rick as they sit on the bench that was specified in the note. Their posture is rigid and it's obvious that there's still some tension between them after their earlier argument. Lizzie just hopes they won't let it affect the way they work together.

She knows that by now Moira will be sitting in her car in the car park watching them from a different angle, ready to help, just as Lizzie is here on the bench.

This is it. They can't fail.

35

RICK

It's four o'clock. Sitting beside him on the bench, Olivia is ramrod straight and rigid with nerves. They've been here only a few minutes, but already Rick's sweating like crazy in his too-tight chauffeur's uniform.

In his peripheral vision he can see Lizzie sitting on the bench furthest away from them, just as they'd planned. Moira had already been in position, sitting in her car in the parking lot, when he'd arrived with Olivia. Aside from them, there's a young family heading out on the trail, and he can hear a couple of car doors slamming back in the parking lot, but it's not busy.

He checks his watch; it's two minutes after four.

'They said they'd message with further instructions,' says Olivia. Her face is pale. Her skin looks paper-thin and, even with the foundation she's applied to try and conceal them, he can still see the dark circles beneath her eyes. Maybe he was wrong to push her with his questioning earlier. Would she look and act this way if she was really in on the abduction? To be honest, he doesn't think so.

'Why haven't they texted me?'

'I don't know,' says Rick, keeping his voice calm, reassuring. 'Maybe they're watching us, making sure we're here without the cops.'

'I guess . . .' says Olivia, although her expression is doubtful. 'I just want this over with and Cody back safe.'

'I know,' says Rick. He needs to keep Olivia calm, but in all honesty he's getting worried too. Ransom demands tend to get followed through by the kidnappers, but on the occasions that they don't it doesn't end well for their captive. 'Just hang in there a bit longer, okay? I'm right here with you.'

'Okay.' Olivia looks down at her hands as she clasps and unclasps them in her lap, trying to stop them from shaking.

Rick checks his watch again. It's now five after four. The young family have disappeared out on to the trail, and behind them the parking lot is quiet. If the abductors were going to appear, this would be the perfect time.

Getting the ransom note out of his pocket, he reads it again.

$1 MILLION. 4PM. BENCH AT START OF SHIMMERING LAKE TRAIL, MIDDLE LAKE NATURE RESERVE. WE'LL TEXT THE TRANSFER DETAILS WHEN YOU SIT ON THE BENCH. YOU'LL HAVE TEN MINUTES TO GET IT DONE. DO IT AND WE RELEASE HIM. DON'T DO IT AND HE DIES. CALL THE COPS – HE DIES.

'Something's wrong, isn't it?' says Olivia, her voice strained. She presses the screen of the cell phone she's holding, but there are no new messages. 'We've done what they told us, so why haven't they messaged me?'

Rick turns in his seat, looking back towards the parking lot. The note says the abductors will release Cody once the ransom is paid, but there are no new cars in the lot, and none of the cars already there look occupied other than Moira's vehicle. He wonders if it's his presence with Olivia that's put them off, but the instructions said no cops, not come alone, and as the chauffeur he should appear fairly unthreatening.

He looks at Olivia. Sees the fear in her eyes and tries to inject as much confidence as he can in his voice as he says, 'They're only five minutes late. Let's give them a bit longer. Something might have happened to delay them. Traffic can be bad at this time of day.'

Olivia nods, but her expression is doubtful.

Rick gets it. A no-show is a big problem. He hopes to hell they're just running late.

36

MOIRA

From her vantage point in the first row of the Middle Lake Nature Reserve car park, Moira watches for any activity that could be the abductors. There are seven vehicles in the parking area and she's memorised the make, model and colour of each of them. Six are definitely empty and the seventh – a white pick-up truck with a double cab – might be. It's hard to tell from this angle as the back passenger windows are made from smoked glass.

Looking forward towards the benches at the start of the Shimmering Lake Trail, Moira can see Lizzie in position on the bench furthest from the trail, and Rick and Olivia seated on the bench closest, just as the ransom note specified.

Moira checks her watch. It's five past four.

She feels nerves fizz in her belly and her senses heighten as adrenaline spikes her blood. It's the feeling she always used to get at the start of an operation – she's always hated the waiting aspect of surveillance, much preferring the action of leading the charge.

Or at least she used to. Now, although she hasn't had a panic attack since she moved to Ocean Mist last spring, she doesn't trust herself to be in the thick of things. It's much safer for Rick to be the one supporting Olivia, and more logical too given the most logical disguise was as a chauffeur and there are far more men in that profession than women. They can't afford for anything to spook the abductors. They need to get Cody Ziegler safe.

Moira checks her watch again. It's 4.06 p.m. That's odd – she hasn't yet seen Olivia reacting or responding to texted instructions. She wonders if the abductors are going to change the process and maybe appear at the benches. Or perhaps they're already here and watching to be sure the coast is clear and that Olivia hasn't involved the police.

She scans the area again. There are a few people walking past the bench where Olivia and Rick are sitting; a couple of young women are laughing together as they stride towards the start of the trail, and an older couple are coming back towards the car park, arm in arm, strolling along with a dachshund trotting beside them. None of them seem to be paying any attention to Olivia, and none look like kidnappers, but then appearances can be deceptive; back in London, Moira learned that lesson in the hardest way.

Glancing in the rear-view mirror, Moira looks to see if there's any activity in the car park behind her. She notices two of the cars – a black Tesla and a silver Dodge – have gone, but no new vehicles have arrived. Checking her watch, she sees it's now 4.07 p.m. It's unusual for ransom exchanges to happen later than the time specified.

Adrenaline spikes her bloodstream again. The nerves fluttering in her belly intensify.

Her phone vibrates in her pocket and she pulls it out, expecting it to be Rick or Lizzie. Her breath catches in her throat as she reads it. It's not a message from her friends. It's come from the unknown number.

STOP. OR YOU WILL REGRET IT.

Her stomach flips. Nausea grips her by the throat.

Then Moira frowns. She doesn't understand the message because she *has* stopped; she left her life in London, her job, her friends, and moved to another country under another identity. She hasn't looked into the old Bobbie Porter case, and she hasn't been in contact with anyone in the UK, since she moved. She stopped everything and ran.

For a moment she wonders if they're telling her to stop looking into the disappearance of Cody Ziegler. Then she realises that cannot be true, because the calls and messages from the unknown number started before she'd even met Olivia Hamilton Ziegler.

It makes no sense.

She clenches her fist tighter around her phone. What the hell do they mean? There's nothing left for her to stop. Anger blooms in her chest as she thinks about what she left behind and why she can never go back. It's not until her nails are going white from the pressure that she realises how tightly she's been holding the phone and relaxes her fingers.

Moira curses under her breath. She's had enough of this. If this is someone from her past, and if they are coming to take her out, then she wishes they'd say it. Enough treading lightly, she's done with that. She wants answers.

With her heart pounding in her chest, Moira types out a reply and presses send before she can reconsider.

WHO ARE YOU? WHAT THE HELL DO YOU WANT??

37

RICK

They wait for an hour. By five o'clock the sun has sunk down behind the trees and dusk is getting ready to turn into night. There haven't been any new visitors to the trail in over a half hour. The only cars in the parking lot belong to him and Moira.

On the bench beside him, Olivia shivers. Turning towards her, Rick thinks she looks even paler now the heat of the sun has dissipated. He puts his hand on her arm. 'I don't think it's going to happen. We should go back.'

'Yes,' says Olivia, biting her lip as her eyes become watery.

He looks over at Lizzie and gives a nod. Giving him a tight smile, she gets up and heads towards them. Standing, Rick waits for Lizzie. There's no point in keeping up the pretence that they're strangers any longer – there's no one else here.

'They didn't text?' says Lizzie, as she reaches them.

'No,' says Olivia. There's a quiver to her voice. 'I kept checking my cell, and I had plenty of cell service, but . . . nothing.'

'What does it mean?' says Lizzie, frowning as she looks at him.

'Something must have made them change their mind,' says Rick. He doesn't want to get drawn into this conversation with Olivia at present. She's looking paler by the moment.

'What, though?' asks Lizzie.

He shakes his head. 'Impossible to say.'

'But if they don't tell me how to pay the ransom, I can't get the money to them. And without the money they'll never release Cody,' says Olivia anxiously. Her eyes dart from side to side. Her whole body is shaking now. 'We need to get him back. They've already hurt him. And they killed poor Pammy. If they don't think they're getting the money, what else will they do? I . . . I can't bear . . .' Olivia's eyes widen as her legs buckle beneath her and she starts to fall.

Rick manages to catch her before she hits the ground. She's paper-light in his arms. Her head is tilted back and her limbs are hanging limp. His voice is gentle but urgent as he says, 'Olivia? Olivia?'

'Is she okay?' says Lizzie, moving closer. 'Olivia, can you hear me?'

Her eyelids flutter but don't open. Picking up Olivia, Rick carries her back towards the jeep. Lizzie hurries along beside them, holding Olivia's hand and talking to her, but as they reach the parking lot Olivia is still out cold.

'Oh God.' Moira leaps out of her car and rushes towards them. 'What happened?'

'She was real upset because the abductors didn't made contact,' says Rick. 'Then she fainted.'

Olivia makes a mumbling sound. Her eyes blink open. As Rick helps her back on to her feet she looks from him to the others, confused. 'I . . . did I?' She frowns. 'But I've never fainted in my life. I've no idea why—'

'It's the stress,' says Moira. 'Our bodies all react differently to it.'

Rick remembers Moira telling him about the panic attacks she's had in stressful situations. He turns to Olivia. 'How do you feel?'

Olivia wrinkles up her nose. 'Kind of spaced out.'

'Let's get you home,' says Rick to her, opening the passenger door of the jeep and helping her slide on to the back seat. It's almost fully dark now and they need to get moving. He turns to Lizzie. 'Can you ride with Olivia?'

'Of course,' says Lizzie, walking around the jeep and climbing on to the back seat through the other door.

Rick turns to look at Moira. 'You going to meet us at Olivia's?'

'I'll stop off and sort out the dogs first, then I'll join you.'

Rick nods. The look on Moira's face lets him know that she's aware how bad this could be. It also reassures him that she won't voice those fears until Olivia is out of earshot. 'See you soon.'

'Be careful,' says Moira, then she turns and walks towards her own car.

Getting into the driver's seat, Rick looks over his shoulder to check the others are okay. Olivia is talking to Lizzie. Her eyes are still half closed, and she still looks dazed, but at least she's conscious.

'Have you eaten today?' says Lizzie, looking concerned. 'You didn't touch the sandwiches at lunchtime, did you?'

Olivia looks sheepish. 'I haven't felt like it.'

'Well, you need to keep up your strength. Cody will need you when he comes home, you can't be fainting all over the place,' says Lizzie. She gets a snack bar out of her bag and gives it to Olivia. 'Eat this, it'll help.'

Firing up the engine, Rick switches on the headlamps and manoeuvres the jeep out on to the highway. Up ahead he can see the tail lights of Moira's car disappearing into the darkness. He's not going to say it to Olivia, but she's right to be worried. He's been involved in a few ransom exchanges in his time – usually drafted in by the local PD or FBI in multi-agency operations. Every time the exchange was aborted, the hostage ended up dead.

Rick glances in the rear-view mirror at Olivia's pale face and fearful expression. The situation is taking its toll on her; she's like a ghost of her former self. He tightens his grip on the steering wheel. He can't let this end badly. He won't lose a hostage. Not on his watch.

He'll do whatever it takes to get Cody Ziegler back safe.

38

MOIRA

Returning to the Ziegler residence after stopping off at home to let the dogs out into the garden for a run and to give them their dinner, Moira finds Lizzie, Rick and Olivia in the kitchen. From the moment she steps into the room, it's clear that tensions are running high.

'But I don't understand why didn't they make contact,' says Olivia, as she paces back and forth between the island unit and the far side of the kitchen. 'We did everything they said, and I'd gotten the bank prepared for the money transfer, so why didn't they contact me?'

'Could be something spooked them,' says Rick, looking up as Moira steps into the room.

'What, though?' says Olivia, her voice increasing in pitch. She throws her hands up. 'We arrived on time. I didn't call the cops. What could have possibly spooked them?'

'It might not have been anything you did,' says Rick.

Olivia frowns, narrowing her gaze as she halts and stares at Rick. 'Do you think they were suspicious of you?'

'It's possible,' he says, shuffling from foot to foot.

Moira can see Rick's feeling awkward. It's a tough one, because it could have been his presence beside Olivia that caused the abductors not to go through with the exchange. But dwelling on that now isn't going to help. She clears her throat. 'We need to—'

'Well, that's no way near good enough. Cody's life is on the line here,' says Olivia, still looking at Rick as she slams her palm down on the kitchen countertop. 'You've had several days working on this and I'm worse off, not better. You even accused *me* of being behind the kidnapping. You need to get out there and—'

'The best thing we can do now is to sit tight and wait for Cody's abductors to make contact,' says Moira firmly. She glances at Rick and Lizzie, knowing they'll be thinking the same as her: that they need to calm this situation. 'We don't know why they changed their mind about the exchange, but if they still want the money – and I'm sure that they do – they'll need to get in touch with you again.'

Olivia switches her attention to Moira. She frowns. 'Then why haven't they? They've got my number – they will have taken it from Cody's phone – so why haven't they texted or called?'

'They've favoured using paper notes previously,' says Lizzie, her expression thoughtful. 'Could be they're going to use that method again.'

Moira nods. 'Yeah, weird as the use of paper is in this day and age, you could be right.'

'If they're going to deliver a note, based on their previous behaviour, it'll either come in tomorrow's mail or get hand-delivered tonight,' says Rick.

Olivia shudders. 'I hate the thought of them coming up to the house again. It's so . . .' She shakes her head. Shivers.

'We'll stay here tonight,' says Rick, his tone confident, calming.

It's a good call, thinks Moira. She nods. 'Yes, we can run surveillance.'

Rick looks over to Lizzie. 'Moira and I can handle things here. It'd be best if you go home so you can debrief Philip when he gets back. Then we'll regroup first thing tomorrow.'

'Okay, fine,' says Lizzie, but she doesn't look too happy.

'Thank you, and I'm sorry for getting so . . .' Olivia drops her gaze to the floor and hugs her arms around herself. She sighs. 'I know you're trying to help, but I feel so . . . powerless. I just want Cody home.'

'That's what we all want,' says Rick, his tone reassuring. 'And we'll do everything we can to make it happen.'

'Although,' says Moira, feeling she has to put the option out there again, 'this could be the right time to go to the police with what we know. Like I said this morning, they'll take you seriously, Olivia, because you've got evidence that he's been taken. And now that they think he's a murder suspect they're already on the hunt for him, but they're probably looking in the wrong places. The information you have will help narrow the focus of that search. They could find Cody faster.'

Olivia hugs herself tighter and says nothing. She looks conflicted.

'It could work,' says Rick. 'But it's your call, Olivia.'

Olivia shakes her head. 'They said no cops or they'll kill Cody. I can't risk that.'

'As long as you're sure,' says Lizzie, putting her hand on Olivia's arm and giving it a squeeze.

Olivia hesitates a brief moment, then nods. 'I am sure. I'm not calling the cops.'

'Okay,' says Rick. 'Then let's work out the plan for tonight.'

Rick takes the first surveillance shift. From the window in the fourth guest bedroom, he has a clear view from the gates, along the driveway and up to the front porch of the house. The CCTV is set to record, although based on previous experience they're expecting the abductors to switch off the feed if they come to the house. That's why having eyes on the approach to the house is so important.

Once Olivia has been persuaded to take a sleeping pill and go to bed, and Rick's set up with his night-vision camera equipment, it's time for Moira to get some rest. She doesn't go right away though, lingering instead as Rick gets settled in the armchair by the window with the best view of the driveway. He looks tired.

'Can I get you a coffee?' she asks him. 'It's going to be a long night.'

He gives her that big smile of his. 'Sure, that'd be great.'

She makes the drinks using the fancy barista-style machine in the kitchen – a coffee for Rick and a green tea for her – then heads back upstairs to their makeshift surveillance room.

Putting Rick's coffee down on the table beside the armchair by the window, Moira stands for a moment, holding her mug in both hands as if she needs the heat from the tea to warm up, as she gazes out of the window and along the dark driveway. She thinks about the threatening messages from the unknown number, the gun in her handbag, and the basic locks on her doors at home. Maybe she should upgrade her home security, but then even with the cameras and alarm here at Olivia's the abductor's bypassed the security. If bad people want to get in, they get in; it's as simple as that. Moira shudders.

Rick looks up at her, cocking his head to the side. 'You doing okay?'

'Yeah,' she says, not meeting his eye.

'You sure?' He lets the question hang in the air between them. 'You had a mighty serious expression just now.'

Moira finds it hard to lie to him. She fiddles with the cuff of her sweatshirt. Exhales hard. 'I've been getting these messages – texts, SMS. And they're . . .' She shakes her head.

'They're what?' says Rick, frowning. There's genuine concern in his expression.

'They're from a number I don't know.' Moira looks at his kind, open face and the sudden urge to tell him everything about who she is, the full story of why she had to retire and run, and what she fears the messages are about becomes overwhelmingly powerful. She takes a breath. Makes a decision. 'They're threatening me, telling me to stop.'

'Stop what?'

Moira bites her lip. Loses her nerve. 'That's the thing, I don't know.'

Rick's frown deepens. 'But if they're threatening you, surely they told you—'

'Sorry,' she says, starting to turn away. 'Look, this isn't your problem, I'll just—'

'You can tell me, Moira. I'm here for you.' Rick reaches out and takes her hand, his huge hand dwarfing hers. It feels nice – comforting. 'You're not alone.'

I should be, though, she thinks. *I shouldn't drag anyone else into this.* But as Moira looks into Rick's eyes, she feels her stomach flip for a different reason. They have a connection. She tries to fight it – pretend it's not there – but it always has been. She can't tell him everything, but maybe a little more of the truth is okay. 'I think the threats could be connected to an operation I led back in London before I retired.'

'The one where your colleagues died?' he asks, still holding her hand.

'Yes.'

'So it's a British number?' says Rick.

'No, that's the thing, I don't know where it's from. It's a weird number – only six digits.' She swallows hard. 'The first calls came at times that would be waking hours in the UK, but that's changed now.'

He frowns. 'So you think they're here, coming after you?'

Moira nods. That's exactly what she fears.

Rick squeezes her hand. Looks thoughtful. 'Look, give me the number. I'll have Hawk run it through the system and see who it's registered to and the location. Even if it's a burner, at least you'll know where it is.'

Moira holds his gaze and lets her hand stay in his. It feels good to have shared her fear, but she feels guilty too. Rick wants to help, and she gets the sense that he wants her to fully let him in – to trust him – but she can't. She won't tell him the rest – the investigation into Bobbie Porter she never finished, the fire and the other attempts on her life, and the fact that her boss and mentor is linked to the criminal kingpin. And she won't tell him about her new identity, or that at some point – now or in the future – she'll probably have to run again. Instead, she forces a smile and says simply, 'I'll think about it.'

◆ ◆ ◆

Moira makes her way to the fifth guest bedroom at the back of the house, which Olivia has said for her and Rick to use to rest when they're not on duty doing surveillance. She tries to put all thoughts of Bobbie Porter and the text messages out of her mind. This case requires her full attention, and she needs to get some sleep so she's ready to take over the watch from Rick in a few hours.

The room is decorated in pastel pink and grey; it's cute in a sophisticated way. Olivia had referred to it as the little bedroom, but it's far bigger than the main bedroom in Moira's house. The soft furnishings are made from luxurious silks, high-thread-count cotton and velvet – a far cry from her own basic but functional decor. She feels a pang of regret that she's not at home with her dogs. Lizzie is going to collect them on her way home and have them stay with her tonight, then she'll take them back to Moira's and feed them in the morning before returning to the Ziegler house. Still, Moira hates to be away from them for this long – it's the first time they've been parted overnight. She hopes that they'll forgive her.

Sitting down on the bed, Moira takes off her trainers and removes her phone from her pocket. That's when she sees she's got a voicemail. Pressing the number for the answering service, she listens to the message as it plays.

'Hi, Moira. This is Jake Malone, the journalist? I'm following up on our conversation to see if the resident you mentioned is willing to speak with me. Let me know, yeah? It's getting kind of urgent. Also, I've done some more digging and found out some stuff I think you'll be interested to hear about. I'm free tomorrow – shall we meet for coffee, say eleven? Call me back on this number.'

His Boston accent seems more pronounced on the voicemail than it did when she was speaking to him yesterday, and from his tone she can tell he's excited by whatever it is that he's discovered about the bad news blackout at The Homestead. With everything that's happened over the last couple of days, she's forgotten to contact Peggy Leggerhorne to see if she'd be willing to speak with Jake. She shakes her head. She doesn't have the energy to do it now, and it's too late anyway, plus she can't meet him tomorrow morning when they're right in the thick of things trying to solve Cody's disappearance.

Moira stifles a yawn. Today's been full on, and tomorrow's not likely to be better.

Tapping her keypad to save the message, she sets her alarm for 2 a.m. and puts the phone on the nightstand. She switches off the light and lies back on the bed. As she closes her eyes, she decides that she'll call Jake Malone tomorrow if there's time.

For now, she needs to focus on finding Cody Ziegler.

39

LIZZIE

The house is too quiet without Philip here. Again, Lizzie goes to the front window and peers out into the darkness, looking for Philip and his Toyota, but there's no sign of him; just as there's been no sign of him the previous fifty-plus times she's checked.

She shakes her head and looks down at Moira's three dogs, who've followed her to the window. 'Where on earth *is* he? It's almost ten o'clock.'

The dogs look up at her. The little one, Pip, sits up on his haunches.

Despite her concerns, Lizzie smiles. She knows the sausage dog is begging for a biscuit and that he isn't allowed one because the vet has put him on a diet. She shakes her head at him. 'Being cute isn't going to help, is it?'

She turns back to the window. It's not like Philip to be gone this long without checking in. It's been hours since his last message about checking out the SUVs on the list. Surely he's not going to continue working through the night?

Padding back across the stone floor to the kitchen with the dogs trotting along behind her, Lizzie removes her phone from the charger and brings up the Retired Detectives Club WhatsApp group. She types a message and presses send.

Lizzie: Philip how are you doing with the SUVs?

Putting the phone down on the counter, Lizzie fills the kettle and sets it to boil. She can feel the anxiety fizzing inside her and needs to stay occupied. Spooning decaffeinated coffee into a mug, she almost spills the spoonful when her phone chirps and buzzes on the counter. Hope flares inside her as she reaches for the handset.

She's crushed when she sees the reply is from Rick rather than her husband.

Rick: Isn't Philip home?

Lizzie: Not yet.

Rick: It's getting late. Hope he's back soon.

Lizzie: Me too. I'm worried.

She knows Philip has always been prone to long hours when he's working a case, and he's lost track of time following leads before, but he was younger then, and employed by the police. He's a retiree now, and he shouldn't be out there running around in unknown neighbourhoods chasing down leads all through the night.

Opening her phone contacts, she presses Philip's name and dials his mobile number. It diverts straight to the voicemail service, the robotic voice inviting her to leave a message. She doesn't. Instead, after hanging up, Lizzie types out a text and presses send.

It's late. Where are you?

She taps her fingers on the counter as she waits for the text to say it's been delivered.

And she keeps waiting, her fingers still tapping. The dogs stay sitting at her feet, watching her attentively. She's still waiting when the phone starts to vibrate and a mobile number flashes up on the screen.

Snatching up the handset, she answers the call. 'Hello?'

'Look lady, I don't know what the hell you want, but you need to stop calling me. My wife is going batshit crazy. Don't call us again, okay?'

Lizzie frowns. 'Bryce Fields?'

'Yep. I'm hanging up now.'

'No, please don't. I need to ask you something.'

There's silence on the call, but at least he doesn't hang up.

'Where are you?' asks Lizzie.

'An exhibition in Tallahassee, not that it's any of your business.'

Lizzie's pulse accelerates. Bryce is in Florida, a few hours' drive from here, but a lot closer than where he lives in San Diego. 'Have you been there long?'

Bryce makes a noise that sounds like a growl. 'What the hell is this? I don't have to answer your questions, lady, but I flew in this morning.'

'And—'

'Like I said, I'm hanging up now. My wife said you were calling on behalf of the Zieglers? Well, you just tell that bitch Olivia to rot in hell, and give my sympathies to that poor bastard husband of hers. You ask me, he should leave her. She's poison.'

'If you could just . . .' The call disconnects and Lizzie is left staring at the phone. When she tries to redial Bryce's mobile phone, she can't get through; he's blocked her.

Using her iPad, Lizzie searches on the internet for exhibitions in Tallahassee. Only one started today – the Refrigeration World Expo. They have a list of exhibitors on the website and she scans the list until she finds the entry she's looking for: Bryce Fields – Senior VP, IceSure Refrigeration.

Exhaling, Lizzie goes over their conversation in her mind. Bryce sounded angry but plausible. He clearly hates Olivia. Lizzie makes a note of everything he said, so she can update the others in the morning. People lie, she knows that, and just because Bryce claims not to have been in Florida when Cody first went missing, it doesn't mean he couldn't have paid someone else to do his dirty work for him.

If Rick can ask his law enforcement contact, Hawk, to get them access to the passenger manifests from this morning's flights from San Diego to Tallahassee, she should be able to confirm Bryce's story about how long he's been here in the Sunshine State. That would be a start. In her mind he's a definite addition to the suspect list. After all, the exhibition could all be part of the misdirection.

She makes a note of the key points to follow up on in the morning, then remembering her text to Philip, she checks her phone again and sees that it still hasn't been delivered. Lizzie bites her lip. She's feeling increasingly uneasy. It's not like Philip to ignore messages and texts, and it's very unlike him to miss a call. The phone going straight to voicemail and the text not delivering indicate his phone is off. He never switches his phone off; she's not even sure he knows how. She supposes he could have run out of battery, but he's always so methodical about charging his phone, and he has a backup charger in the car.

Lizzie swallows hard and fear engulfs her like a straitjacket being fastened too tight. Things haven't gone well today – first the ransom exchange, now Philip not coming home.

She bites her lip again.

Lizzie's got a bad feeling about this.

40

PHILIP

Everything hurts.

Correction. Not everything. His arms and lower legs are numb and he can't feel his fingers or toes. But the rest, the rest of him really hurts. There's something across his mouth – tape, he assumes – keeping his lips together. He can hear his own breathing. He's snuffling, his nose feels half blocked. Every breath is a challenge.

Slowly, Philip tries to open his eyes. They feel sticky, and the corners itch, but he manages to prise his lids apart. There's no big pay-off for his efforts, though; all he can see is darkness.

Where the hell is he?

Blinking, he tries to adjust to the gloom. Even the small movement makes the pounding in his head worsen. He swallows back the pain and waits a moment, eyes closed, for the throbbing to stop before he tries again.

This time his eyes adjust faster. They feel scratchy, dry, and his vision is hazy and unfocused, but he slowly looks at his surroundings. He's in some kind of building – not a house, but a garage or an outbuilding. The floor is cracked grey concrete and the walls are made of cinder block. There are no windows or doors in his eyeline, although he assumes there must be a door somewhere behind him at the very least.

He can't look round to check, though. Layers of silver duct tape have been wrapped around him, from his neck to his ankles, binding him to the chair he's sitting on. He's fixed in position, unable to move. A prisoner.

Philip exhales hard and his eyes water from the sudden pain in his nose.

He's really messed up. This is hopeless. He'd hoped Lizzie was going to be impressed by his discovery, but now he's got himself captured he's useless. Worse than useless. Now he's a blasted liability. He hangs his head and pain vibrates through his skull from the movement. He's failed the group and he's failed himself. Lizzie will love him even less now.

Then he hears a muffled groan and he's pretty sure he didn't make it. Sitting stock still, he tries to breathe quieter as he listens out for another sound.

A couple of minutes later he hears it: another groan. It sounds like a man and as if he's somewhere to Philip's right. Turning his head, Philip tries to look, but the tape around his neck is so tight that he can't move more than a couple of inches.

It just won't do. It won't do at all.

Leaning forward, Philip tilts his weight until only the front legs of the chair are on the floor and his feet are positioned flat on the crumbling concrete. He holds the position. At first he can't feel his feet, but after ten seconds or so, pins and needles start to spread up his toes and along the soles of his feet, the feeling intensifying with every second.

He needs to move, but he doesn't know whether his weakened legs will hold his weight. He can't wait around though. He has to try.

Tilting forward more, he puts more weight on to his feet.

So far, so good.

The groan came from his right. Philip leans his weight on to his right foot and tries to lift and move the left-side chair legs around to the right. The floor is uneven, and the chair legs catch on the concrete. Philip grits his teeth. Keeps trying.

It's awkward moving the chair when he's taped to it; extremely awkward. His legs start to shake from the effort, but he feels some movement. The chair legs move a half inch. Philip sits back down and gives himself a moment to rest. Then he repeats the process.

It takes a while, but he perseveres. The chair legs scrape across the floor as he moves them, half inch by half inch. The sound is deafening in the silence. The movement makes his head pound harder and his stomach flip. Sweat runs down his face, stinging his eyes. Nausea rises in his throat. Acid bile hits the back of his throat and he retches from the pain.

This is bad, really bad. He can't vomit while his mouth is taped shut.

Fighting back the nausea, he keeps going. Keeps moving the chair. Eventually he's done. He collapses back into the chair, legs shaking and breathing hard. Eyes closed, he fights to catch his breath.

When he opens them, he sees he was right; it was a man groaning. He's tied to another chair, bound with duct tape just as Philip is. The man's face has a bloom of purple and black bruising across the nose, cheekbones and jaw, and there's a deep gash over one of his eyebrows that's crusted with dried blood. But even with his injuries, Philip recognises the man. He's found Cody Ziegler.

Philip's triumph at being right, and finding Cody, is somewhat dampened by the fact he himself is also captive. He needs to tell the others – give them the location of the out-of-town property and have them come here to storm the place. If he can work one of his hands free, he can call them on his mobile.

He looks down at his shirt pocket. The pocket is empty – his phone gone. Philip slams his feet down hard on to the broken concrete floor in frustration. The sound echoes around the room. The jolt vibrates up his legs and his spine to his head, making everything hurt more.

Philip roars with anger into the duct tape. He shakes his head and stamps his feet again, despite the pain. Tied here, unable to move – to do anything – he feels impotent. Useless. Furious.

That's when he sees it. High up on the wall behind where Cody is sitting there's a long rectangular window. There's no curtain or blind, so Philip can see out through the dusty glass. It's dark outside and through the branches of the trees he can make out a handful of stars and a quarter crescent moon.

Philip's breath catches in his throat. What time is it?

The ransom was due to be paid and the exchange due to be made at four o'clock that afternoon. At this time of year in central Florida the sun sets around five, and with the sky so dark now it must be well after sundown.

This doesn't make sense. It's too late in the day – Cody shouldn't be here.

Did something go wrong?

Philip thinks back to the conversation in Olivia Hamilton Ziegler's kitchen early that morning. The ransom note had been very clear: if Olivia didn't deliver the ransom, Cody would die. And if Olivia told the cops, Cody would die.

He shudders and looks again at Cody's battered, unconscious face. He flinches as he remembers the violence directed at himself by the man who attacked him in the shipping container. These people are ruthless. If Olivia Hamilton Ziegler didn't play ball, or if Lizzie and his friends somehow messed up the trade, there's no saying what they'd do to retaliate.

Then it hits him. Maybe it wasn't anything that Olivia or his friends did. Maybe the reason the trade didn't happen is because the abductors found him, Philip, snooping around. Maybe *he* screwed everything up. If that's true, Lizzie and the others would have gone in good faith to deliver the ransom and walked right into a trap.

Oh dear God no.

Guilt makes nausea rise in his stomach. His pulse pounds at his temples.

He's never much been into God. He's always favoured science and logic over religion and faith, but not any more. Now he wants to believe in a higher power. He needs their help. Clasping his hands into fists, Philip starts to pray.

With tears streaming down his face, Philip prays that his Lizzie, his love, is safe and unharmed. He prays that he'll get the chance to see her again, to give her the explanation she's deserved for so long and to tell her what an idiot he's been and that he's sorry. He's so very sorry.

Philip prays that he'll get the chance to make things right.

41

MOIRA

The beeping of the alarm jerks her awake. Sitting up, Moira silences it and switches on the bedside light, blinking as her eyes adjust to the brightness. She feels groggy from the sudden wake-up call and lack of sleep – more tired than she did earlier before she'd slept. But there's no time to dwell on that. She has to get up and relieve Rick at the surveillance post.

Pulling on her navy hoodie, she goes to the bathroom and splashes water on her face, then pads quietly along the dark hallway towards the front of the house. It's very silent – eerie almost – with no audible movement in the house and no road noise from outside.

The bedroom that faces out over the driveway towards the gates is straight ahead at the end of the hallway. The door is ajar a few inches. Stopping in front of it, she pushes the door open wider. The room is in darkness. It has to be, otherwise anyone coming up the driveway would be able to see there was a person in the room.

Moira keeps her voice low, not wanting to risk disturbing Olivia's rest in the next room. 'Rick?'

There's no answer and no sound of movement.

Peering into the gloom, Moira steps further inside. Her heart starts to quicken. This feels wrong. The room is too still. She wonders if Rick's gone downstairs to get a coffee or something. 'Rick, are you in here?'

That's when she hears it, a loud snore, coming from the navy velvet armchair facing the window in the far corner of the room. Hurrying towards the noise, Moira finds Rick slumped in the chair, his head tilted back and his mouth open. Asleep.

Cursing under her breath, she puts her hand on his shoulder and gives him a shake. 'Rick, Rick, what the hell . . . ?'

He wakes fast, grabbing her hand and twisting it up and back at an awkward angle as if she's an attacker that he's trying to disarm. She cries out, but his grip tightens.

'Rick, it's me, Moira, stop it,' she says, her voice firm, urgent. 'Let go!'

He drops her hand. Blinking, Rick rubs his face. 'What were you . . . ?'

'You were asleep.' Moira doesn't disguise the annoyance in her voice. Sleeping on surveillance duty is very poor form. 'I was trying to wake you.'

'I . . . I didn't . . . I must have . . .' Rick looks back at the armchair, confused. Shakes his head. 'I'm sorry.'

'Has there been any action?' asks Moira, glancing out towards the drive and the gates beyond. Sorry isn't really good enough. Rick knows that; she can see it in his eyes.

'Not that I saw . . .' Rick looks sheepish as his voice trails off.

Moira's not surprised he's embarrassed – falling asleep is a rookie error and Rick's a retiree rather than a rookie. She knows he's well past middle age, but if he thought there was a danger of him dozing off, he should have told her. Still, she doesn't say that. What's most important now is to make sure they haven't missed anything. 'How long were you asleep?'

'I don't know.' Rick looks thoughtful as he runs his hand through his hair. 'I remember a few cars passed down the road

243

around 12.40 a.m., and a cat walked across the driveway just after 1 a.m., but aside from that . . .' He shakes his head again.

'It's just after 2 a.m. now,' says Moira, the irritation clear in her tone. 'So we could have almost an hour unaccounted for.'

'I'll check the cameras,' says Rick, barely meeting her gaze. 'See if they caught anything in the last hour.'

Moira nods. 'Okay. Go. I'll keep watch from here.'

◆ ◆ ◆

Five minutes later, Moira opens a text from Rick and learns that things are far worse than she'd feared. The CCTV live recording was turned off remotely at 1.27 a.m. The security system has been tampered with remotely too, and the access log on the gates is showing that Cody Ziegler's login was used to open them at 1.29 a.m. As she's reading, a second message appears from him.

> We've got a problem. Meet me at the front door.

Trying not to make any noise as she hurries past the closed door to Olivia's room, Moira goes downstairs to join Rick.

He's standing beside the mat. As she reaches him, he bends down and picks up an envelope. 'Seems they left something.'

Of course they did, thinks Moira, shaking her head. This is a disaster. If Rick hadn't fallen asleep, he'd have got a good look at whoever delivered the envelope. As it is, they've got nothing on the person or people who did this. 'What does it say?'

Carefully, he undoes the seal and pulls out a single sheet of paper. Moira sees his eyes widen.

'It's real bad,' he says, handing her the paper.

She scans the page. There's a new picture of Cody Ziegler, this time taken side on. He's tied to a chair. His face is a mottled patchwork of purple and black bruising, and there's what looks like fresh blood coming from a deep gash in the side of his head. Beneath the photo is a typed note:

> DON'T TRY TO FIND HIM, OR HE DIES.

> DON'T CALL THE COPS, OR HE DIES.

> THE RANSOM IS NOW $10 MILLION.

> BLUE HARBOR DRIVE. 10AM. THE BENCH BY No.2256.

> COME ALONE. OR HE DIES.

Moira swears.

'I'm sorry,' says Rick, guilt thick in his voice. 'I totally dropped the ball here and—'

'Yes, you did.' Moira holds his gaze and he seems to deflate right in front of her. She shakes her head. 'But what's done is done and so there's no point focusing on that. What we need to do right now is work out how to fix this.'

As they make their way back upstairs, Moira has a nasty feeling that this isn't going to end well. The note threatens Cody's life multiple times. The ransom demand has increased tenfold. And they want Olivia to make the exchange alone.

She looks at Rick. 'Do you think Olivia has access to this amount of money?'

Rick looks thoughtful. 'I don't know for sure, but the $1 million ransom didn't seem to faze her, and she mentioned multiple offshore accounts but only used one for the previous ransom demand, so I'd say there's a good chance she could get the cash together.'

Moira nods. It's good to know Olivia should be able to raise the money, but she wonders if the abductors ever intend to release Cody. They've beaten him badly, and the violence is escalating. To her, it seems more likely that they intend to kill him once they have the money.

She clenches her fists. They've got eight hours until the new ransom exchange is due to take place and they have to figure out a way to ensure Cody's safety before then.

Once again, the clock is ticking.

42

LIZZIE

Lizzie wakes with a jolt.

Her heart's pounding. Her pulse is racing. Her fingers grip the duvet vice-tight.

There's a blood-curdling scream from outside – high-pitched and wailing – that sends her pulse racing faster. It's followed by another yowl, this one at a lower pitch and more menacing. This noise – it's what must have woken her. Downstairs in the kitchen, Moira's dogs start to bark.

Looking across the darkened room towards the double-width window, she sees that there's light leeching out from around the edge of the blackout blind. *That's odd*, thinks Lizzie. The floodlights in the back garden are motion sensor operated. If they're on, it means someone's outside in the garden.

With her heart still going nineteen to the dozen, she flings off the duvet and hurries across to the window. Pulling up the blind, she peers outside. She's right – the floodlights have been activated and the back garden is fully illuminated. In the middle of the lawn are two cats.

Lizzie laughs with relief and then immediately curses under her breath at the cats for waking her. She watches them – a tabby and a ginger cat – circling each other. The fur on their backs is standing upright, and their arched-back posture is stiff and tense. They make her think of how she and Philip have been behaving around one another these past few weeks.

She's surprised the cats – and now the dogs barking – haven't woken Philip, but maybe he got back so late that he's crashed out in a deeper sleep than usual – that must be it, as he hadn't got home when she went to bed. Normally he'd be banging on the window and shouting at them to be quiet. He's always complaining about the neighbourhood cats using their garden as a dirt tray. Once he turned the hosepipe on a big tortoiseshell cat he caught in the act, although it managed to sprint across the lawn and over the fence before the water hit it, thankfully.

Out on the lawn now, the tabby makes a yowling noise and the ginger a deep, guttural moan. Both are motionless aside from their furiously twitching tails. Lizzie wonders how this will end.

Suddenly, they both turn to face the fence that leads to the next-door neighbour's garden. There's movement at the top of the fence, and Lizzie sees a large black and white cat appear. In unison, the ginger and tabby turn and hurtle off across the lawn, away from the newcomer. Jumping down from the fence, the black and white cat slinks across the lawn to the place where the two cats had been previously, and sits down, claiming the territory. The tabby and ginger cat are nowhere to be seen now. Lizzie guesses that's the end of the noise.

As she lowers the blind, Lizzie shivers. The air conditioning is still going full blast and the sheen of sweat on her skin has turned cold and clammy now she's outside the warmth of the duvet. She frowns. Philip usually turns off the central air when he goes to bed.

Putting on her dressing gown and slippers, Lizzie opens her bedroom door and walks along the hallway to Philip's room. The door is slightly ajar and the room looks dark inside.

'Philip?' she says softly.

There's no answer so Lizzie moves closer to the door. It's only open a couple of inches and she can't see the bed from here. She listens for a few seconds but she can't hear any noise, so she pushes the door wider and steps inside. 'Philip, are you . . . ?'

The bed is empty. It's neatly made – the navy pillows plumped, and the navy duvet smooth and crease-free. It doesn't look like it's been slept in. Her heart rate accelerates again as she realises what's happened.

Philip hasn't come home.

43

MOIRA

'Someone's out there,' says Moira, grabbing the night-vision binoculars and peering down the driveway to the gates. There's a woman staring up at the CCTV camera. Her long white hair is pulled up on to the top of her head in a messy bun, and she's wearing leggings and a sweatshirt. Moira frowns. 'It's Lizzie. She's on foot – must have got an Uber.'

'But it's barely five o'clock. What's she doing here?' Rick says, squinting in the direction of the gates. 'And why didn't she have Philip drive her?'

Moira shakes her head. 'No idea, but we need to let her in.'

Rick uses the remote control to unlock the gates. As they start to swing open, Moira watches as Lizzie pushes between them and runs up the driveway.

'She looks panicked,' says Moira, getting up and hurrying downstairs. She opens the front door just as Lizzie jumps up the steps on to the porch. 'Lizzie, are you—?'

'I've been calling you. Don't either of you ever answer your phones?' says Lizzie as she storms into the house. 'I've been trying to get hold of you for ages.'

Rick, standing in the foyer, shakes his head. 'I didn't—'

'I called at least twenty times,' says Lizzie, her tone accusatory. 'What the hell were you doing?'

Moira glances at Rick. She doesn't want to tell Lizzie he fell asleep when he was on surveillance duty, especially not while she's in this mood. 'We've got a bit of a situation here, there was a—'

'Well, I've got a situation going on too. Philip didn't come home. He's not answered any of my messages and when I call his phone it's going straight to voicemail,' says Lizzie, the anxiety clear in her voice. 'He *never* turns his phone off, but the messages I'm sending aren't being delivered. Something is wrong.'

Moira has to agree it doesn't sound like Philip's usual behaviour. She knows Lizzie and Philip have been having problems, but he's never up and left before. 'You think it's connected to his search for the SUV?'

'Yes I do. We should have worried more about him yesterday when he didn't turn up for the ransom exchange. *I* should have worried,' says Lizzie, striding into the kitchen and getting her iPad from her messenger bag. Putting the tablet on the counter, she wakes the screen and taps to open one of the apps. 'Philip had a GPS tracker fitted to our car so we'd get a lower insurance premium, and the Find My Cellphone tracker app is activated on both our phones too. I'd forgotten he'd done it, but when I realised he wasn't back this morning I remembered, and after searching for the login details – which took a while to find – I was able to download his last locations and plot them on this map.'

Moira and Rick lean forward, looking at the screen.

Lizzie points to a pink dot on the screen. 'Our Toyota was parked in this location for an hour just after lunchtime yesterday.' She moves her finger across the screen to where a red dot is flashing. 'And this is where the car is now. It's been there ever since it moved from the previous location.'

'What's there?' asks Rick.

'It's the car park of the new Sunshine Rise Outlet Mall.' Lizzie shakes her head. 'But I very much doubt Philip has been shopping for the past thirteen hours.'

'What about this dot?' says Moira, pointing to a blue dot on the screen that's barely a centimetre from the original pink one.

'That's where Philip's phone was the last time the tracker recorded its location,' says Lizzie, turning to Moira. 'His phone was switched off at the same time the car was moved from the place marked with the pink dot to the location of the red dot.'

That doesn't sound good, thinks Moira.

Lizzie glances at Rick. 'Do you still have that list of SUV addresses that you sent to Philip?'

'Sure,' says Rick. 'They're in my cell. I'll go get it.'

As Rick goes upstairs to fetch his phone, Moira looks at the map again. 'Can I see the phone tracking app? It'd be good to see the exact locations it recorded.'

'Okay' says Lizzie, swiping to another app and opening it. On screen is a satellite image. She zooms in on a cluster of dots concentrated around a small area of ground.

'Where is that?' asks Moira.

Lizzie traces her finger along a road. 'This is Cattails Road.' She taps her nail against the street by the high concentration of dots. 'These record the phone being on Cattails Road, and in the garden of this property – the last one before this big orange farm. It's Philip's last recorded location.'

'Is there an SUV registered to an address in Cattails Road?' asks Moira as Rick returns to the kitchen.

Leaning against the counter, Rick opens the list of SUVs on his phone. Nods. 'Yeah, it's 1281 Cattails Road.'

Moira's heart rate accelerates. She shifts her gaze from Rick to Lizzie. She can see from their expressions that they're thinking the same as her. She points to the cluster of dots on the map. The location is remote, with no close neighbours, and from the outlines on the map it looks like there are a number of outbuildings as well as the house. 'Philip might have found the people that took Cody. This could be the place.'

44

MOIRA

They decide not to wake Olivia. She's still asleep – the sleeping pills have worked their magic – and checking out the location of Philip's car and the last place his phone registered a location is less risky without her. So Moira writes a note telling her that they're following up a lead, and they'll call her as soon as they have any news. She includes the new ransom note – and says that if for any reason they don't return in time, Olivia should go to the exchange without them. She just hopes Rick is right, and Olivia does have access to $10 million to pay the ransom.

Taking one last glance at Olivia's sleeping form – her slender frame tiny in the huge super king bed – Moira props the note against the alarm clock on Olivia's bedside table and quietly leaves the room.

What they're doing is risky, but it's the right call. Moira's sure of it.

Hurrying outside, she runs across the driveway and gets into the back seat of Rick's jeep. Rick and Lizzie are already in the front.

Rick glances at her in the rear-view mirror. 'You all set?'

'Yes,' says Moira, fastening her seat belt. She thinks of Olivia now alone in the house. Remembers her fear the previous night, before she and Rick said that they'd stay. 'Can you activate the house alarm and the CCTV recording?'

'Already have,' says Rick, putting the jeep into drive and pulling away down the driveway. 'And Lizzie's put the co-ordinates into the navigator. We'll visit the parking lot of Sunshine Rise Outlet Mall first, to double-check Philip isn't there. Then head to Cattails Road.'

'The mall is on our way, so we shouldn't lose much time,' says Lizzie, looking round from the front passenger seat. 'And we need to make sure they haven't left Philip in the car . . .' Her voice gets quieter. '. . . locked in the boot or something.'

'Agreed,' says Moira. It makes sense. If they find Philip, he might be able to give them vital information about what he discovered. Although given the violence the abductors have already directed towards Cody, and the fact that they killed Pamela Blake, Moira dreads to think what they would do to someone they found snooping around.

Shivering, she glances at Lizzie. There's a muscle pulsing in her jaw, and her posture looks rigid and tense. Moira guesses that her friend is thinking the same thing: that they might not find Philip alive.

There's only one way to know. Anxious to get to the mall, Moira leans forward and says to Rick, 'Can you go any faster?'

'I'm on the speed limit,' says Rick, shaking his head. 'I don't want to get us pulled over.'

Lizzie mutters something under her breath.

'What was that?' says Rick.

'I said, we should have guessed Philip was in trouble,' says Lizzie. There's a tremble in her voice. '*I* should have guessed. Instead, I thought he was upset or angry with me and was staying out late to spite me.'

Moira reaches forward and gives Lizzie's shoulder a squeeze. 'It'll be okay, we'll find him.'

Lizzie nods, but says nothing.

They drive on. Everyone's tense. No one speaks. There's just the sound of the wheels on the asphalt, the low-volume mumbling of the radio, and the occasional sniff from Lizzie as she tries to hold back tears.

Even though the Sunshine Rise Outlet Mall is closed for the night, the car park is lit up by powerful street lights. It's a huge area, but impossible to get into with the jeep as the automatic barriers at each entrance are down and padlocked. Instead, they park on a side street nearby and jog back to the car park.

From the map and GPS locator, Lizzie has worked out where the Toyota is parked. With her iPad in hand, she leads the way. There are only a handful of cars parked here and all of them have parking tickets stuck to their windscreens, along with a 24-hour tow notice.

'There,' says Lizzie, pointing diagonally across the car park to the furthest corner.

Moira looks in the direction Lizzie's pointing and sees a dark-coloured car parked on its own. Picking up the pace, they head towards it. As they get closer, Moira can see it's definitely Philip's Toyota. Rick arrives at it first and tries the doors – they're locked.

Moira turns to Lizzie, opening her mouth to speak.

'I brought the spare,' says Lizzie, pre-empting Moira's question and producing a key fob from her pocket. She presses a button and the Toyota's lights flash as the car unlocks.

Rick opens the driver's door and he and Lizzie peer inside. Moira doesn't wait to find out what they can see; instead, she hurries to the boot and opens it, knowing if something bad has happened to Philip, and he's in the car, the boot is the most likely place he'll be.

Moira holds her breath as the boot opens. Exhales hard as she looks inside.

'Anything?' asks Rick.

She shakes her head. 'It's clear.'

'Okay, okay,' says Lizzie, talking half to them and half to herself. 'He's not here. That's okay.' She looks at Moira and Rick. 'We need to go to the Cattails location. He has to be there.'

'Agreed,' says Moira. They do need to check the location, but she doesn't have the heart to point out the obvious to Lizzie – that just because it's the last known location of Philip's phone, it doesn't mean he's still there.

They jog back to Rick's jeep and he sets the navigator to Cattails Road. As he drives through the built-up area towards the outskirts of town, they make a plan.

'I think it's best if we approach the location from this direction,' says Rick, tapping the map on the navigator. 'There are no properties along this stretch of the road and we can get closer to the property without being seen.'

Moira nods. She'd been thinking the same. 'We should split up as well, and come at the place from different angles.'

'Good idea,' says Lizzie. She looks at Rick. 'You can drop me and Moira off before we get close to the property, and we can cut across the scrubland.'

'I could,' says Rick, not sounding very certain about it. 'But we're more vulnerable if we split up. These people are violent, and we've seen from what they did to Pamela Blake that they're ruthless. We're not armed. So we need to tread real careful.'

Moira nods and clutches her bag tighter. This would be the moment to tell them that she's got a gun with her, yet something stops her. Maybe it's because she tried to make light of the threatening messages she's received. If she tells them about the gun, Rick will realise how worried she really is. So she doesn't mention the weapon and instead says, 'I agree with Lizzie, we can cover a larger search area if we split up.'

'Well, okay, I guess,' says Rick. 'But we should aim to check the outbuildings first. The pictures they've sent of Cody don't look like they were taken in a house. If Philip's managed to find him, it's possible they're being kept in the same location.'

Moira glances at him. He's frowning, and doesn't seem as positive and focused as usual. His point about the outbuildings is a good one, but she's missing his usual decisiveness and wonders whether he's still feeling on the back foot because he fell asleep during surveillance.

Turning to Lizzie, Moira says, 'Agreed. Rick can approach from the road, I can loop around the back of the property and come into the area with the outbuildings here.' She points to what looks like a shipping container on the satellite image on Lizzie's iPad, then moves her finger across to what looks like a brick outbuilding. 'And you can take the shallower route through the trees to here.'

'Deal,' says Lizzie.

'We can keep in contact via Messenger and send updates on what we see and find,' says Moira.

'Okay,' says Lizzie. 'Sounds like a plan.'

Rick looks grim-faced, but nods in agreement.

'Good.' Moira takes a breath. The operation is planned. With the limited preparation time and the unknown location there's a lot that could go wrong, but they've done what they can with the information they have.

She thinks about the panic attack she had on her last job in London, and how she'd almost had another when she'd chased down the killer responsible for the murder in Manatee Park just a couple of months ago. She'd managed to get her breathing back under control and prevent a full-blown panic attack that time, but she can't afford for it to happen again. If Philip and Cody are being held hostage on the property, there's only going to be one chance to save them. If they fail, she has no doubt that the abductors will kill them.

She can't let that happen.

Moira looks at Rick – his hands are clenched tight around the steering wheel, and his brow is creased into a deep frown – and at Lizzie, who is fiddling with the three rings on her wedding finger, twisting them around and around. Although the three of them might be older, and they aren't officially in law enforcement any more, they'll all do whatever it takes to get Philip and Cody out of danger.

Live or die – it's down to them.

45

RICK

After letting Moira and Lizzie out by the orange groves, Rick drives the jeep, lights off, along the road for a quarter mile past the house and then parks up outside another property. Jumping out of the vehicle, he closes the door quietly and jogs back along the road towards the house.

He slows his pace as he reaches the property. It's dark here, with just a smattering of stars and a slim crescent moon giving a glint of light. But even in the darkness, he can tell before he steps off the blacktop that this place is a real dive. What should be the front yard is so beat up the grass has turned to dirt and weeds, and the front porch is leaning at a crazy angle so that it makes the ranch-style house look as if it's a drunk who's about to fall over. The worst of it is how overgrown the property is.

Not wanting to get too close to the house in case they've gotten a camera doorbell or other security devices out front, Rick ducks down low and skirts around the perimeter fence – a rusty chain link. He can't go as fast as he'd like due to all the crap that's littered around: old gas cans, a kitchen sink without a faucet, an old toilet and a bunch of rotten packing crates.

As he draws level with the porch, he catches his foot on the handle of an upturned lawnmower. Hopping as he struggles to stay upright, he just manages to stop himself cussing out loud. Stepping around the ancient mower, he continues, more steadily, along the side of the house towards the outbuildings. There's no sign of any cameras.

Unlike the front of the house, which is in darkness, there's a light on in one of the back rooms and no blind has been pulled across. Ducking lower, Rick hurries across the overgrown yard towards the house and drops to the ground beneath the window. He can't miss this opportunity to check out what's going on inside.

As long as he doesn't make any sudden moves, he should be camouflaged by the darkness. Slowly, taking care not to make a sound, he straightens up enough to peer over the termite-riddled sill and through the window.

There are five men inside. Two are sitting on a sagging and stained couch with their backs to him, one is leaning up against the wall on the far side of the room, putting a Tupperware container into a rusty-looking microwave, and the other two are seated on a couple of deckchairs. There's a farmhouse table that's completely covered in dirty plates, glasses, beer bottles and takeout cartons. Rick's real glad he can't smell inside.

The thing he's not glad for is that at least three of the men have weapons – their firearms either tucked in the back of their jeans or in side holsters – and he'd wager that the two men sitting with their backs to the window will have guns as well. It's bad news. They're already outnumbered, and with five weapons to zero this is not going to be a fair fight. Rick cusses to himself, wishing he'd insisted that they stop off at his place on the way so he could get the handgun he keeps for personal protection. He should have said something, or thought about fetching the gun earlier, but he didn't. What with that, and falling asleep on surveillance duty, he feels like he's losing his edge.

Ducking back below the window, Rick crouches in the bare dirt at the side of the tumbledown house and thinks. Back in the day, when he was at the top of his game and young enough to believe himself invincible, he'd have stormed this place anyways, but he's sixty-seven years old now and he's come to learn his body has a few limitations. Hell, he fell asleep when he should've been taking watch. Could be he's not fit to do even the most basic operational stuff any longer. Taking on a group of armed assholes would be a death wish. Rick grimaces. He needs to think of another way to get Cody and Philip out if they are being held here; one that limits the body count to none.

He's still thinking on it as he moves, as stealthily as he can, across the trash-strewn yard towards the outbuildings. The trees seem to have grown up around a large, ancient-looking brick outbuilding and a rusty old shipping container. Both look busted and beat up, but that doesn't mean they're not being used.

Slowing his pace and squinting into the darker gloom beneath the trees, Rick sees the brick outbuilding has a shiny new padlock on the door that looks real heavy-duty. He'd bet money on this being the place where Cody and Philip are being held.

He looks for any devices that could alert the men inside to his presence – cameras, trip wires and the like – but sees nothing. Approaching the door of the outbuilding, he pulls on the padlock, testing the security of the door and frame. Nothing budges. Whoever owns this place has made sure the door is solid, unlike the crumbling roof.

Rick turns to walk around the building, then stops, his heart pumping hard. He stays very still. Listening. Then he hears it again. A faint, muffled groan, coming from inside.

Scooting around the side of the outbuilding, Rick looks for a window that could give him a look-see inside. The place looks like an old garage or workshop. It should have a window and maybe even another door. On the backside of the building, he gets lucky – a long, narrow window that's far too high to be up to building code.

Finding a battered but solid packing crate in the undergrowth nearby, Rick carries it across to just below the window and steps on to it. It's a little wobbly, but he pays that no mind. Cupping his hands around his eyes, he peers through the grimy glass.

A rush of adrenaline spikes his blood as he sees them. Inside, tied to chairs in the centre of the outbuilding, are two men. One is definitely Philip, the other looks like Cody Ziegler. Squinting through the gloom, he can just make out that both have been badly beaten; their faces are a patchwork of bruises and blood. And although they're slumped in the chairs, held in place by layers of duct tape, he's hopeful that they're both still alive.

They've done it; they've found them. Rick clenches his fists. He's going to get them out. Then he remembers his failure to stay awake on surveillance and shudders.

People are relying on him. He just hopes he's still up to the job.

46

LIZZIE

The images from inside the outbuilding are burned into her mind's eye and impossible to look away from. Fumbling with her phone, Lizzie dials the number and waits for it to be answered. She'd volunteered to do this – left Moira and Rick by the outbuilding and come away across the scrubland to make the call without danger of being overheard by the men in the house – anything to try and dampen the guilt she's feeling. Poor Philip. Poor Cody. She hopes it's not too late.

'911. What's your emergency?'

'There's a domestic disturbance at 1281 Cattails Road,' says Lizzie. Her voice is hushed. Her tone urgent. 'A man is being beaten.'

Lizzie gives the emergency despatcher the address of the house Philip and Cody are being held at. She knows that Rick will already have got in touch with his law enforcement contact – Hawk – to give him the heads-up that an emergency call about 1281 Cattails Road is about to come in and that anything he can do to get the cops out here fast will be appreciated. Lizzie's withheld her number and she doesn't give her name. She's about to hang up when the despatcher asks her another question.

'Are you in danger, ma'am?'

Lizzie sees Philip's battered and bloody face in her mind's eye and thinks she's going to be sick. She can't say that, though; needs to remain anonymous. So instead she says, 'No . . . no, I'm fine, but the man . . . his wounds . . . oh God . . . tell them to hurry, please. I think they're going to kill him.'

The despatcher is asking another question as Lizzie ends the call. She can't keep chatting. Needs to get back to the outbuilding – to Philip. She has to know that he's okay.

She runs through the weeds and scrub. It's too dark with just the dim moonlight to see the undergrowth clearly, but she can feel branches and thorns pulling at her clothes as she runs. She grits her teeth as she stumbles on the uneven ground. Keeps going. She needs to be back with the others and Philip. She can't allow anything awful to happen.

Up ahead, Lizzie sees the outlines of the outbuildings and the shipping container come into view and slows her pace. There's a lot of junk littering the ground and, as she picks her way through piles of old bricks and wood, an upturned pram, bagfuls of rubbish and rusty car parts, she's careful to be as quiet as possible. They'll need the element of surprise if the plan is going to work.

Rick and Moira are around the back of the brick outbuilding, next to the window. They look serious and grim-faced as Lizzie joins them.

'Did you make the call?' mouths Rick.

Lizzie gives him the thumbs up.

'Great,' he mouths. 'I've told Hawk to alert his patrol friends – they're close by and should get here fast.'

Lizzie hopes so. Stepping up on to the packing crate, she rises up on to her tiptoes and peers through the bottom of the grimy window. Inside, through the gloom, she can just make out the motionless forms of Philip and Cody, both still tied to the chairs in the centre of the space. Philip is closest to her. He's slumped forward in the chair, unconscious. Kept upright only by the duct tape that's been wrapped around him from his legs, up his body, to his neck. She shudders as she sees the mottled bruising across his face and a deep gash on his forehead that looks as if it's dripping blood.

Her eyes water and she clenches her fists, fighting back the tears. Where are the cops? They need to get here now – to get Philip safe. She needs him to be safe. Because even with everything that's happened – the things he hasn't told her and the anger she feels at him – she knows one thing for sure.

She still loves him.

47

MOIRA

They've pulled back, away from the outbuilding, to the cover of the trees. From here, in the darkness, it's hard to tell what's happening. Moira hears footsteps, light and fast, across the dirt, whispered commands and the click of service weapons being readied.

'We should move closer,' says Lizzie, shuffling forward a couple of steps.

Rick reaches out to stop her. Shakes his head. 'Don't, Lizzie. If anything, we're still too close here.'

Moira agrees. Although the urge to join in with the raid is strong, she fights it. They're better staying where they are – on the periphery of the property, behind the trees, watching the operation go down. If they try to get involved they'll confuse the cops at best, and maybe even distract them from the actual perpetrators. No, staying back here is best. But even though Moira knows the logic is sound, a part of her still wishes she were on the team breaking down the doors and making arrests.

Her heart hammers against her ribs as she waits, crouched in the undergrowth in the wooded area, waiting for the officers to make their move. Clutching her bag tighter, she feels the hard shape of the gun inside, but she doesn't remove it. Not yet. Not unless it becomes absolutely necessary.

'I can't see,' says Lizzie, shaking off Rick's hand. 'I need to be sure Philip's okay. If they hurt him, or he gets mixed up in a fight . . .' She steps forward through the trees towards the outbuilding.

'Lizzie,' says Rick. He turns to Moira, who's started to follow Lizzie, and gives a brief shake of his head. 'It's not safe.'

'I know,' says Moira, but she continues going after Lizzie anyway. They're a team and they need to stick together. She hears Rick sigh, then the sound of him following.

They reach the edge of the trees. From here they have a better view of what's happening. They can just make out the outlines of the officers standing motionless outside the house and the outbuildings, their black kit almost blending into the darkness.

She doesn't see the signal. It must have been given via their radios, because suddenly the silence is broken as the doors of the house and the outbuilding are bashed down in unison. Moira hears metal snapping and wood splintering, then a loud crash as a door hits the ground, followed quickly by another. One of the police teams charges into the house and a second raids the brick outbuilding. There's shouting, a lot of shouting, and although the words are muffled by the distance, she's still able to make out some of them.

'Police! . . . on the ground now! Hands on your head . . .'

'Kitchen, clear . . . Hallway, clear . . .'

'Stay where you are . . . don't move . . . I said freeze!'

Through the windows, Moira sees lights moving through the house as the cops continue to search the premises.

'I have to go to Philip,' whispers Lizzie, edging forward from the treeline.

'Don't,' says Moira, pulling her back. 'You'll confuse things and put yourself in danger – Philip wouldn't want that. Wait until the property is secured.'

'Do you think he's okay?' asks Lizzie. Her voice has a tremble to it.

Moira nods, although in truth she has no idea. They know his captors are armed, and if they raise their firearms at the cops it could turn into a firefight. 'Let's hope so.'

On her left, Rick stands statue still. His gaze focused on the action around the house.

'What is it?' Moira asks.

'They've left the side windows exposed,' says Rick, his voice low. 'The team has covered front and back, but there's a lot of windows and a door along the side, that's a lot of potential exits.'

Moira follows his gaze and realises he's right. The house is a ranch-style home – single storey going back several rooms deep on to the plot. As she scans the length of the building, movement behind one of the windows catches her attention. Squinting through the darkness, she thinks she can see the outline of a person behind the glass. She points it out to Rick. 'Is that . . . ?'

She doesn't finish her sentence. As they're watching, the window unlatches and a slim man dressed in workout gear with a beanie hat pulled down low over his brow climbs out. The window isn't huge, and at first it looks as if he's going to get stuck. Then he manages to twist his leg up and around, and drops lightly to the ground.

'You seeing this?' Moira whispers.

'Sure am,' says Rick.

There's no shouting from inside the house. No cops appear at the window. It looks as if the man has managed to give them the slip. The man stays low, crouching, as he runs towards the wooded area.

Moira doesn't think. Doesn't hesitate. Leaping up, she sprints after the man. Behind her, she hears footsteps following; Rick partnering with her on the chase, just like last time.

The ground is uneven and she has to dodge around the debris that's littering the property: an old motorcycle, a pair of tractor tyres, a pile of bricks and a rusty metal dog kennel. It's hard to see in the hazy dawn light – it's still more night than day – and she stumbles a couple of times as she runs.

Up ahead, the man glances backwards, checking to see if he's been spotted. Moira doesn't get a good look at his face, but it's obvious he's seen her and Rick when he accelerates faster and disappears around a cluster of overgrown crape myrtle trees.

Chasing around the crape myrtles, they hurtle out on to a path that leads through the trees and then curves around towards the orange groves. The shortest route to head off the guy is across a patch of scrub. Moira plunges into the mess of weeds and overgrown bushes. Rick follows.

They're halfway across and gaining on the guy when, behind her, Rick cries out. There's a cracking noise. Some cursing. And the sound of shattering glass.

'Goddammit,' Rick shouts, sounding angry rather than hurt.

Moira glances over her shoulder, checking he's okay. It looks like he's fallen on an old microwave and the glass door has smashed from the impact. She can't see any blood and he's up on his feet but hobbling. There's no sign of Lizzie.

It's up to her alone to catch this guy.

Moira pushes herself faster. Jumps over a stack of rotting crates and an old air-conditioning unit. Pumps her arms quicker, willing herself forward as she jumps out of the scrub and on to the path just a few yards behind the suspect.

Her lungs are burning. Her breath comes in gasps. Moira hopes this isn't the start of a panic attack. She can't have one now, she just can't. She *has* to catch this guy.

Closing the distance between them, Moira summons every last bit of energy she has and leaps up on to the man's back in a dodgy rugby-style tackle. Clamping her arms around his neck, she uses her weight and momentum to push him off balance.

They fall forward as one and land hard, Moira on top, on the dirt path. The man lets out a loud grunt as he hits the dirt. As he wheezes beneath her, Moira pins him to the ground with her knees. She pulls a rope dog lead from her bag and loops it around the man's wrists to secure him. 'Hold still.'

'What the . . . get the hell . . . !' yells the man, trying to wriggle free.

Moira recognises that voice, but she doesn't let it distract her. Holding him firm, she ties the lead in place, then releases her knees from his back and pulls him over so he's face up. Yanking off the beanie that's obscuring part of his face, she looks at the man's deep tan and blond hair, and can't believe what she's seeing.

'I knew you'd be trouble when you showed up at the office asking all those questions,' says the man. 'But I was nice, yeah? I answered them. So come on, let me go.'

'Let you go? Why the hell would—?'

'I've got a lot of money stashed away.' The man gives Moira a wide, ultra-white-toothed smile. 'Let me go and I'll see you right.'

Moira wrinkles her nose, disgusted. 'That's never going to happen.'

'Come on, sweetheart, everyone's got a price,' he says. His tone is still cajoling, but the megawatt smile has started to dim.

She fixes him with a no-bullshit expression. 'Not me. And don't call me sweetheart, arsehole.'

Rick has hobbled over to join her. Raising his eyebrows, he looks from the man to Moira. 'You know this guy?'

'Yeah,' says Moira, shaking her head. 'This poor excuse for a human being is Cody's Vice President and so-called friend – Brad George.'

48

PHILIP

He's sitting on a gurney in the ambulance with a silver space blanket around his shoulders when Detective James R Golding arrives. He can't see Golding – the ambulance's windowless sides block his view – but he can hear the man, barking off orders to his subordinates.

Philip grimaces. He's locked horns with Detective Golding before when he and the team solved the murder at Manatee Park that Golding was officially leading on. To be fair, they'd tried to give Golding the information they'd discovered, but he ignored them, so they'd taken the investigation into their own hands. There'd been a lot of animosity between Philip and Golding, and although they called an uneasy truce once the murder at Manatee Park case was solved, it wouldn't take much to upset the situation.

Outside, Golding's voice is getting louder. He sounds angry as he asks, 'Where the hell is he?'

'In the ambulance,' replies a male voice – a uniformed copper, Philip guesses.

Moments later, Golding appears in the open doorway at the back of the ambulance. He's wearing a black suit and has aviator shades on; the outfit makes him look more FBI than local PD, but maybe that's the point. Running his hand through his rather unruly brown hair, he looks over the top of his shades at Philip and scowls. 'Well, shit. I thought we had ourselves an understanding, Sweetman? And yet here we are again.'

'Detective,' says Philip. He keeps his tone clipped and professional even though sitting in the back of the ambulance like an invalid while Golding's outside blocking the only exit makes him feel at a disadvantage. Sliding off the gurney on to his feet, Philip removes the silver space blanket. His vision swirls and the inside of the ambulance seems to be spinning. He reaches out, holding the edge of the gurney until the dizzy spell passes. Then, slowly, he walks across the ambulance floor and down the steps to join Golding outside. From the shock on Golding's face, Philip knows he must look pretty bad.

The detective narrows his gaze. 'This is another police investigation you've meddled in, Sweetman.'

'It's another case we've solved for your boys, don't you mean, Golding?' Philip counters, his tone hard, determined.

'What the hell were you thinking?' Golding gestures back towards the outbuilding where Philip and Cody had been held. 'I mean, goddamn, this was quite the stunt you pulled today. Why is it every time I'm called to a shitstorm, you're right at the centre of it?'

'I get stuff done,' says Philip, puffing out his chest. He looks across to the entrance of the shipping container where Lizzie is talking to Moira and Rick. '*We* get things done.'

'Yeah?' says Golding, his tone making it clear he doesn't believe Philip. 'I'm going to speak with Cody Ziegler and his wife.' The detective shakes his head. 'But these Hollywood types are very litigious. I'd be surprised if they don't sue you.'

'Cody's been taken to the hospital already,' says Philip, wondering on what grounds the Zieglers could possibly sue him and the team. 'He was beaten badly. I said I didn't need to go.'

Golding gives a look that implies he thinks Philip should have gone to the hospital too. His tone is condescending as he says, 'Well, I guess we'll see about that when I speak to the Zieglers. But you should know I'm thinking of charging you with obstruction of justice and impeding an active investigation, and that's just for starters.'

'Arrest *me*?' says Philip, shaking his head and setting off another dizzy spell. 'Ridiculous.'

Over by the shipping container, Lizzie stops talking to the others and looks across at him. There's concern on her face.

'For sure,' says Golding. 'Read you your rights and sling your meddling ass in a holding cell.'

Philip's shorter than Golding by a couple of inches and doesn't like the way the detective is looking down on him. He stands as tall as he can, trying not to wince at the sharp twinge in his lower back. He's not getting any younger, and although the paramedics said his heart rate and blood pressure are okay considering what he's just been through, he's feeling quite out of sorts. He doesn't want Golding to see that, though; can't show any weakness. The detective has already made it clear he believes Philip and his retired friends are well past their sell-by dates. 'But I found Cody Ziegler. And we solved his kidnapping. Why would you—'

'Yeah, well.' Golding shakes his head. His expression is grim. 'I was prepared to let what happened a few months back slide, but what's happened here today, this is on a whole other level. It's a real problem for me having you seniors running around playing detective. Someone could have been killed, Sweetman. Hell, it could have been you. You're becoming a real liability and I'm—'

'We got the job done,' says Philip firmly. His head's pounding, and his vision is hazy – Golding is going blurry around the edges – but he can't let the detective put him and the team down this way. He has to stand up for himself, and he tries, but as he speaks his own voice sounds weak and distant. The words are hard to form somehow. 'Something . . . some . . . thing your officers . . . failed to do.'

'They didn't fail,' says Golding, his voice getting louder and his tone more irritated. 'They didn't have the chance to—'

'They had plenty of chances,' says Lizzie, joining them and standing closely beside Philip. 'Olivia Hamilton Ziegler called the cops to tell them her husband was missing two days ago. They did nothing. And when Cody's car was found sunk in a lake with a poor young woman dead inside, they decided *he* was the killer and marked him as a fugitive.'

'With all due respect, ma'am, they were following due process and—'

'That's bullshit and we all know it,' says Lizzie.

Despite the nausea rising in his stomach, Philip raises his eyebrows as he turns to look at his wife. She's not usually one to curse or swear. He wants to say something, but his brain feels sluggish, and he can't find the words.

'No,' says Lizzie, putting her hand on his arm and giving it a little stroke. 'My husband risked his life to find Cody Ziegler and get him safe, while your officers ate doughnuts and did nothing.' She shakes her head, her voice rising in pitch and volume. 'Actually, they did worse than nothing. Officer Schofield mocked Olivia Hamilton Ziegler, implying her younger husband must have run off with a younger woman, and then smirked, actually smirked, when a woman was found dead in Cody's car. Do you know how repulsive that behaviour is? How utterly disgusting?'

Golding's cheeks redden and he glances away, looking uncomfortable. 'Well, ma'am, I'm sure they didn't mean to—'

'They *did* mean to. And if it had been down to them, Cody Ziegler would still be missing, maybe even dead,' says Lizzie. She glances at Philip and squeezes his arm before looking back at

Golding. 'So don't you dare imply that my husband is anything other than a hero. Olivia Hamilton Ziegler is a friend of ours, and if you so much as suggest again that my husband could be arrested, I'm sure she'll change her mind about suing the police department for negligence and unleash her lawyers and the media.'

'Yes, ma'am,' says Golding, grimacing and bowing his head. 'I'm sure it won't be necessary for her to do that.'

Philip looks from his wife to Golding and back again, his vision tilting and swirling from the movement of his head. He knows the paramedics gave him a shot of strong painkillers, but he's pretty sure Lizzie just stood up for him. Maybe she hates him a little less than she did. He hopes so.

'Yes, ma'am, and then what?' says Lizzie. 'You should be thanking us, not threatening arrest.'

Golding exhales hard and curses under his breath. He looks from Lizzie to Philip. He holds his gaze. 'Look, I can't agree with your methods, Sweetman, but your results are good, I'll give you that.'

Philip supposes that's as close to a thank you as they're likely to get.

A wave of tiredness hits him. He leans into Lizzie. The pounding in his head is accelerating. His legs feel weak, wobbly. Turning to his wife, he says, 'I'm so sorry. I should have told you about my . . . health problems all those years ago. I was wrong to hide it. Really wrong . . . an idiot. I wish I could . . .'

'Philip, are you okay?' says Lizzie, frowning. 'Philip?'

She's talking to him, but it sounds as if they're underwater. Everything is blurred and black spots are dancing across his vision. 'I . . .'

'Philip, Philip?' There's alarm in Lizzie's voice now, but she sounds a long way away.

He reaches out towards her, but his fingers grasp at air. Nausea rises.

'Philip, stay with me.' There's panic in Lizzie's tone. She's shouting now. 'Quick, get the paramedics!'

He's falling. There's a jolt as he hits the ground. He smells the dirt and mouldy leaves beneath him. Hears voices somewhere high above. Footsteps are running closer.

Then everything goes black.

49

RICK

Philip gave them a scare passing out like that. He came around pretty fast, but he's on his way to hospital now and Lizzie's gone with him in the ambulance. That's left Rick and Moira at the scene of the rescue and so the cops are focusing their attention on them.

Rick knows he has to be economical with the truth. The young cop taking his statement in the mobile operations unit seems like a good guy, but he's a wet-behind-the-ears rookie and is sticking to the script he learned at the academy, rather than pressing Rick harder on some of the vagueness he's dishing out. It probably doesn't help that they've both been up most of the night. Rick can see the tiredness in the cop's red-rimmed eyes and pallid complexion. He figures this guy must be scheduled on permanent night shift; it's rare to see a Florida cop who isn't tanned.

But even though this guy is a rookie, Rick knows he needs to tread real careful, especially now that Detective James R Golding is on scene. The man's had a love-hate relationship with them ever since they solved the murder of the woman in Manatee Park a few months back, and if he got the chance, Rick's pretty sure Golding would be happy to slap on the cuffs and throw his ass in jail.

Maybe that's what makes him feel so alive when he's on a case – not just the search for justice and truth that's always motivated him, but also the thrill of a forbidden adventure and operating just a little outside the law. Whatever it is, he'd hate to have to give it up. Doing this has given him new purpose and made him feel young again; at least, it had right up until the moment he fell asleep on duty last night.

The officer clears his throat as he consults his notes. 'So, Mr Denver, you say that you were walking nearby and you heard screams?'

'Sounds about right,' says Rick, his tone neutral.

The officer frowns. 'You often go out walking with two, erm, lady friends in the middle of the night?'

'By my reckoning, six thirty in the morning isn't the middle of the night, sir. I tend to suffer from insomnia and I'm an early riser too. If you ask my opinion, then the hour before dawn is when the sky is at its most beautiful. It's my favourite part of the day.'

The officer gives him a look that makes it clear he thinks what Rick's saying is nonsense. Rick doesn't care a damn, though. They got Philip safe and found Cody. That's a great kind of two-for-one deal in his book. It don't matter if some rookie cop thinks different.

'And you just happened to be walking in the area that your buddy was being held hostage?'

Rick hesitates. He can't afford to stretch the truth too far; what he says has to be plausible. 'We knew the location our friend's cell phone had last been switched on was around this area.' He gestures out of the window of the operations unit, towards the orange groves. 'So we thought we'd take a walk out this way and see if we could find him.'

'But you didn't think to look for him earlier?'

'Well, like I said before, it wasn't until my friend Lizzie – his wife – woke up this morning that she realised he didn't come home the previous night. We came out here as soon as we knew.' He fixes an earnest expression on his face. 'Philip has had a few . . . mobility problems recently. We were worried he might have fallen and not been able to get up.'

The rookie cop nods and makes a few notes. 'And this anonymous tip-off – that anything to do with you?'

Rick doesn't answer right away. He looks past him at the beige wall of the mobile operations unit. It was, in reality, a large RV that'd been divided up into several small meeting rooms. The whole decor was beige – walls, ceiling, vinyl floor and even the chairs and table. That's how their story needs to be – beige and unremarkable, and as close to the truth as possible, without causing the cops to believe they withheld information that should have gone to them earlier. He meets the cop's gaze. 'It was Lizzie, my friend, who made the call.'

The young cop nods. He gives a slight smile and Rick guesses that the cop's been able to match the story he's just given him with Moira's and Lizzie's. That's good for them, but the rookie really needs to work more on his poker face.

◆ ◆ ◆

Rick's free and clear within another fifteen minutes. His witness statement is signed and Detective Golding even gave him a smile as they passed on the steps of the mobile operations unit, which is rather disconcerting if Rick's honest.

Moira's waiting for him back along the road by the jeep. She waves as he limps towards her, trying not to let the pain in his leg from the fall earlier show too much.

He raises his hand, waving back. 'Hey there.'

'We did it,' says Moira, her smile widening into a grin. 'We got Cody safe, and we found Philip.'

Rick doesn't quite meet her eye. He can't. Not after falling asleep on surveillance. It's embarrassing. Makes him think, even though he loves investigating, he should permanently hang up his detective badge and take up racquetball or something. 'We sure did.'

'I'm sorry about earlier,' she says. 'I overreacted. It'd been a long day. I should have taken the first surveillance shift. You'd been—'

'You don't need to make excuses for me,' he says softly. 'I screwed up, and that's the fact of the matter.'

'It happens,' says Moira. 'And, like I said, I overreacted.'

He knows she's being kind. It shouldn't have happened, that's for sure, but he's thankful for her kindness. 'Well, it won't happen again, ma'am.'

Moira laughs. 'Deal.'

Although she's laughing, Rick can see there's still tension behind her smile. He remembers the conversation they'd had back at the start of last night, up in the room they were using for surveillance. Looks serious. 'You still getting those messages?'

Her smile fades. 'Yes.'

'That ain't good.' Rick runs his hand over the stubble on his jaw. 'We need to get to the bottom of it.'

'It's okay, I—'

'It's not okay, because it's stressing you, and that's not right.' He puts his hand on Moira's arm and tries to ignore the way touching her skin makes his fingertips ping with electricity. 'Like I said back at Olivia's last night, if you give me the unknown number, I'll find out who's behind this.'

She closes her eyes for a moment as she exhales, then looks back at him. For a moment he thinks she's going to brush away his offer to help again, but she nods once and hands him her cell phone with the messages from the unknown number on-screen. 'Okay.'

Holding Moira's cell in one hand, Rick uses his own to make a call. Even at this early hour, and after Hawk has already been woken

281

much earlier that morning for assistance, it rings only a couple of times before being picked up.

'Congrats and all that. I hear the operation was a big success,' says Hawk on the other end of the call. He's chewing gum as ever.

'Sure was,' says Rick, giving Moira, who is leaning up against the bumper of the jeep, a reassuring smile. 'Thanks for your help.'

'No problem, but I'm guessing you're not calling so early to shoot the breeze?'

'You got that right, buddy. I've got a favour to ask you.' Rick looks at Moira. The tension is clear in her face. He needs to sort this.

'Another one?' says Hawk, the chewing noise speeding up. 'You're going to owe me a pair of season tickets, y'know?'

'I guess I am,' says Rick, knowing Hawk will hold him to it, but not caring because it'll be worth it to get to the truth of whoever the hell is harassing Moira.

'Okay then,' says Hawk. 'Tell me what you need.'

50

MOIRA

A couple of days later, Moira and Rick are back in Millionaires' Row, sitting in the great room at Olivia's on a squishy cream leather sofa. Cody is slowly lowering himself down on to the matching sofa opposite. From the grimace on his face, Moira can see he's still in pain from his injuries. Despite the challenges of the past few days, he's smartly dressed in chinos and a designer polo shirt, and clean-shaven. *Neat and tidy*, thinks Moira. *Just like his office space.*

Olivia has brought in a pitcher of iced tea and some glasses. She pours the tea and sets each glass on the coffee table within easy reach. It's the first opportunity they've had to get together since the raid on the property where Cody and Philip had been held hostage, the previous couple of days having passed in a blur of police interviews for all of them, and medical treatment for Cody, Philip and Rick.

Rick leans forward to pick up a glass of iced tea, wincing as the movement puts pressure on his stitches. They'd not realised during the chase and capture of Brad George, but when Rick had fallen over the microwave hidden in the scrub, he'd suffered multiple cuts to his legs and side from the shattered glass.

Cody's face is a collage of purple and yellow bruising and Moira can see that he's sitting awkwardly, his injuries making it difficult to get comfortable. He'd spent the first twenty-four hours after his rescue in the hospital, but once they were happy that his vitals were stable and his injuries treated and on the mend, he was released.

Olivia looks better rested and seems back to her usual energetic self as she fusses around Cody, making sure he's as comfortable as he can be by propping cushions behind him. When she finally sits down, she looks across at Moira. 'How's Philip doing? And Lizzie?'

'They're okay,' says Moira. She knows Lizzie spent time with Olivia during the investigation, but doubts that she'd have mentioned her marital issues so keeps things professional. 'Philip's still in the hospital, but he's hopefully getting discharged this morning. Lizzie's gone over to pick him up.'

'He was very brave,' says Olivia, reaching for Cody's hand. 'If he hadn't found where they were holding Cody and you hadn't used his phone and vehicle trackers to locate him, I don't know what would have happened.'

'I owe him, and you, my life,' says Cody. 'Olivia's told me how much you helped her. If things had been left up to the cops then I'd still be a prisoner, or worse, like Pammy.'

Olivia shudders and pats Cody's hand. She looks across at Rick and Moira. 'I'm so grateful, to all of you.'

'You're very welcome, ma'am,' says Rick. 'We're glad to have helped.'

'And we're very sorry for your loss,' says Moira. 'For Pamela.'

There's sadness in Cody's eyes. 'Pammy was a good friend. I thought maybe she'd become more than a friend in time but . . .' He shakes his head. 'I only found out they'd killed her when the police spoke to me. Why they couldn't let her go I just . . .'

'Like Moira says, we're real sorry for your loss,' says Rick.

Moira feels a wave of sympathy for Cody; going through the trauma of being kidnapped and then finding out about the senseless murder of someone he clearly cared about must be a lot to process. She's about to say something when her phone buzzes in her pocket and she flinches. She wonders if it's another message – another threat – from the unknown number. The thought makes her stomach flip and a sour-tasting queasiness tickle at the back of her throat. She tries to ignore it and focus instead on Cody. Other than giving their statements to the cops, they've had nothing: no details of what Brad had planned, and no information about the other men involved. Even Rick's law enforcement contact hadn't managed to get the details yet. So although they'd solved the abduction mystery, the case still feels unresolved in her mind. She needs the motive to get closure. She needs to know why. 'Can I ask you something, Cody?'

'Sure, ask away,' says Cody, taking a sip of iced tea and wincing as the liquid stings his cracked lips.

There's no delicate way to ask, so she jumps right in. 'Why did Brad do it? He earned a lot of money, didn't he? And with the company expansion plans he'd be in line for a load more. What made him risk it all?'

'He always did love the high life. I guess he got greedy,' says Cody, giving a sad shake of his head. 'A number of weeks ago I was alerted to some accounting anomalies by a junior colleague. At first, I didn't think much of it – they'd already left the company and at a glance it seemed like a couple of innocent errors, a few thousand dollars here or another couple of thousand there, misdirected to the wrong project budget code. I mentioned it to Brad and he said it was easy enough to fix.' Cody exhales hard. 'But then I learned the errors weren't a one-off, and the money missing wasn't just a few thousand. It was happening month on month, and year on year. For almost the whole time we'd been in business, money had been misappropriated. On the face of it, everything had seemed above board because the money didn't go missing, it got transferred out to stakeholder accounts for working projects. Except once I started looking into the projects, I realised some had never produced a shooting script, or engaged talent, or shot any frames. They weren't real projects and every one of them – and their shell companies – led back to one single person . . .'

'Brad George?' says Moira.

'Yep, you got that right.'

'What about the notes you received?' asks Rick.

'Yeah, about them, the first one arrived two days after I told Brad I thought the anomalies in the project budgeting had been happening for a while and I was going to look into it further. I didn't put the timing together back then, but it all makes sense now.'

Olivia frowns. 'If he'd already stolen thousands, why did he abduct you and not just run?'

'Because he got greedy, especially when he realised I was on to him. He always thought he was smarter than me and—'

'He's not smarter than you. He's a self-important ass,' says Olivia, interrupting. 'He was charming for sure, but it was all a veneer, like the teeth. Underneath, he was rotten. I've seen plenty of people that way – Hollywood's full of them.'

Moira doesn't disagree. There'd been more than a whiff of pompousness to Brad when she'd interviewed him. She's just mad at herself for not seeing past his charming act to the truth. 'So you confronted him, is that what triggered the abduction?'

'Yeah. I told him on the phone after the conference call briefing about the Skyline project. I said I knew what he'd done, I'd got evidence and I was going to the cops. He denied it all, of course, and made out that the errors were due to the project teams and the admins coding the budgets wrong. He told me if I came into the office a little early before my meeting, we could talk and he'd show me the paperwork that proved it. Said it'd only take a few minutes.'

Cody looks from Moira to Rick. 'Sucker that I am, I agreed. I guess, after working with him for so long, I really wanted to believe he was clean.'

'So how did they get you off the road by the Lucky Lagoons?' asks Moira. 'Did they ram you?'

Cody gives a single laugh. 'It was nothing so dramatic. I found Brad at the side of the road, his car's hood up, looking like he'd gotten engine trouble.'

'And you stopped?' says Moira.

'That I did.' Cody shakes his head. 'But Brad wasn't alone. His mates jumped me when I was leaning over the engine taking a look for the problem. They must have knocked me out, as the next thing I remember is waking up in that outbuilding. Pammy had been sitting in the car while I helped Brad, but she'd seen his face, and I guess she also saw his mates.' He looks across at Olivia. 'I didn't even know the car had been dumped in the lake, or that Pammy was dead, until the police told me. I fell for the oldest trick in the book, and Pammy died because of it.'

'You trusted someone you thought was a friend and colleague,' says Rick. 'You can't blame yourself. Brad George is the villain here.'

Moira bites her tongue. Trust makes you vulnerable. Makes it harder to see the shit before it hits the fan. She learned that the hard way back in London. After all his years in the DEA, she's surprised that Rick hasn't learned it too, but then maybe he has and he's just trying to help reduce the guilt Cody's obviously feeling about Pamela's death.

Cody nods. 'I put my trust in a—' A knock on the front door interrupts Cody. 'Ah great, he's here.'

Olivia gets up and leaves the room. Moira hears the front door opening and Olivia greeting someone. Cody takes a sip of his iced tea.

Beside her, Rick leans forward to put his now empty glass back on the coffee table. He winces at the stretch and his cheeks flush red. Moira would help, but she knows Rick likes to be the tough guy. Instead, she says, 'You okay?'

'Hanging in there,' he says.

When Olivia re-enters the room, she is with a twenty-some-thing, super-slim, scruffy-haired guy with glasses. Moira has no idea who he is, but she can see recognition on Rick's face.

As Rick's eyes meet the new guy's, the younger man halts abruptly. He runs his hand through his messy hair, tugging on the back nervously. 'Oh man, what is this, I didn't know you'd called the—'

'Relax, Dirk,' says Cody. 'We're all friends here.'

'Dirk?' says Moira, putting it together – this is Dirk Baldwin, the guy who'd filed a lawsuit against Cody Ziegler and his com-pany, and the man who'd refused to speak to Rick and Philip when they'd visited his home. She looks at Cody, frowning. 'You're on good terms?'

'It was Dirk who first alerted me to the anomalies in the accounting, and later on helped me pull together evidence of what had been happening for years,' says Cody. 'He joined us as a project assistant, but his masters was in computers – he was able to get into the back end of the systems and see who was behind the budget coding issues.'

'But you got fired?' says Rick, frowning. 'Was that for show, to throw Brad off?'

'Not exactly,' says Cody. 'Brad had already fired Dirk before I knew about the anomalies. He said it was for poor performance, but it happened after Dirk had alerted Brad to the anomalies in the budgets, and when I checked into Dirk's performance from his team leader's perspective, I was told he'd been one of their top employees.'

'I contacted Cody direct, away from the office,' says Dirk, with a shrug. 'He'd always been good to me, and there was something about the way Brad acted that made me figure he didn't want Cody to know about the accounting issues. He'd already screwed me over, I didn't want him doing it to the big boss too.'

'Once I'd seen the proof that the anomalies weren't the one-offs I'd been led to believe, I pulled the files for the projects that the money had been wrongly transferred to and told Brad I was doing it. Like I said, it was a couple of days later that I started getting threats in the mail to my home.'

'What I don't understand is why he used paper notes for the threats and ransom,' says Olivia. 'It seems very old-fashioned.'

Moira shrugs. 'It could have been to avoid an electronic trail, or maybe he's just fond of old crime shows.'

'Could be,' says Cody. 'Anyways, I hadn't made the connection to Brad at that point, but given the notes I figured things might get dangerous and I didn't want Dirk caught in the crossfire. I gave him external access to the systems and he filed the lawsuit against DVIZION and me personally.'

'Smart,' says Moira. She's about to say more, but her phone vibrating again in her pocket makes her hesitate. She wonders who is messaging her; fearing it's the unknown number again. Her stomach flips. The case of Cody Ziegler's disappearance might be solved, but she's still got the problem of the threats towards her and what to do about them.

Rick narrows his eyes and looks at Dirk. 'It would've been a whole lot easier if you'd told me this when I came knocking the other day. We could have gotten Cody safe faster.'

'I didn't know who you were, man,' says Dirk, his right leg jigging up and down as if he's fighting the urge to run. 'I tried calling Cody after you'd gone, but his phone went straight to voicemail, so I figured it best to say nothing. That'd been our deal – say nothing except to Cody. Trust no one else.'

'But you should have trusted me,' says Olivia, looking at Cody. 'I don't get why you didn't just tell me what was going on with the money and those letters instead of shutting yourself away in the study and worrying about it alone.'

'You'd already done so much,' says Cody, giving her hand a squeeze. 'You invested all that money in the business and I didn't want you to worry. I wanted to get it sorted and then tell you.'

'You were the investor?' says Moira, raising her eyebrows. 'That's something Brad used to throw us off his trail. He said Cody had kept the identity of the new investor a secret and he was worried Cody'd got involved with the Mob. It was clearly meant to misdirect us.'

Rick nods. 'Luckily, we've had dealings with Mob cases before, and yours had none of the usual hallmarks, so we discounted that line of enquiry fast.'

'It's such bullshit – he knew exactly who the investor was and why she didn't want it made public, even in the office.' Cody looks at Olivia. 'It was my wife being her usual generous self. She bailed us out, and she didn't want any credit.'

'I didn't know Brad had told you that,' says Olivia, frowning. 'If I'd known, I'd have put you right straight away.'

Moira nods. If they'd suspected Brad's story, then they could have tailed him. He would have led them right to Cody and Philip. But Olivia's right – Moira hadn't mentioned what Brad had said about the mystery investor and his Mob suspicions within her earshot, as she'd feared it would push Olivia's anxiety higher. Moira looks from Olivia to Cody. 'There were a couple more loose ends we'd like to tie up. It'll just take a few more questions, if that's okay?'

'Of course,' says Cody. 'Ask away.'

'When we looked at your alarm system, it seemed the backup battery pack had been removed. Do you—'

'That was me,' says Cody ruefully. 'I'd removed it to charge the battery, but hadn't gotten the opportunity to reattach it before everything kicked off.'

Moira nods and glances towards Rick.

'That makes sense,' says Rick. He looks from Cody to Olivia. 'We noticed some strange behaviour from your gardener. He seemed to be spying on us while we were here during the investigation. For a while we had him listed as a possible person of interest, but there's not been any evidence to suggest he was involved. Still, we thought it best to warn you.'

'What, Earl?' Olivia laughs, shaking her head. 'No, he'd never be mixed up in something like that. He likes to keep a watch on me, for sure, like a self-appointed bodyguard. And he's a little over-protective, perhaps, but entirely harmless. He just doesn't trust strangers.'

Rick smiles. 'Well, okay, that's good to hear, ma'am.'

'So what's happening with Brad now?' asks Moira. 'Are the police keeping you informed?'

'He's been charged with one homicide, two counts of abduction and they're building a separate case around the embezzlement. They recovered my briefcase from the property where Brad's goons were holding me, and it still had the paper evidence trail inside. The lead detective, James Golding, says the District Attorney is confident they'll get convictions on all counts. Brad is going to jail for a really long time.' Cody glances at Olivia, then clears his throat as he looks back at Moira and Rick. 'The detective did say you guys having been involved, and being there at the rescue, had made things a little more complicated, but that they think it'll all work out okay.'

Olivia balls her hands into fists. 'If they hadn't been involved, you'd still be tied to a chair in that outbuilding, or worse.'

'It's okay,' says Rick. His tone is calm and reassuring. 'I think what Detective Golding means is that some embarrassing truths about his department are likely to come out as part of the trial.'

Moira nods. 'They've already flagged that they're going to need all four of us to give evidence. Their inaction is going to come up and they won't like it when the media gets hold of it, which of course they will, because there's so much media interest already in the case.'

'Well, that's karma for you,' says Olivia, with a small smile. 'They should have behaved better.'

Rick raises his glass towards Olivia, before drinking the last of the iced tea. 'Amen to that.'

51

MOIRA

After saying their goodbyes to Olivia and Cody, they walk back down the driveway to where the jeep is parked. Rick's phone rings and, as he answers it, Moira pulls her own phone from her pocket and checks the screen. She's got a message. Her pulse starts to race; it's from the unknown number.

DON'T TALK TO THE MEDIA OR ELSE.

She frowns as she stares at the message. It makes no sense that the criminal gang from London would tell her to not talk to the media. No sense at all. Surely, if she'd have been going to do that, she would have done it already rather than leaving the country?

Beside her, Rick is still speaking on the phone. He says, 'I think it's best if you talk to her direct.' And then holds out his mobile to her. 'It's Hawk. He's traced that unknown number.'

Anxiety tightens across her chest as she takes the phone from Rick. She wants to know where the threats are coming from, but she's also afraid of what the truth might be. Her voice sounds thin, half strangled, as she says, 'Hi, Hawk. This is Moira.'

'I ran that trace Rick asked for,' says the voice on the phone – a slightly nasal-sounding guy with a stronger American accent than

Rick. 'The number is registered to a Leena Alsope. The registered address is in Clermont, Florida, but that's not the interesting thing.'

'Leena Alsope, okay. Who is she?' says Moira. Her heart is hammering in her chest as she waits for Hawk to tell her this person is connected to a UK criminal gang.

'She's an office manager at Perfect PR.'

'What?' says Moira, not understanding why that's of any significance.

'Perfect PR run the marketing and press campaigns for The Homestead. In fact, The Homestead is their biggest client.'

It takes Moira a moment to speak. 'The Homestead?'

'That's right,' says Hawk. 'You live there like Rick does, yeah?'

'I do. I . . . okay, thanks for letting me know.' Moira passes the phone back to Rick. She feels like she's in a daze. The threats are nothing to do with what happened in London. It's hard to take in and process. She'd never thought someone connected to The Homestead would threaten her.

Rick nods as Hawk says something on the other end of the line. 'Appreciate it, buddy. See you then.' Ending the call, he looks at Moira. 'So what's your next move?'

The surprise at the identity of the person threatening her is giving way to anger. She's feared for her life these past couple of days; she's armed herself and mentally prepared herself for fighting back or giving up the new life she's made here and running. And she's told Rick far more about what happened in London than she ever intended to. Clenching her fingers tighter around her phone, she looks up at Rick. 'I'm going to call them out on this bullshit.'

She taps out a message to the unknown number and presses send.

HELLO LEENA ALSOPE. I KNOW WHO YOU
ARE. I KNOW YOU WORK FOR PERFECT PR.

AND I KNOW THE HOMESTEAD IS YOUR
BIGGEST CLIENT. IF YOU DON'T STOP
HARASSING ME I'LL TELL THE COPS AND
THE PRESS.

She waits a minute. The message shows first as *delivered* and then a few seconds later as *read*, but no reply comes. Moira decides to add an additional message.

CONFIRM YOU UNDERSTAND. CONFIRM
THIS HARASSMENT WILL STOP.

She wants this woman to respond – but when she presses send, the new message doesn't go through. Moira frowns. Then her phone vibrates and a message appears beneath the one she's just tried to send.

Message Not Delivered

Her frown deepening, Moira holds the phone towards Rick to show him the screen. 'My messages aren't getting through any more. Looks like this Leena woman has blocked me.'

'For sure,' says Rick, looking at the screen. 'So what are you going to do now you know who was sending the threats?'

Moira thinks for a moment, remembering the voicemail Jake Malone, the journalist, had left her a few days ago. With all the drama that's happened around finding Cody and Philip, she still hasn't replied to him. 'Something they're *really* not going to like.'

Finding the number in her contacts, she sends Jake Malone a message.

Sorry I've not been in touch – was busy with a
job. It's finished now and I'm keen to get to the

> bottom of the bad news blackout (and I've got
> some more information that will interest you). I
> can meet tomorrow. 10am. The Coffee Shack.
> Let me know if that works.

The reply is almost instant.

> Great. See you tomorrow.

Putting her phone back in her pocket, Moira looks up at Rick and smiles. 'Thanks for getting Hawk to look into the number. I guess The Homestead really don't want me looking into the bad news blackout.'

'Maybe there's something more that they're worried you'll find,' says Rick, looking thoughtful. 'It's real weird how the police haven't given much thought to either of the two cases we've worked. They've done less than the minimum right up until we've finished the job for them by finding the perpetrator. Seems an odd coincidence.'

'I don't believe in coincidence,' says Moira. Rick's right. It could be that this isn't just about suppressing bad news in order to not put off prospective residents. Maybe there's something even more unsavoury to it. There's determination in her voice as she says, 'Whatever's going on, I'm going to get to the bottom of it. We live here – we need the truth.'

'And I don't doubt you'll find it,' says Rick, smiling. He puts his arm around her shoulders and pulls her to him in a friendly bear hug.

Moira relaxes into his embrace. Inhaling his citrusy aftershave, she smiles. It feels good to have him so close. She just wishes she could tell him everything about her past; about who she is, the attempts on her life and why her ex-boss and Bobbie Porter are unlikely to rest until she's dead. She's happy here, but she can never properly relax. Because deep down, Moira knows it's only a matter of time before they discover her new identity and come for her. This time it might have been a false alarm, but she will never be safe as long as Bobbie Porter is out there in the world.

Still, in this moment, with Rick's muscular arms wrapped around her and his kind, handsome face looking down at her, she hopes she can stay here in Florida, being Moira Flynn, for a very long time. For the first time, she lets herself admit it: she'd like some romance on her tabula rasa.

Rick smiles. Raises an eyebrow. 'You okay there?'

'Very,' says Moira.

Then she stands on her tiptoes and kisses him.

52

LIZZIE

They choose a table beside the lake. What with the traffic from Orlando Medical Center not being as bad as Lizzie had anticipated, they're a few minutes early, so Moira and Rick haven't arrived yet. An old pop song from the eighties is playing over the speakers, one she recognises that the kids liked – Madonna or Cyndi Lauper, perhaps. It's an upbeat tempo, far quicker than the speed she's walking to accommodate Philip.

Philip stays silent as they cross the patio to the closest unoccupied table for four. She lets him stay slightly ahead of her, and watches – making sure he doesn't stumble with the unfamiliar walking stick the hospital have given him, and need her help.

Most of the tables they pass are occupied – Betty, in her signature lilac twinset and pearls, and her more flamboyantly dressed companion Alfred, who's wearing a red and orange Pucci print silk shirt with skinny jeans and flip-flops, are taking coffee and pastries; the twin professors – Mark and Jack – are having pancake stacks; and the ladies of the Pickleball Club have commandeered several tables, thrown down their sports bags in a heap beside them, and are brunching on eggs Benedict, toast and Buck's Fizz. Jayne Barratt is seated at the Pickleball Club table, her cheeks flushed from the recent game. When she sees Lizzie and Philip, she raises her hand in greeting. Lizzie smiles back, and waves, thinking she must invite Jayne round for coffee soon.

Alfred, seeing Philip's slow, limping progress across the patio, starts to clap and cheer. Betty joins in, quickly followed by Jayne and the ladies of the Pickleball Club and a number of other people breakfasting at the surrounding tables.

'Well done,' says Mark, pushing his sunglasses off his nose and on to the top of his head, making his ginger hair stick out at a funny angle. 'What you did was over and above, man.'

Philip nods graciously. 'Thank you, but I only did what anyone would've done in that situation.'

'You put yourself in danger for a fellow Homestead resident,' says Mark's twin brother, Jack, patting Philip on the back, his beaded bracelets jingling from the movement. 'You're a goddamn hero, is what you are.'

It surprises Lizzie that Philip looks awkward, as if he isn't enjoying the attention. He's always loved the glory of solving a case. Right now, it looks as if he can't wait to get away from the twins.

'Shall we go to our table and sit?' says Lizzie to Philip, giving a warm smile to Mark and Jack to soften the question. 'The doctors did say you shouldn't walk around too much too soon.'

'Yes, yes,' says Philip, looking almost grateful. He raises his free hand in a wave to the twins. 'Good to see you both.'

Lizzie watches Philip limp stiffly around the table and hook over the back of his chair the stick he's been using since he was beaten and held captive. Just an hour ago she'd collected him from the hospital where he'd been an inpatient for the last couple of days and driven him here to Crystal Waters Plaza in the Ocean Mist district of The Homestead. He's been subdued since the incident, but she'd thought that would have worn off by now.

They didn't speak much on the drive and that bothers her. Philip's usually chatty. He's always liked the sound of his own voice, and she'd have thought that after a couple of days cooped up in a private hospital room, he'd have been keen to talk about what happened.

She tries not to feel disappointed. Before he'd passed out at the scene, he'd told her he'd been wrong to keep his medical issues from her and he'd finally apologised for what he'd done. Now she wonders if he even remembers saying it.

Philip sits down and lets out a long sigh. 'It's good to be back.'

'It's good to have you home,' says Lizzie, but her voice sounds forced, tense. The physical reminders of what happened in the out-building at the hands of Cody Ziegler's captors are stark and Lizzie forces herself not to wince as she looks at her husband. The bruises are mottled purples and yellows across his face and there are lacerations on his neck and wrists from the tape. Beneath his shirt she knows there's strapping to protect his cracked ribs, and he's wearing an ankle brace to help the torn ligaments in his lower leg heal faster.

Philip says nothing, just gives a quick nod and looks away across the lake.

This is hopeless, thinks Lizzie. She needs to say something. She can't keep up this surface-level politeness. There are more important things to discuss. They'll never move on if they don't talk about the issue that's a block between them. She can't wait any longer. Clearing her throat, she says, 'Philip, look, is—'

'Sorry we're late.' Rick's voice booms across the veranda.

Turning, Lizzie sees Rick and Moira striding towards them. Rick's grinning and Moira has a real glow to her.

Rick brandishes the stack of newspapers he's holding. 'We stopped off to get these. Olivia's on the front page of most of them.'

Good for her, thinks Lizzie. It's impressive to still be pulling headlines in your mid-eighties, although she imagines Olivia would rather have done without the drama of the past few days. 'How is she?'

'Olivia?' says Moira, as she takes a seat opposite Lizzie. 'She's doing okay. We dropped in to check on her and Cody this morning. Cody's sad about the murder of his friend, obviously, but physically he's healing well and they've upgraded their security and camera systems.'

'That's good,' says Lizzie.

Rick sits down next to Moira and puts the papers on the table. Lizzie glances at the front page of the one closest to her. There's a big picture of Olivia and Cody taken in their lounge. Cody's sitting in an armchair, his bruises obvious despite the make-up and lighting, and Olivia is standing beside him with her hand on his shoulder. They look happy. She reads the first paragraph of the story and looks back at Rick and Moira. Is it her imagination or have the pair moved their chairs closer together? Their elbows are practically touching. 'It says here Olivia's landed a new role?'

Moira nods. 'Yes, kind of, she told us about it this morning. It's a reality show, like an *At Home with the Zieglers* or something like that. Cody's going to be in it too and it'll be filmed here at The Homestead.'

'Jeez, that sounds awful,' says Rick. 'Having cameras shoved in your face all the time as you go about your business. Sure isn't my kind of thing.'

Moira grimaces. 'Sounds like my idea of hell.'

'Mine too,' says Lizzie. She scans the rest of the story – it says the reality show will star Olivia and Cody, and they'll co-produce it. Cody is quoted as saying he's very excited to be going in front of the camera for the first time. Lizzie wonders if that's why Olivia's agreed to the show – for Cody. She remembers how Olivia had called him her rock, and said she'd never have coped with the death of her lover if he hadn't been there to support her. She remembers how she'd said any partnership needs give and take on both sides.

'Hello there, folks, and welcome to Crystal Waters Coffee N Brunch. I'm Alexia and I'll be your server.'

Lizzie looks up from the newspaper to see standing beside her the fresh-faced, ponytailed server, Alexia, in a green uniform with a 'Welcome to Ocean Mist District – The Homestead' badge pinned to her lapel. 'Hi, Alexia.'

Alexia takes a step closer to the table and lowers her voice. 'You're the Retired Detectives, aren't you? The seniors' group that solves crimes faster than the cops?'

Rick and Moira smile. Philip looks down at the table.

Lizzie smiles at the young woman. 'We are.'

'That's so cool,' says Alexia. 'It's my pleasure to serve you today and my boss said if it was you then your order is on the house, so what can I get for you?'

'Well, that's very kind,' says Lizzie. 'I'll have a coffee and a cin-namon bagel, please.'

'For sure,' says Alexia, beaming. She looks over at Philip. 'And for you, sir?'

'Just coffee, please,' says Philip. He doesn't make eye contact and his voice is unusually flat.

'You got it,' says Alexia, not seeming to notice as she makes a note of the order on her pad.

As Rick and Moira give their orders, Lizzie leans closer to Philip. 'You've been ever so quiet since I picked you up. Are you okay?'

He glances down and fiddles with his napkin. 'I didn't want to hassle you.' He looks up and meets her gaze. His eyes search hers. 'I meant what I said before. I've been stupid, selfish. I know I was wrong to keep my health issues from you and my bosses, and I should have talked to you about it afterwards – properly talked. I'm sorry that I didn't. I have to live with the consequences of what happened that awful day for the rest of my life. I'll always feel the

302

guilt – I should have told you that.' He looks down again. His voice gets quieter. 'And I understand if you want a divorce.'

Lizzie looks at him, surprised. He *does* remember that he'd apologised, and he *had* meant it. She looks into his eyes, past the bruised face and the tension between them, trying to connect with the man she'd met all those years ago and fallen in love with.

She still loves him now.

Almost losing Philip has dimmed her anger at him for holding back telling her about his medical issues. Yes, he'd lied by omission, to her and his bosses, but he hadn't intended it to hurt anyone. What he'd done was wrong, very wrong. He'd been selfish and secretive and he's acknowledged that. The child died because he'd delayed passing on the tip-off, and that was heartbreaking and awful, but he hadn't deliberately set out to cause tragedy. Philip does have to live with the consequences of his delay for the rest of his life. But Lizzie knows now, having come so close to losing him, that she doesn't want to be without him. He's flawed – pompous and bossy and sometimes selfish – but he's also kind and community-minded and driven to get justice, even if it almost kills him.

She puts her hand on his. 'I don't want a divorce.'

Philip frowns, confused. 'No? But I thought—'

'Let's start over,' she tells him. 'We can start by visiting Jennifer in Australia, she's desperate for us to visit. We can travel around too – see the sights together. I'll book us some flights.'

Philip's eyes are watery and she can see the emotion in them. 'I'd really love that.'

'Great,' says Lizzie, giving Philip's hand a squeeze.

We're going to be all right, she thinks. *Everything will work out okay.*

ACKNOWLEDGEMENTS

Firstly, thank you for reading this book – I hope you enjoyed this second adventure of the Retired Detectives Club as much as I did writing it.

The crime-writing and -reading community is such a fantastic place and I'd like to say a massive thank you to all the readers, bloggers, reviewers, fellow crime writers and everyone who has supported me – you are all wonderful!

I'd like to give a special shout-out to Jayne Barratt, who generously bid and won the Young Lives vs Cancer Good Books 2022 auction to have her name in this book. I hope you enjoyed starring as one of The Homestead's top community patrollers – and providing key intel to the retired detectives as they conducted their investigation.

I am super lucky to work with a fantastic bunch of people. To the Thomas & Mercer team – you are a dream to work with. Massive thanks to my editor – the fabulous and ever enthusiastic Leodora Darlington – whose insights and wise guidance have helped develop this book from first draft through to the finished article. Working with you is always the most fun.

Another huge thank you goes to the great Ian Pindar, whose structural editing powers are second to none, and who is always a delight to work with. Big thanks to Jenni Davis and Ian Critchley for your great work in copy editing and proofing, and to @black-sheep-uk.com for the fantastic cover design. And an enormous thank you to the lovely Nicole Wagner, and the marketing and PR teams, for all your support.

As always, a gigantic thank you goes to my fantastic agent, Oli Munson – a legend and a wise adviser – to whom I owe so much. And to all at A M Heath, for always being brilliant.

As ever, a huge thank you goes out to all my family and friends for your encouragement and support (and understanding when I lock myself away writing for hours on end). Plus a special shout-out to Andy for all the book chat and support, and to Red for sitting patiently at my feet as I write, always hopeful that it's nearly walk time.

If you'd like to find out more about me, you can hop over to my website at www.stephbroadribb.com or get in touch via Twitter (@crimethrillgirl) or Facebook (@CrimeThrillerGirl) – it's always great to connect.

And, if it's not too cheeky to ask, if you enjoyed reading this book, I'd really love it if you'd leave a review.

Until next time . . .

Steph x

FREE *CONFESSIONS* BOX SET

ABOUT THE AUTHOR

Steph Broadribb was born in Birmingham and grew up in Buckinghamshire. A prolific reader, she adored crime fiction from the moment she first read Sherlock Holmes as a child. She's worked in the UK and the US, has an MA in Creative Writing (Crime Fiction) and trained as a bounty hunter in California.

Her other novels include the first book in the Retired Detectives Club – *Death in the Sunshine* – which was a bestseller in the UK, USA, Australia and Canada, along with the Lori Anderson bounty hunter series and the Starke/Bell psychological police procedural books (writing as Stephanie Marland). Her books have been shortlisted for the eDunnit eBook of the year award, the ITW Best First Novel award, the Dead Good Reader Awards for Fearless Female Character and Most Exceptional Debut, and longlisted for the *Guardian* 'Not The Booker' Prize.

Along with other female authors, she provides coaching for new crime writers via www.crimefictioncoach.com.

You can find out more about Steph at www.stephbroadribb.com, and get in touch via Facebook (@CrimeThrillerGirl) and Twitter (@crimethrillgirl).